ALSO BY GEORGIA

The Billionaire Banker Series

Owned

42 Days

Besotted

Seduce Me

Love's Sacrifice

Masquerade

Pretty Wicked (novella)

Disfigured Love

Hypnotized

Crystal Jake

Sexy Beast

Wounded Beast

Beautiful Beast

Dirty Aristocrat

You Don't Own Me 1 & 2

The Bad Boy Wants Me

You Don't Know Me

Beauty and the Dark

Click on the link below to receive news of my latest releases and exclusive content.

http://bit.ly/1Oe9WdE

Editors: Caryl Milton, Elizabeth Burns

Contributors: IS Creations

Cover Designer:
http://www.bookcoverbydesign.co.uk

Proofreader: http://
http://nicolarheadediting.com/

Submitting To The Billionaire

Published by Georgia Le Carre

ISBN: 978-1-910575-50-5

You can discover more information about
Georgia Le Carre and future releases here.

https://www.facebook.com/georgia.lecarre

https://twitter.com/georgiaLeCarre

http://www.goodreads.com/GeorgiaLeCarre

Appreciations

I wish to extend my deepest and most profound gratitude to:

Caryl Milton

Elizabeth Burns

Nicola Rhead

Tracy Gray

Brittany Urbaniak

One

Nikolai

https://www.youtube.com/watch?v=PcKo
YGNjoBU

Something Inside So Strong

Thump, thump, thump.

Fucking hell! Someone take my head out of
the drum of this washing machine. The wash
cycle continues as my cell phone vibrates against
the surface of the bedside table. The sound is
like a nail gun going crazy. I unglue my eyes.

My lofty, gilded ceiling comes into view.

I stretch out my arm, fumble around, locate
the blasted thing, hold it over my face, and
squint at it. The blue light from the screen blinds
me. Screwing my eyes, I hit the green button and
put it to my ear.

"Boss, I've been pushing the bell for some
time, and didn't get a response. Are you okay?"
Semyon's alarmed, booming voice tips the
washing machine into the spin cycle.

"What time is it?"

"After seven, Boss."

"So?"

"At night, Boss."

"What?"

I took four pills and decided to lie down for a few minutes, but I must have been more wiped out than I thought. I should have been at the club by seven.

"Bring the car around to the front in fifteen," I instruct, pulling myself off the bed.

My shoes are haphazardly kicked in two different directions, but I'm still in my clothes. Rolling my shoulders, I make my way to the bathroom. I open my mirrored cabinet, and reach for a new box of tablets. Discarding the plastic wrapper, I go into the drawing room and head for the bar. It's an antique, made from wood reclaimed from a Russian church.

Warning. Do not take more than twelve tablets in any twenty-four hour period.

Fuck that. I pop out eight pills into the palm of my hand. Grabbing a bottle of Grey Goose, I unscrew the top, and take a generous swig of neat vodka. Nice one.

Fortified by the best legal anesthetic available, I go swiftly to the bathroom. In ten minutes, I'm showered and dressed in a fine Saville Row black tailored suit.

I grab my phone and wallet, and glance in the hall mirror. No time to shave. Still the five

o'clock shadow suits how I feel. I open the door, and cool autumn air fills my lungs.

"I've called ahead and informed Vanessa that you're running late and to have dinner ready for 8:30, Boss" Semyon says, as he opens the rear door of the Maybach.

I nod my approval and slide into the limousine's luxurious leather interior. The air is scented with expensive perfume, and over the smooth purring of the engine, classical music plays. Semyon closes the door for me, and climbs into the front passenger seat. Immediately, Zohar, my stone-faced driver sets off for the club. I let my body ease back into the seat. Shutting my eyes, I rest my throbbing head on the plush headrest.

Were it midweek I sure as hell would not have left the house, but it's Friday. It's the one night I never miss being at the club. It's not the truth, but I tell everybody that it's because Friday night is sucker's night. It's time the dreamers, the hopers and the scammers will all be along. They go because, of course, life is a complete fantasy-fucking-land.

In their tiny, greedy bird-brains they think they're just gonna stroll into my club, and a few fun-filled hours later, hit the £100,000 Free Stake (which has the same lure of fresh blood for the Great White shark). Sure, the odd one does good, gets to hold it in sweaty palms ... for a bit, but that's when the big hook comes out to play.

It's the glittering, sweet-smelling, dream ticket out of their miserable, pathetic lives: the irresistible £5,000,000 Free Stake. The idea? Put a hundred K in there that didn't belong to you in the first place, and win five million. It fucking fries their brains. Even the most cautious, most level-headed gambler will forget that he walked through *my* front door, the man who never loses.

What does the man who never loses, rush to his club like a slave running to his master, on a Friday night for, you ask? Even when his head is fucking killing him?

Awww ... look at you. All curious.

Stick around, cupcake, and maybe you'll see me get it.

Two

Nikolai

Roman and Andrei, both over six foot five, retired Special Forces soldiers, and the most loyal and reliable of my security team, are already waiting outside the entrance of Zigurat. You're thinking because I'm a Russian billionaire, it's fancy and probably built in a pseudo pyramid style, aren't you?

Nah.

The location is discreet, and it's sandwiched between some plain, gray offices on a deserted backstreet. There are no bright lights to announce its existence. In fact, the nicest thing you could say about the entrance is it's nondescript. No cameras, or reporters hanging around. Exactly the way I like it. We neither advertise nor court any attention.

One has to be recommended by another member to enter, then there is a rigorous vetting process. Before a punter can step a foot through our door he must understand exactly what's on offer inside ... and the risks ... of non-payment. This way there are no, well, let's call it, misunderstandings.

Roman opens my door. I slide out, and stand on the sidewalk for an instant, while

Roman and Semyon with military precision step into place on either side of me. Their cold, expressionless eyes dart around, alert and wary. Andrei, he's always scowling, remains holding the front door open. I shoot my cuffs before heading for the door, my bodyguards closely shadowing me.

It sounds like too much?

Trust me, you can't be too careful in my business. I have more enemies than friends. Come to think of it. I have no friends. They are all enemies in disguise.

It's a different world inside the plain black door. Rich velvet curtains, glossy marble floors, chandeliers, and burnished gold fittings. It's every nouveau riche oligarch's wet dream. I walk through the splendor without seeing it. Anastasia, who mans the front desk, nods and smiles at me. She doesn't expect me to smile back. I don't.

I head upstairs to the first floor. Roman remains on my heels. He enjoys his job and takes his task of protecting me very seriously, which I am rather pleased about.

"Good evening, Mr. Smirnov," a cocktail waitress, greets me on the landing. Her smile is wide and promises all kinds of things. She is tall, willowy, and very beautiful, quite honestly, catwalk material. She licks her lips. Ah, that age-old invitation.

She's new, but she'll learn soon enough. I don't ever mix business with pleasure. As a

matter of fact, I don't mix anything with business. I haven't had a girlfriend since I was seventeen. That's twenty years ago.

In my world, everything has a price. If I want pussy, I don't chase it around the room. That's bullshit. I just pay for it. That way I get exactly what I want, when I want it. It's worked real well so far.

"How many in the Blue Room?" I ask her.

"Six, Mr. Smirnov."

"And next door?"

"Six as well."

"Excellent."

"Thank you, Mr. Smirnov."

I look at my watch. Eight-thirty on the nail. I head downstairs and make my way to the purple room, where I normally dine, and where, very occasionally, the richest punters are invited to dine too, but never with me, obviously.

Vanessa, a sweet little thing, greets me. "Good evening, Sir."

I take a seat. With military precision, a glass of Chateau Petrus arrives. I let its opulence slide over my tongue. Yes, this is the life. In five minutes Vanessa brings seared fillet mignon and girolles in truffle sauce. My head has stopped banging so I enjoy the food. It's Friday, and I have a good feeling about today. A very good feeling.

I skip dessert, but accept the small, strong expresso she puts in front of me. Standing up, I

make my way back upstairs to my offices. Roman follows silently at my heels.

Passing through reception again I see a number of punters milling around waiting to hand their coats over to the cloakroom staff. Some stare, some attempt to make eye contact, others are oblivious, one tries to dash over to shake my hand. He is one of those fools who hope that knowing me personally will make his situation somewhat more favorable should he lose. He is wrong. It doesn't.

Roman ensures there is no contact, and I keep moving.

I pass the main gambling room. As I put my foot on the first step of the stairs that lead to my office, my ears tune in to a loud voice. Every sinew in my body tightens. Here is another one of those fools. Slowly, I turn around and look towards the commotion. Nigel Harrington. Look at him. In his sharp pinstripe suit.

"Nico," he calls. Looking directly at me, he attempts to barge past security and come to me.

Three feet away from me Andrei slaps his huge palm on his chest, effectively stopping him in his tracks. Well, well, who knew today was the day. I walk towards him, my face wiped clean of the joy and excitement surging in my veins. This is it. This is the moment I have been waiting for.

"You got my money?" I ask.

Nigel's facial expression doesn't alter. "I will. By tonight. I promise."

I raise one eyebrow. "By tonight?"

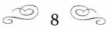

"Yes, yes, by tonight. You have to let me play tonight and I'll be able to pay you back."

"You don't have the money now."

"No."

I turn towards Roman.

"Wait," Nigel shouts desperately.

I turn back towards him.

"You see, I had a dream. I dreamt that I would win big tonight, so I will. I will win it all back. I can feel it in my bones. You'll get it all back, Mr. Smirnov."

"Take him to the pit," I instruct.

Roman and Andrei oblige by grabbing his forearms and shoulders. "Hey," he screams in a panicked voice. He is still shouting when they quickly frog-march him down the hall to the cellar. I walk behind, keeping a small distance. Nigel pleads over his shoulder. There is nothing in the cellar but a badly stained pool table and a couple of chairs. They have already pushed him down onto a chair by the time I go in.

I close the door quietly behind me and stand for a moment looking at him. Every time I see him I am shocked by how unbelievably pathetic he is. I don't speak, and he rushes to fill the dank silence.

"What are you going to do to me?" he asks, wild fear in his eyes.

I shrug. "Nothing ... if I get my money."

I watch him lean forward in the chair and shuffle his feet. "You're going to get your money, Mr. Smirnov. I told you, I had a dream. It was so

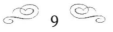

vivid. I was playing in this very club, and I just couldn't lose. I won a lot of money. Much more than I owe you. You just need to let me play tonight. Please, I won't lose, I swear. You'll see."

Sudden laughter erupts from my throat. Roman and Andrei join in. Our laughter reverberates around the carpetless, curtainless room.

I stop laughing suddenly and step closer. I remove my jacket and hold it out. Roman steps forward to take it from me. I roll up the shirt sleeve of my left arm, and then my right arm. It's just drama. Adds nicely to the tension. Actually, I've never done this before. I suppose I could be a gangster. It's not too bad if I only had to knock off whiney excuses for human beings like him. Nigel's eyes dart anxiously from me to my men and back to me. His hands are trembling.

"I'll pay you back. You know I'm good for it."

"Do I look like a fool to you?" I ask pleasantly.

"No. Not at all."

"You must think I'm a fool. You actually thought you could come here without my money, and I would let you play again."

"I know you're not a fool. It was an honest mistake."

I raise an eyebrow. "An honest mistake?"

"Look, I won't play tonight, all right? I'll leave this club, get the money, and come here tonight."

"How will you get the money?"

"I ... have the money."

"You have the money?"

"Well, not, right now. But, I ... I ... can get it. Just give me one day."

"One day?"

"I'll get it by tomorrow."

I shake my head. "That's not the deal, Nigel. The rules are clear. Every member has three months. Run up as big a debt as you want during that time. Then you have to settle in full. Your three months was up last night."

"But I can settle it tonight. If you just let me play. My dream ..."

"This is no dream, Nigel. This is your fucking reality." I stare at him. "Put him on the table."

Before the sniveling liar can say another word, he is thrown face down on the pool table.

"Hold his right hand out." Roman takes one and Andrei the other. I walk slowly towards the wall cabinet and pick up a hammer. My staff have a sick sense of humor, there is blood still on it. I go back and hold the hammer close enough so that he can see the blood. His eyes bulge with terror. Ridiculous fool.

"Please, please, Mr. Smirnov. I'll get you the money," he begs.

I lift the hammer above my head.

"Wait, wait," he screams. "You can have my Mercedes. It's the latest model, worth one hundred and fifty grand." Sweat is pouring down his pale face, and there is a wild tick in his jaw. I try not to smile as I lower the hammer and drag the metal claw against his face. How could he fall for this shit?

"You owe four hundred and fifty grand you piece of shit. What else do you have?"

"Take my house. It's worth one point eight million. You can have everything. Anything. Just let me go," he cries wildly.

That's the thing about gamblers. Even when they're in danger of taking their last fucking breath they'll try to con you.

"Is that all you have?"

"I swear, Mr. Smirnov, that's everything I own. I only owe less than half a million, but you can have it all. Everything I own."

I walk across the room and stand with my back to him. For a few moments, I let the silence ride while I turn inwards. Why Nikolai you've won. You've played the game, you never flinched or gave up, and you won again. I smile. Yeah, I won. I wipe the smile off my face, turn around and walk back to him.

"Well, Nigel, in that case, you are completely fucked. We both know the bank owns everything you have offered me. Break his hands, boys," I snarl.

"No, no," he sobs. "I beg you don't hurt me. Please."

"I don't understand," he wails. "If you know I have nothing why do you keep asking for what I haven't got? What do you really want?"

I grab a fistful of his sweaty hair and raise his head. His eyes search mine, hoping for a glimmer of vulnerability. He sees none. Only icy cold eyes. He knows this is one debt he must pay. I smile coldly.

"I want your wife, Nigel."

Three

Star

It's still dark when I wake up. The first thing I do is glance at my mobile phone. No messages from the hospital during the night. Good. No news is good news.

Relieved, I slowly turn my head and look at Nigel. He is sleeping on his side and facing my direction. A lock of his dark hair has fallen over his forehead, and the little lines of stress around his eyes and mouth are less noticeable, making his boyishly handsome face look almost sulky. The sight makes me smile.

No matter how bad things are with Dad at the moment, all I have to do is look at Nigel's face to make me realize just how incredibly lucky I am. I have everything I have ever dreamed of. The perfect husband. The ability to spend my days doing the thing I love; writing. Never having to worry about financial problems. Living in my beautiful house tucked away in a leafy area of fashionable Fulham. I sometimes even think I live in a little slice of heaven.

And ...

Next year, I will be twenty-three, and that is the age Nigel and I have earmarked to start our family. Nigel wants six children. Obviously, we won't have that many. I think I'll be happy with four, or even three for that matter. Gently, I brush the lock of hair off his forehead. He is a deep sleeper and doesn't stir. I hope all my children have his gloriously dark hair. Especially the boys.

A little flutter sets up in my stomach at that thought.

After all these years, six to be precise, my love for him has settled into a delicious warmth inside my chest. Of course, I don't pretend to understand the hectic world Nigel inhabits when he gets into his suit and walks out of our front door.

In fact, if I can help it, I don't want to know that world. Once when we were first married, I travelled into the city to meet him at a swanky bar. At first, he seemed to be the Nigel I knew. Then, without any warning, right before my astonished eyes, he morphed. He was unrecognizable. Veins bulged in his neck, his face became red, and his eyes filled with murderous rage. The most foul language imaginable began to pour out of his mouth. He even used the C word. Absolutely horrified, I watched him mercilessly rip into a poor barrista. All that fury and venom because the man had let too much water run into his coffee!

I couldn't say a word. I was too shocked. I had never seen that side of him before. All I could do was stare blankly while he explained to me that to succeed in the city one has to be willing to unleash the ugliest, cruelest and most intolerant version of oneself, and watch it run wild.

I felt horrible.

I told him that I didn't care if he didn't bring home as much money as he did. I didn't want him to have to do that. I offered to get a job and help with the household finances if he wanted to take a different career path than the high-pressured world of being a broker.

He laughed and said he wouldn't give up what he did for the world. That it was actually a liberating thing to be wild and cruel and ferocious. I can even remember his exact words.

"Especially, when you haven't slept all night, and you have ten callers lined up, and you know every one of those fuckers wants to call you a four-letter word."

No, I don't understand his world at all, but I love him dearly so I try and do anything I can to make his life better.

I reach up and gently kiss his naked shoulder.

He is so tired he doesn't respond, but I have a vague stirring between my legs, probably because of what he did last night. He had to work late and by the time he came home I was already asleep.

He woke me up with butterfly kisses all over my body, and then he made love to me. Mad, passionate love. It's been a very long time since he was that hungry for me. He couldn't get enough.

When it was over and I had come hard, he held my face gently between his palms and whispered that I was the most important thing in his life. That he would die for me. It reminded me of how it was at the beginning when we were in the first flush of love.

He was thirty-four and I had just turned sixteen when we met. I had gone to a friend's birthday party and her uncle came along. The uncle was Nigel. He was so crazy for me he would wait outside my school. At first I wasn't sure, but he was so handsome and so experienced that from the moment he kissed me I was a goner. Since I was so young we had to keep it a secret from my father.

I hated that, but I think the idea of our relationship being taboo turned him on. I feel like a dirty old pervert he used to say as he had me in lifts and the toilets of nightclubs. Then I turned seventeen, and I refused to hide it anymore.

I told my dad.

Oh, my, he was furious. He called Nigel every awful name in the book and said he was going to call the police. I told him if he did that I would run away from home and he and Mum would never see me again. It was Nigel or no one else for me. So, we carried on uneasily. Me sleeping over at Nigel's at the weekends, and Dad huffing and puffing when I returned home.

When I was eighteen Nigel asked me to marry him. The next day, I brought him home and introduced him to my father. Dad distrusted him on sight and never took to him. It made me unhappy, but what could I do? I loved Nigel. When Dad walked me down the aisle, there were tears in his eyes, and he told me my wedding day was the saddest day of his life.

Dad was wrong. Nigel has been good to me. The real irony is that it's Nigel's money that's keeping Dad alive now. That hospital room he is staying in costs thousands per week.

Four

Star

Quietly, so I don't wake Nigel, I slip out of bed. I tie my robe, lift my phone off the bedside table, and go downstairs. In the kitchen I switch on the coffee machine and set the dining table for two before pulling open the heavy curtains.

Outside daylight is beginning to appear and I sigh with pleasure. The garden always looks best at this time of the year when the honeysuckle, freesia, sunflowers and roses are all out. I open the French doors and go out into the cool, fresh air. This is my favorite time of the day. When Nigel is asleep upstairs, the air is filled with the sounds of birds, and my mind can plot out my storyline. My phone rings. I take it out of my pocket and look at the screen.

"Hi, Nan."

"Good morning, Love," she greets brightly. Nan is like me. An early bird. Sometimes she'll get up at five in the morning and start cleaning out the garden shed. It drives my granddad crazy.

"You all right?" I ask.

"Other than my dodgy knees and your granddad's dodgy mouth, I'm just fine. I swear

that man has moved me to thoughts of murder more often than I've had cooked dinners."

I smile as I turn around and go back into the house.

"Are you going to see your father today?" she asks.

"Of course," I say as I step into the kitchen.

"I'd like to come with you. Will you drop by and pick me up, then?"

I pour some bird seed into a small container "Sure. I'm going before lunch. Is about ten o'clock okay with you?"

"I'll be ready, Love."

We chat a little more as I tear some bread into small pieces and add it to the bird seed. Finishing the call, I go out into the garden and toss the mix onto the roof of the shed. I go back inside, and to my surprise I hear Nigel's footsteps in the bathroom above.

How strange. He never wakes up this early on a Saturday. Nigel works very long hours during the week, and the weekends are the only times he gets to relax a little. In fact, I usually get hours of writing time in before he wakes up.

If he's awake I know he'll be down in about fifteen minutes so I start to prepare eggs and toast for two. Neither of us are big on breakfast. Nigel appears in the doorway as I am cracking the eggs. His hair is tousled, and the sight puts a big, sloppy smile on my face.

"Good morning, you gorgeous Sex God you."

Nigel is not a morning person, but even so his expression is particularly mournful as he returns my greeting. "Morning."

"Breakfast will be ready in five minutes," I tell him.

"I'm not hungry, Star."

My smile slips a notch. Nigel is not a man to skip breakfast. "Fine, sit down, and I'll get your expresso."

He forces a smile and, turning around, heads towards the dining room. Now I know for sure: something is very wrong. Abandoning the eggs, I make his expresso the way he likes it, and follow him into the dining room. I place his coffee on the table, and take the seat next to him. He thanks me quietly, but does not look my way.

For a few moments neither of us speaks.

I clasp my hands in my lap and watch him sip his coffee. All of this is so unlike Nigel. He is a man on the go. He wakes, showers, gets dressed and eats breakfast whilst he reads the morning paper or checks his emails. When he's running late he'll shout down the stairs for me to make his coffee, down it in one hit, peck me on the cheeks and disappear out the door.

"What's going on, Nigel? Why are you acting so strangely?" I ask quietly.

He shakes his head the way someone who has lost everything would do.

"What's the matter? Don't you feel well?"

"I feel sick to my stomach with what I've done."

My stomach drops. "What have you done, Nigel?"

He slaps his hands on his cheeks and looks at me, his eyes distraught. "I have to tell you something, Star," he says, his voice cracking.

In a split second two scenarios cross my mind. He's lost a lot of money at the brokerage, or, oh God, he's got another woman. I'm strong enough to handle the money thing, but not the other woman.

"What is it?" I ask nervously.

"I'm in trouble."

"What kind of trouble?"

"Big trouble," he says swallowing a large mouthful of air. "I've been such a fool, Star. Such a colossal fucking fool."

For a moment, the horror of anticipating what he is going to tell me, dumbfounds me. In my mind I hear him saying I cheated on you, Star. It was just a one-night stand. Or worse. I've fallen for someone else and I'm leaving you.

I just stare at him, hardly daring to breathe.

He opens his mouth. "I owe money. A lot of money."

My breath comes out in a rush of sheer relief. Okay. This, I can deal with. I take a few shallow breaths and straighten my spine. This I can definitely handle. "Do your bosses know yet?"

He frowns. "Bosses?"

I stare at him. "At work?"

He shakes his head slightly. "This is not work, Star. This is my personal debt."

"A personal debt?" I ask. I feel confused and frightened suddenly, as if I am standing on shifting sand. "Why did you need a personal debt, Nigel?"

He doesn't answer me straight away. Instead, he stretches out a hand to cover mine.

"Nigel?"

He removes his hand, and my skin feels cold and empty. My mind goes blank as I watch him buy time by swallowing the last cold coffee dregs.

"I'm a gambler, Star. I owe four hundred and fifty thousand pounds."

Five

Star

https://www.youtube.com/watch?v=TR3Vdo5et
CQ
Don't Speak

His words don't even register. I shake my head. I can't have heard right. "What?"

"Oh, darling," he croons. "Don't look at me like that. You know I can't take it."

"What are you talking about, Nigel?" I ask slowly.

"I'm an addict. I'm addicted to gambling," he mutters.

"Gambling?" I repeat stupidly.

He nods, a pained expression on his face. "What? At work?"

"No." He exhales loudly. "In casinos."

I stare at him blankly. Nothing makes sense. We've been to a casino once. Two years ago. We sat together at a blackjack table. Nigel refused to play, but I did. He looked on with a slightly disapproving expression as I played three rounds and gleefully collected my winnings. Three hundred pounds. "But you don't even like gambling!"

He runs his fingers through his hair. "I like it too much."

"Since when?"

He shrugs. "Recently. It started off as just a little fun, small amounts, letting off some stress. You know the intense stress I'm under in the city."

"Stress?" I echo.

"You have no idea how much stress I have to cope with at work. It wrecks you."

"What? I begged you to leave your job, but you insisted that you thrived on the high-powered stress. Your exact words were, 'Thank God stress is not a woman, or I'd have to fuck her.' So don't you dare tell me that you started gambling because of the stress."

"Well, whatever the reason was, I started gambling, okay," he cries. "It's not really my fault. I was only gambling small amounts. Everything would have been fine if this stupid guy at work didn't tell me about a place where we could make a killing. That's where it all went wrong. I was so sure I'd get it all back. I was so close to winning, Star. You don't know how close. If only I could have had another chance ..."

"I don't believe this," I whisper to myself.

"I wanted to tell you."

I gaze into his eyes. There is a hint of recklessness in them. The ability to put everything on one throw of the dice. I wonder why I never noticed it before. "So why didn't you?"

"I was afraid. I didn't want you to love me less. I love you so much, Star."

"Who do we owe this money to?"

Something flashes in his eyes. "You don't owe anyone, Star. It's me and only me, who owes this debt."

"No, everything that happens to you, happens to us." My voice sounds louder, more secure. I can already feel my backbone straightening with steely determination to make it right. I'm like my Nan. When bad things happen, I pick myself up, dust myself off, and I'm ready to carry on with the journey. Yes, it's a setback to my lovely plans, but we'll work through it. We'll get professional help for Nigel to beat his addiction. We'll get back on our feet in time.

"We'll sell this house. There must be more than enough equity in it by now to cover that debt," I say.

He drops his eyes guiltily.

"What?"

"There's no equity in it," he says quietly.

"How can that be? We've had it for five years."

He looks at me beseechingly. "I remortgaged it."

"You remortgaged it without telling me?" I gasp.

He drops his eyes again and nods slowly.

"Christ, Nigel."

"I know. I know. I fucked up."

I just cannot believe what I am hearing. "What about our savings account? We still have that. Right?"

"No." His voice is so quiet it is a whisper.

My hand flies up to cover my mouth. "The apartment you bought for me in Spain?"

He screws his eyes shut. "Sold," he says in an anguished voice.

"How could you sell it? It was in my name?"

"I forged your signature," he admits, looking ashamed.

I press my palms to my temples. This can't be happening. Closing my eyes, I take slow breaths through my mouth. When I open my eyes, I will wake up from this nightmare. In, out. In, out. I lift my eyelids. My husband is staring at me with that I've-been-a-naughty-little-puppy-but-please-don't-scold-me-cause-that's-what-we-puppies-do expression. I feel sick. I should be angry, but I must be too shocked, because I don't feel anything.

He reaches out a hand and touches mine, and I feel that first flare of boiling rage. He refused to let me work because he said it was his job to take care of his woman, and look what he has done. I snatch my hand away.

"Jesus, Star. Don't pull away from me."

"What the hell did you expect from me after you tell me you've been living a life of deceit, and you've gambled away every last bit of wealth we had?"

"Maybe if I thought you would have reacted differently I would have told you about my problem sooner."

My eyes widen. "Are you trying to blame *me* for your gambling habit?" I explode incredulously.

"Of course not, but if you weren't such a paragon of virtue it might have been easier to confide in you."

I gasp at the unfair accusation.

"Do you know how difficult it is to confess an addiction to someone as blameless and perfect as you are? You have no vices, no weaknesses, no bad habits at all. You don't drink, you don't swear, you don't smoke, you don't gamble, you don't tell lies, fuck, you don't even watch porn."

I shake my head in disbelief. "You selfish bastard. How dare you blame me for being a good and loyal wife to you?"

He opens his mouth to argue and I raise my hand. "I don't want your money. You earned it. You want to blow it all away. Go ahead, but we were supposed to have a baby next year."

He starts as if he has completely forgotten that we've earmarked next year as the time we start our family. As if he doesn't know that I've already began to paint the little bedroom next to ours yellow.

"I gave up my independence because you said I'd want for nothing. You promised we could start a family next year. How could you do this to me?" I shout.

"I'm sorry, Star, I never meant to hurt you."

"Well, you have, Nigel. You've stuck a knife in my heart."

"Hell, Star. I know I messed up bad, but I'm trying to be straight with you now. You're right, I was a selfish bastard. You're too good for me. I know, I don't deserve you, but please. I don't want to argue with you. I don't blame you at all. You are the best thing that's ever happened to me. I want to tell you everything. No more lies. No more secrets. Please, Star. Everyone deserves a second chance."

I try to rein in my growing anger. Instead of recriminations I should be trying to help. We need to talk. To work this out. This is bigger than my hurt or anger. "Okay, let's talk."

"You have no idea how fucking sorry I am. I wanted to just end it all last night."

I take a deep breath. The shock of his words makes me feel almost light-headed. He actually thought about ending it all. Leaving me here to carry on without him. I look at him with new eyes. In a few minutes, my whole world has been turned inside out, everything I believed has been proved to be lies.

He looks back at me sadly. "But I knew that I would only be leaving you in a bigger mess because the money has to be paid back. One way or another."

"Who do you owe the money to, Nigel?" My voice sounds distant, calm, rational, even though I feel as if we are standing at the roof edge of a sky-scraper in high winds.

He pauses and clasps his hands so tightly, his knuckles become white. When he speaks, there is an odd expression in his eyes. "Nikolai Smirnov."

My brow furrows. "Who is he?"

His eyes narrow. "You don't know him?"

"Why would I know him?" I ask, confused.

His mouth turns down at the corners. It's a strangely sulky expression, and my brain notes it with surprise.

"You tell me," he says.

"Stop playing games, Nigel. What the hell are you talking about?" I ask, barely holding onto my temper.

"Maybe you know him by a different name? Russian, tall, at least six feet three or four. Broad, very fit—"

I shake my head impatiently and interrupt him. "I don't meet men. You know that. Why would you think I would know him, anyway?"

He makes a dismissive movement with his head. "Forget it. He's the owner of the gambling club I was telling you about before. I've met cold bastards before, but he fucking takes the cake."

My eyes widen. "Did he threaten you?"

His voice is bitter and a touch frightened "Yes, he wants his money. I told him I'd get it somehow. I just needed a bit of time, but he had his men grab me and hold me down on a smelly pool table. You don't know how terrified I was. He came close to breaking my hands with a fucking hammer."

At that strange, surreal moment, I feel no love in my heart for my husband. He seems like a stranger. Someone I never knew. Someone who just smashed my wonderful life into a thousand pieces. "Why didn't he, then?"

He looks down at the table and his hands become fists. "Because ..."

That coldness in my heart grows. "Because what, Nigel?"

30

Tears crawl down his cheeks. "Because he wants you."

Six

Star

His words don't make sense. My whole body feels like it is on fire. I'm an ordinary girl. I live an ordinary life. All of this is unbelievable stuff. Stuff of gangster movies.

"What?"

"He wants you," he repeats glumly.

"Me? What do you mean me?"

He covers his face. "Fuck, Star. Do I have to spell it out to you? He wants you ... your body."

I frown. "My body? Why would the owner of a gambling club want my body?"

"You don't need me to tell you why."

"But he doesn't know who I am. I could be a frumpy, middle-aged housewife for all he knows."

His brow furrows. "I'm beginning to think that someone is jealous of me. They know that the most important thing in my life is you, and the best way to destroy me is to get to you."

Nigel goes on talking, but I stop hearing him.

"He didn't use the hammer because you agreed to let him have me, didn't you?" I ask, my body crawling with revulsion.

"No," he denies, looking at me with wide eyes, and shaking his head vigorously.

"Oh, my God. You damn coward. That's what last night was all about, wasn't it? You thought you could manipulate me into selling my body to pay off your gambling debts."

Suddenly, the light goes out of his eyes. He just looks defeated. "No, Star. I meant it all. Every word I said. I'm not giving you away to anyone. I love you. He let me walk because I told him I would persuade you, but I have a different plan."

"What plan?" I spit. I don't believe him anymore. He's lied again so much I feel as if I've been married to a stranger.

He looks me in the eye. "Last night was me saying goodbye. My life insurance is worth one million. If I die in an accident tomorrow the mortgage on this house will be fully paid, and you will be the beneficiary of a million pounds. You'll be able to pay my debt off and still have half a million and some change in your bank account." He smiles.

I stare at him in utter disbelief. This is just becoming more and more surreal. "Are you completely mad?"

"Far from it. I want to make it right for you."

"You want to make it right by killing yourself, and leaving me a widow?"

He stares into my eyes. "This is the only way to save your father."

I feel that like a shot in my solar plexus. My dad. Oh, God. My dad.

"Remember, I always said I'd die for you. You always used to scoff that you'd have to see it

33

to believe it. Now you know that I meant every word."

"This is madness. I can't believe this."

"I haven't been a good man. I've been wrapped up in myself, my own needs and pleasure, but for the first time in my life I'm the one willingly making the sacrifice. I feel good about my decision. I'm putting you before me"

"No," I shout.

"There is no other option, Star."

I take a lungful of air. My chest feels too tight. "There is another option."

He shoots up so suddenly, his chair falls backwards, making me jump. He looks down at me, his eyes hard. "What kind of man do you think I am? As long as there's breath in my body I'll never let him have you. God, even the thought makes my skin crawl."

I stand up too, and words I never dreamed I would ever say, stream out of my mouth. "What kind of woman do you think I am? Do you think I'll let you die to pay a debt when all I have to do is spread my legs once?"

"Besides the fact that it wouldn't be just once, I couldn't live with myself if my wife had to pay my debts with her pure body. I might as well be dead if I allow you to do that."

I swallow hard. "How many times would it be?"

"For fuck's sake, Star."

"Answer me."

"Why? It's not an option. I'm not going to let you do it."

My fists clench. "Answer me, goddamn you," I scream.

He looks shocked. I've never raised my voice like that to him. "A month," he whispers.

"I'd just go to him every night for a month?" I say coldly.

He flinches. "You'll have to stay with him."

"Will anything be down in writing?"

He kicks the fallen chair. "There's a contract."

"Will it just be straight sex, or will ... there be other kinky things I'll have to do?"

"He let me look at the contract. Nothing will happen without your consent."

My legs suddenly feel like jelly and I flop back into the chair. I look up at him. "I'll do it."

He sits down and covers my shaking hand with his own. His hand is warm. "Please, Star. I don't want you to do this."

I get off my chair. I can't bear him touching me right now. I begin to pace the dining room. He doesn't move, he just sits with his head in his hands. I take deep breaths to calm my thoughts. If my Dad knew? I think of my father lying in hospital fighting for his life and just like that, my decision is made. I go back to the table and stand in front of Nigel. "We've got no savings so if you die, the insurance company needs at least a few months to issue a check, don't they?"

He nods.

"What happens to Dad until then?"

"Can't you ask your mother, or your sister to help?" His voice trembles.

I bite my lip and close my eyes so he will not see how much he has hurt me. *I won't let you down, Dad.*

"When do I need to go to his house?" I ask when I open my eyes.

He buries his face in his hands again. "I can't let you do this."

"It's tonight, isn't it?"

He nods brokenly.

"Contact him. Arrange for me to go there tonight. Make sure the contract is ready for me to sign."

He grabs my hand. "I can handle this. I just need a bit of time. I don't want you to do this for me."

"Rest easy, dear husband of mine. I'm not doing this for you. I'm doing it for my dad," I say coldly.

He flinches as if I have hit him. "I won't let you do this," he blurts out suddenly.

"You don't get to tell me what to do anymore. You lost that right when you deceived me and put us in this mess."

I snatch my hand away from him and stand up. Quick as lightning, he catches it again. "Where are you going?"

"I need to shower, Nigel." My voice sounds dead and flat.

"Look, I'm going to try and arrange a temporary loan."

I look at him with bitter eyes. "Don't bother. You'll just be jumping from the frying pan into the fire. Here's the deal. You will get on the phone right now and you will make an

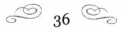

appointment to seek help with your addiction. Until you have been cured you will come straight back after work to this house every night. Do you understand?"

He nods.

I lean in closer. "What's more, if you visit another club, or place another bet again, do not expect me to be here for you."

He swallows and nods again.

"Good."

"I love you," he says softly, his eyes glistening with tears.

That stops me in my tracks. I have never seen Nigel cry. Not even when his mother died last year. "I love you too, Nigel, but you've really hurt me with this one. I never saw it coming. I feel as if I don't even know you."

He grabs my hand with both of his. "You know me. I am the man you fell in love with. I've just been a fool. I was lost. Now when I look back I can't believe I did what I did."

"It's okay. We'll work through this," I say dully.

"There has to be another way."

"The other way is both you and my father die."

"This is such a fucking mess. I'm sorry, Star. I'm so sorry."

"So am I," I say softly. The truth is I feel completely numb. I actually feel nothing. Not fear, sadness, horror, revulsion, not even anger. Maybe, I'm in shock, but everything feels unreal. Like a dream that I will wake up from.

"I don't care what I lose as long as I don't lose you," he cries.

I nod, too numb to care. Then I break away and go upstairs.

Seven

Star

https://www.youtube.com/watch?v=QH3Fx41J
pl4
(Sinnerman)

When I get out of the shower Nigel is waiting for me in the bedroom.

I walk past him without looking at him and go to my wardrobe.

"Star?"

I open my underwear drawer. "Have you called him?"

"No."

"I've got to pick up Nan now. I'll be back this afternoon. Please make that call by then."

"We need to talk," he says.

I let my towel drop and pull on my panties. "No, we don't."

"Our marriage ..."

"Shame you didn't think about it while you were happily gambling away everything we have," I spit.

He walks towards me. "Please, Star."

In the mirror, I see him standing behind me. His hand reaches out, and I watch

transfixed, as his fingers caress my breast. His hand is a few shades darker than my skin.

The image is erotic.

I carry on watching him. Surprised at how I feel absolutely nothing. He slides around to the front of me and latches his mouth onto my nipple. I look down at him suckling at my breast. Like a … vampire. He looks up and our eyes meet. The expression in my face makes him freeze. He pulls his mouth away and straightens.

"I'll be late," I tell him.

"I love you," he says.

"Yeah, you said." I side-step him and pick up the first pair of jeans my hands fall upon.

"I'm sorry. I am really, really sorry. If I could turn back the clock I'd do everything differently," he wails.

"Shame, then, that you can't turn back the clock."

"I'm going to find another way."

I look at him expressionlessly. "Like I said, I'll be home after lunch. Make sure you either have the four hundred and fifty thousand pounds ready to pay off your debt, or you've made an appointment for me to see the Russian this evening."

"You're pretty eager to give yourself to him," he says bitterly.

I turn around and slap him hard across the face. So hard his face jerks all the way to the side, and the palm of my hand stings. I look at the white imprint of my palm on his cheek. I have never hit anyone before.

"Get out," I snarl.

"I'm sorry. I shouldn't have said that."

"The longer you stand here the more respect I'm losing for you."

He holds his face and walks out of the room.

I get dressed and go downstairs. He comes out into the hallway. Totally ignoring him, I walk out of the front door. Once I'm outside, I feel the tears start stinging behind my eyes. I blink them back. No matter what happens Nan or Dad must never know. I get into my car and drive down to Nan's house. Grandad opens the door.

"What's up, Love?" he asks, patting my shoulder. "You look a bit pale."

"Nothing. I think I might be coming down with a cold. I don't feel that well."

"Is that Star?" Nan shouts from the bedroom.

"Who else would it be?" he shouts back.

"Come in. Come in," Grandad invites.

I walk through the hallway. "Nan, I'm not feeling too well. Is it okay if I get you a taxi? I'll go see Dad tomorrow."

"What's wrong with you, Love?"

"I must be coming down with something. Whatever it is, I definitely don't want to give it to Dad."

"No, no, definitely not. Sit down and I'll make you a cup of tea."

I smile weakly at her. "No, I won't stay. I think I'll just go back and get back in bed."

"You shouldn't have come around. You should have just called."

"I only started to feel bad in the car." It's partly true. The true enormity of the situation only started to hit home while I was driving over.

I take my phone out and call Uber and arrange for Nan's transport to the hospital. Then I get back into my car and drive to Hyde Park. I park in a place I shouldn't, but quite frankly, I don't care if I get a ticket.

It is a dull, overcast day, and rain is forecast, but I go into the park. Sitting down on an unoccupied bench, I google 'gambling addiction' on my cellphone. Over four million pages on the subject. I start clicking on the links and find out the most important thing to remember is not to lose faith if a loved one wants to overcome addiction.

That a support system is absolutely vital for the recovery process. It is a difficult road to travel, but the way to make the process easier and more successful is to recognize that it is actually an illness. A mental illness. I learn that addictions can change the way the brain functions. It skews perceived needs so that the addiction becomes the top priority, and that is what leads to the compulsive, uncontrollable behavior.

Apparently, there are millions of people who have a gambling addiction. Some to a lesser degree, but for some it is bad enough to wreck marriages and families.

I scroll down and read about other people's experiences. Wives who have left their husbands. Wives who have stayed and supported them through the hell. The main advice they all offer is to be a support system, but not to become the enabler.

The most important aspect of support is communicating in an open and honest way and creating boundaries, they say, by telling your loved one what you are and aren't willing to do. Being consistent in your expression of loving them and wanting to help. Replacing bad environments with good ones and changing routines. Joining a support group is highly recommended. Feelings of isolation can creep in so a support group is vital.

I close my phone and stare at some kids playing in the distance. I think of my yellow room with its painted daffodils. It was a stupid idea, anyway. A baby's room should be blue or pink. I'll repaint it in a month's time. Or maybe I'll wait until I know the sex of the baby. I think of myself walking by the Bonpoint store in Soho, a French label that makes gorgeously over-the-top clothes for children and babies. I had to fight the temptation to go in. But once I gave in and pushed open the door ... oh, it was a treasure trove of wonderful things.

Nikolai.

The name flashes into my mind. Who is this man? Why does he want to hurt Nigel so much that he would take his wife for a month? At the thought of someone wanting to hurt Nigel a deep sense of protective instinct for Nigel kicks in.

I remember the day he proposed. He hired the whole Café du Paris and filled it with can-can dancers that he had flown in from Paris. One of

the dancers came and called me up to the stage. I didn't know what was going on. Blood was pounding in my ears. Then the curtain of dancers parted and I saw him get on one knee.

I thought I would die with happiness.

Yeah, it was showy, but I was young and that was the happiest day of my life. Until my wedding day arrived, that is. Nothing will ever top that. We were both so excited about the future. Not even my parents' long faces could dim our happiness. How handsome he was standing in his blue morning suit.

When he turned to look at me, I almost fainted with happiness.

I stood in that small, sunlit church and promised for better or worse. Now Nigel is ill. An addiction is just as much a disease as cancer is.

I'll stand by Nigel as long as he wants to change. Other women have stood by their husbands and won the battle against this disease. If this Russian thinks he will destroy what I have with Nigel, he can think again.

My phone rings, startling me out of my thoughts.

Eight

Star

"**W**anna do breakfast?" Rosa, my best friend, asks. I've know her since we were in primary school, and she's always taken it upon herself to look out for me. She doesn't sound quite awake yet.

"Yes," I say automatically.

"What's up?"

"Nothing."

"Bullshit."

"What makes you so sure something's up?" I ask.

"Let's call it tone."

"I'll tell you when I see you."

"But you're all right?"

"Yes."

"Sure?" she insists.

"Sure."

"Lucianos?"

"Okay."

"Can you get there in twenty minutes?"

"I can get there in ten," I tell her.

"See you in ten, then."

As I park the car it starts pouring down with rain so I hold my bag over my head and run into the café. As I stand inside the doorway brushing my hands down my light jacket, I spot Rosa. You cannot miss her.

She is stick-thin with flaming red hair cut into a smooth bob. She is wearing scarlet lipstick and what looks like a lace trimmed camisole over a long-sleeved, fitting, dove-gray T-shirt. Must be the latest fashion, or what everybody will be wearing come autumn. Rosa works for a fashion magazine. She is one of those people who actually sits around a long glass table with a bunch of her colleagues and decides what will be the new look for the next season. A bangle glints on her arm. I walk up to her table.

"I like your top," I say as I reach her.

"I threw a T-shirt under my nightie so it wouldn't look like I just rolled out of some random dude's bed," she says as she stands and throws her skinny arms around me.

"Did you?" I ask.

"I should be so lucky," she says close to my ear.

The familiar spicy-rose notes of her Serge Luten's perfume fills my nostrils, and I don't want to let go of her thin body. Just being in her warm, scented embrace makes me want to bawl my eyes out. This morning I've had all my dreams crushed. I could stay in her arms a lot longer, but she pulls away, and eyes me warily.

"Out with it. What's eating you?"

With a sigh, I sink into the chair opposite hers. She reclines back, arms folded.

I hesitate.

"Spill the beans, Star," she prompts with her usual no-nonsense attitude.

"It's Nigel," I blurt out.

 46

"He's cheating on you, isn't he?" she snaps, leaning forward, her face livid.

"No. No it's not that."

She narrows her eyes, and looks ready to do battle on my behalf. "What's the crooked asshole done then?"

This is going to be harder than I thought. I fidget with the buckle on my bag. "He's in big trouble, Rosa."

A waitress comes to take our orders, but Rosa waves her away impatiently. "What kind of big trouble?"

I take a deep breath. "He's lost a lot of money."

"How much?" she asks curiously.

I clear my throat. "Four hundred and fifty thousand pounds."

She frowns. "That's nothing. Don't brokers routinely lose millions?"

"It's not his clients' money, Rosa. This is personal. He took a loan and he can't pay it back."

Her eyes bulge. "Christ," she swears. "You mean he didn't lose it at work. He actually owes it to someone?"

I nod miserably.

"Who the fuck would lend almost half-a-million to that useless husband of yours?"

"There's no need to be rude about him," I mumble.

She looks at me incredulously. "You're still defending that piece of shit?"

I know I shouldn't, but it's become a habit. Whenever Rosa and my family insult him I

47

instantly rush to his defense. Until this morning, I could do it without sounding like a fool. I look down at the table.

"Who does he owe the money to?" she asks again.

"I didn't catch his last name. Nikolai something ..."

"Nikolai? That's a Russian name."

I nod.

"So clueless Nigel owes some Russian guy four-hundred-and-fifty thousand pounds. Couldn't have happened to a more worthless man," she says heartlessly.

"It's not funny, Rosa. Nigel is really scared."

She looks at me without any compassion in her eyes. "Good. He should be. People get killed for much less."

As soon as Rosa mentions being killed, the seriousness of the situation sets like a lump of concrete in my chest. I've been so angry, shocked, and hurt that I didn't fully comprehend the situation: Nigel could have been killed last night. Goosebumps crawl over my body. I stare at Rosa with wide eyes.

"Why does Nigel owe the Russian?"

I clear my throat. "He lost the money gambling at his club."

Her eyes widen. "Nigel's a gambler?"

I nod.

She shakes her head in wonder. "He's like one of those vicious vegans who will shake their fist at you and call you a murderer for eating an egg, and then get up in the middle of the night to secretly feast on veal chops."

"He swears he only started gambling recently."

"Justify his behavior all you want, Star. He's a fucking fake."

I press my fingers into my temples. "Stop with all the snarky comments and quips, please. I can't handle it today, okay?"

She shrugs. "Quite frankly, I don't know why you're so cut up over this. Sure, half-a-million is a lot of money, but you guys have got five years worth of equity in your house. And Nigel does earn good money—"

"Nigel has re-mortgaged our house. There's no equity in it," I interrupt flatly.

This time her mouth drops open.

I swallow hard. "And he's emptied our savings account." I see the astonished fury building in her face and hurry on with the rest of my bad news. "He's even sold the apartment in Spain. We have no assets left to liquidate."

"I could cheerfully kill that bastard," she spits.

"So there is no money to pay the debt, and this man threatened Nigel with violence last night if he does not settle it immediately."

"Well, the solution to your problem is obvious. Just let the Russian beat the shit out of him," she suggests callously.

"There is another way the debt can get written off." I pause. I can barely let the words leave my mouth.

"Yeah? I'm all ears."

 49

"If ... if ... I go to him."

Rosa's eyebrows look like they could shoot completely off her face. "What the fuck? You can't be serious," she splutters.

I just stare at her dumbfounded face.

"Are you telling me that some Russian mobster is willing to write off a loan worth half-a-million in exchange for sex with you?"

"The deal is I have to stay with him for a month."

She leans forward, her eyes glittering. "Do you know this man?"

"No."

Her forehead furrows. "Does he even know what you look like?"

"No."

She leans back and exhales. "How strange. A man who can let one customer run a debt that massive can have all the pussy in the world he wants, why would he agree to an arrangement where he doesn't even know what the woman looks like. No offence, but you could be a frumpy old bag."

"It doesn't make sense to me either," I say slowly. "But Nigel thinks that someone is out to get him."

Her face twists with sarcasm. "Sorry, but how is it revenge on Nigel if you're the one being punished?"

"Don't you see this is their way of hurting him. Everyone knows the best way to hurt Nigel is to hurt me."

She rolls her eyes. "That's very subtle of Nigel's enemy. Still, someone should tell them

that Nigel is an opportunist. If you fell off the earth tomorrow, he would find a replacement the day after. The best way to hurt Nigel is to hurt Nigel. Not you."

"What other explanation can there be?"

"Coming to that conclusion based on what you've told me is like concluding that birds don't eat tigers; therefore, they must eat lions. There could be any number of reasons why you are part of this sick deal. I won't be in the least surprised if it was Nigel who offered you up to save his cowardly skin."

Nine

Star

I gasp. "That is low. Even for you, Rosa. Nigel is absolutely devastated. You would be shocked if I told you what his original plan to sort out this mess was."

Rosa folds her arms and looks at me steadily. "Be good enough to share his brilliant plan with me."

"He was going to arrange for an accident … for himself so that I could collect on his life insurance money."

Even saying the words is painful to me, but Rosa bursts out laughing. "And you believed him?"

The way she laughs makes me feel foolish, but I straighten my spine. Rosa can't be objective about Nigel. Until this morning, Nigel has always been good to me. "Yes, I did. You should have seen the state he was in this morning."

"I love you, Star, but honestly, when it comes to Nigel you are just unbelievably naive. I mean, if I hadn't met you before you got entangled with him, I would have written you off as an irredeemable bimbo. You think the sun shines out of his ass. Look at you. Defending him when he has proven without doubt that you cannot trust a single word that comes out of his corrupt mouth."

"I know you think I'm really stupid for the way I feel about Nigel, and I'm fine with that, but how you feel is not the issue here now. I have to do something. I can't let this man hurt him. He's still my husband, and I love him."

"Yes, I don't like him. In fact, I detest him. As far as I'm concerned Nigel is the best reason why I would never support any legislation that attempts to reduce the age of consent. Adults should never ever be allowed to have sex with children. It fucks their heads forever."

"I was not a child when Nigel met me," I can't help saying.

"Star," she says fiercely. "You were so damn innocent you hadn't even made out with a guy properly. He came along, and ruthlessly chased you, turning your head with his flashy car, expensive presents and bullshit. It was not enough that he had you, he then set about controlling you, and completely brainwashing you into his way of thinking."

"He doesn't control me," I say hotly.

"No? Hmm ... Let's see." It is obvious she has a list of accusations and she starts ticking the first one off on her thumb. "He didn't let you carry on studying."

"I didn't want to study."

"If you had been living at your dad's house, I know for a fact that you would have carried on with your studies."

I say nothing.

"He doesn't allow you to work."

"Only because I'd just be earning peanuts compared to what he earns," I defend.

"That should be your decision, not his."

"To be honest I agree with him. There's no point in me working as a clerk somewhere bringing home so little it won't even pay for a good pair of shoes," I say quietly.

"Yes, you'd be earning peanuts because he stopped you from getting a good qualification. Fine. Moving on. He doesn't let you go out at night without him."

"Yes, he does."

"He acts all moody and hurt if you do and makes it so unpleasant you'd rather not."

I stare at the table.

"He doesn't let you wear anything that reveals your cleavage, or your legs, or anything that shows off your shape."

"I don't like dressing too sexily, anyway."

"How would you know what you like? He decided it for you when you were sixteen years old." She raises her eyebrows in a waiting expression, but when I say nothing, carries on counting off on her fingers. "He vets your friends and doesn't allow you to have any men friends."

"I don't want men friends."

"The point is he wouldn't allow it even if you did. He just about tolerates your women friends."

"That's not true."

"Really? How many friends have you got, Star?"

I frown. "There's you and Cindy."

"Yeah, Cindy and me because we are as tenacious as pitbulls. Ask yourself why everybody else has dropped off?"

I shift in my chair. "What do you mean?"

"Did you know that Nigel makes little digs at us when you're not around."

I stare at her. "He does?"

"'Don't you have a home to go to?' he once asked me."

My jaw hangs open. I know Nigel doesn't really like Rosa, but I never imagined he would have been so rude to her. "Why didn't you tell me he said that?"

"That's because I understand your husband better than you do. I knew exactly what he was doing. He wanted me to run to you and complain. Then you would be forced to choose between him and me. And of course, being your husband you'll eventually have to choose him. Psychopaths like him are always trying to remove their victim's entire support system so I wouldn't give him the satisfaction. Cindy and I decided we'd play the waiting game. Men like him have no staying power. We knew the day would come when he'd find another impressionable teenager, or the scales would fall from your eyes, and you would need us."

I exhale. It seems I understood nothing of the world around me.

"Worse than anything else he's done, is the fact that he stopped you from pursuing your dream of being a writer."

"I still write," I say quickly.

"Yeah, secretly. When he's not at home."

"It's not because he disapproves or anything. He just doesn't want to share the time he has with me with my writing."

Ten

Star

"**S**hare you?" She throws her hands up in disgust. "This is what I mean by saying he's brainwashed you. He is an arch manipulator who doesn't care for anybody but himself. Nigel loves Nigel. Even now, it may appear to you as if you are making all the decisions, but believe me you're being played by him. He wants you to offer yourself up to pay his bill."

"You're wrong, Rosa. An addiction is a disease. Even though you can't see it, it is a real disease."

I watch her to see if there are any signs she is softening, but there are none.

"Yes, he's screwed up badly, but that's after seven wonderful years. I can't just walk away the first time something goes wrong. He deserves a second chance."

"Live in denial if it helps you. Nigel is no good."

I squeeze the metal buckle of my handbag until it hurts. "Nigel is truly sorry and he's promised me that he's going to get professional help."

Another waitress approaches us, and Rosa turns around and growls at her. "In your

professional opinion does it look to you like we're ready to order?"

The poor girl backs off with a shocked expression.

"Will you please calm down, Rosa. You're making a scene," I whisper.

"Just listen to yourself! He's a bloody liar. I don't believe he's going to change for one instant. You dig him out of this hole and he'll find himself back in another as soon as he can. Someone who started gambling recently doesn't lose this kind of big money. He's obviously been gambling for God knows how long!"

By now Rosa has become so agitated the table next to us can barely keep their focus on their food.

"Let's not do this now," I urge. My heart feels heavy. I am frightened. Afraid that I have been fooling myself. Afraid that she is right. Terrified that my father was right all along. And I'm not even allowing myself to think of what will happen when I meet the Russian.

"When are you going to face the truth, Star? Your husband has saddled you with his bullshit and you want to apologize for him and expect me to say nothing. What would you do if our positions were reversed?"

The couple at the next table stand up to leave. The woman swings by our table. "For what it's worth, I think your friend is right," she tells me.

I look up at her, surprised.

"If my husband had done that to me, I'd let the Russian break his gambling legs. That'll teach him a lesson," she says heartily, and moves away.

"So what are you going to do now?" Rosa asks.

"I'm going to go to the Russian tonight."

"Tonight?" she explodes. She's so shocked she almost jumps out of her chair. "You're as crazy as your husband."

"It may seem like I'm crazy, but I love my husband, Rosa. Whatever you might think of him, he has taken care of me, *good care* of me, for the last five years."

I feel myself begin to choke up and swallow hard.

"And as hard as it might be for you to believe Nigel really did try everything in his power to stop me from going tonight, but I have no choice. It's all very well saying he needs a good beating, but the truth is we have no savings or assets squirrelled away, and there is no equity in our house, so we need all the earnings that Nigel brings in. If Nigel doesn't bring in his paycheck I won't be able to keep my father in the hospital." As soon as I think of my father my eyes fill with tears and start rolling down my face.

Rosa deflates suddenly. She comes around to my side and hugs me tight. "I'm sorry, babe. I'm such an insensitive witch sometimes."

"It's okay. I know I'd probably say the same things to you if the shoe was on the other foot," I sniff.

She crouches down beside my chair. "Do you know anything about this guy? You can't just go in blind. He could be a sadist, or anything."

"He has drawn up a contract. Everything we do has to be consensual."

Something flashes in Rosa's eyes.

"What?"

"You won't like what I was thinking."

"Doesn't matter. Just say it, anyway."

"The Russian sounds more fair than your husband. What else do you know about him?"

"I only know what Nigel told me. He's six feet four and very fit."

Rosa sits back on her heels and stares at me.

"What?"

"Jesus, Star. You're going to have sex with a six-feet tall, very fit billionaire."

I frown. "And ..."

"That's my fucking ideal guy."

I blink. "Are you serious?"

She grins. "Of course, I am. You know what I always say. When a door closes God always leaves a window with a faulty hinge. Nigel is no good and this could well be Fate's way of getting you out of his clutches."

"I don't think that's funny, Rosa."

"I wasn't trying to be funny. Serves Nigel right that you'll finally get to spread your wings

60

somewhere else. Quite frankly, I'm beginning to think that this is the best thing that could have ever happened to you. Ever since you met that creep you've been walking around with blinkers on your eyes. This will be good for you. You're being forced to interact with a real man and you'll see Nigel as he really is. A lying, shallow, rotten to the core, self-obsessed Svengali."

"I'm afraid, Rosa," I whisper.

"Don't be, sweetie. Trust me. Something good will come out of this."

I bite my lip to stop it from trembling.

"Remember when I went to New York to work as an intern for Vogue and those bitchy women there who just hated my guts? The first time I made a mistake one of them fired me on the spot. Just like that. I ran to the washroom in tears. I thought my life was over."

She smiles at the memory.

"The woman cleaning the toilets was this big black mama. We'd just exchanged smiles until then. She asked me what was wrong and I told her I'd been fired. 'Lawwwd, Lawwwd. Folk crazy. Never you mind them stuck up hoes, child. You'll find another job,' she dismissed cheerfully. 'What if I end up homeless and living in the streets?' I wailed. And you know what she told me?"

"What?" I asked, intrigued, in spite of all my troubles.

"Well, I've never forgotten it. She said, 'And what an amazing adventure that will be.' Ever since then, I've learned to see everything new as a new adventure. Sometimes we are so comfortable in our little cages that someone has to come along, rip open the door and destroy the whole cage before we will look around us and realize that there is a whole world out there outside our little cage."

I stare at her. "You're serious? You think this is some sort of … opportunity?"

"Yes, I do. Anything that gets you away from Nigel's influence for even a brief time can only be good for you."

Outside, the sun starts shining through the clouds.

"I should go back," I say softly.

She stands and beckons to the waitress she growled at earlier. The girl comes towards us hesitantly. Rosa smiles at her. "We won't be eating today, but this is for you. I can be a right bitch sometimes, but my bark is worse than my bite," she says, and hands the girl a twenty-pound note.

The girl's eyes widen. "Thank you, very much," she says happily, and heads back to her station with a spring in her step.

I touch Rosa's hand. "I know I seem weak and naïve to you, but I truly do love Nigel."

"I know you think that, but I'm not sure what you feel for him is love. The sooner you realize it the better."

"I'm sorry Nigel was rude to you, Rosa."

"You're not responsible for that prick. Don't apologize on his behalf."

"I love you, Rosa."

"Me too. Never forget that I'm always here for you, okay?"

I nod.

"I want you to get the address of this guy and text it to me before you leave tonight. When you get there, I want you to send me a text and tell me that everything is all right. And if you need for anything. Anything at all. At any time, day or night. Just call me."

I nod again. Maybe this is all I wanted. To know that Rosa knows where I am. Rosa, whom I trust more than Nigel, to know exactly where I am if anything goes wrong.

Eleven

Star

When I get back home, Nigel is in the front room slumped on the sofa. The atmosphere is tense and strange, and there is an open bottle of whiskey on the coffee table.

"You switched your phone off," he says, standing up and coming to me. His hair is ruffled and his face is pale and stressed. I've never seen him look so unhappy and depressed. "Why?"

"I didn't want to speak to anybody." My voice is wooden.

"Where have you been?"

"Out," I say briefly.

There is a flash of something in his eyes. "Where?"

I want to say, none of your business, but I can't. This is my Nigel. My hero for so many years. Turns out my idol has feet of clay, but he is still my husband. "I met Rosa for coffee," I reply, as I brush past him to go upstairs.

"Did you tell her about me?" he asks in a strange tone.

I turn around to look at him, surprised that he'd even ask. "Yes."

"I bet she was delighted," he says bitterly.

"Why on earth would you think that?"

"Because that woman is insanely jealous of you. She has been ever since we hooked up."

For the first time since I met Nigel I look at him and I don't see my knight in shining armor, but a terribly flawed man. "What a strange idea. Rosa's not jealous of me at all. She has a wonderful life and if she had to exchange places with me she would go crazy with boredom."

He looks at me as if I have slapped him. "Are you bored?"

"No, I'm not bored. I'm, I was very happy, but Rosa wouldn't be if she had to live my life of hardly meeting anyone, hardly going anywhere except if it is out with you."

His eyes narrow. "She's already poisoned you."

I sigh. "I don't think Rosa is where your energy should be targeted right now."

"I'm sorry, Star. It's just that I don't like her. I never have. There's a nasty streak in her. You can say what you want, but you've got something she'll never have."

"What? You?" I ask, sarcastically.

"You're still mad at me," he accuses. Fumes of alcohol waft from his breath.

"Mad at you? Whatever would make you think that? No. I'm super happy with you, Nigel. Why wouldn't I be?"

"You don't have to do this, Star. I've been sitting here, lost. I can't bear the thought of that bastard touching you. Don't go, please," he pleads.

"Well you should have thought of the consequences of your actions while you were gambling away everything we had," I say sharply.

He reaches out to grab my hand. I yank mine quickly away.

"I know and I'm sorry. I never thought anything like this would happen."

"I'm not in the mood for this discussion, Nigel."

He looks guiltily at me and I want him to feel guilt. I want him to understand the enormity of the situation he has put us into. Rosa can call it an adventure, but I don't see it that way at all. My sweet little life, the one that I adored and would have been content living out for the rest of my life, is about to be changed forever. I feel fury in my stomach with Nigel for doing this. I quickly change the subject. "Have you spoken to the Russian?"

"Yes."

"What did he say?"

"He will send a car for you at seven."

I blink with shock. A car for me. As if I am a hooker.

"You don't have to do this," Nigel says softly. "I can figure something else out," he says, but this time I feel that there is a lack of conviction in his voice and I sense that it is only a lame attempt to discourage me from doing what we both know is the only real solution.

"How will this work? Do I pack a suitcase?"

"No," he says quickly. "You are to take nothing with you."

"What do you mean? What about my clothes and things?"

"Everything will be provided. The contract is very clear. You are to go tonight and take nothing with you."

"Where will I be living?"

"Windlesham."

"Where is that?"

"In Surrey. It's just over an hour from here."

"Will I see you during the month?"

"We'll figure something out. There is no way I can survive a whole month without seeing you at least a couple of times."

I nod.

"We'll speak on the phone all the time, okay?" he says reassuringly.

"Okay."

He touches my hand gently. "We'll make it through this, and we'll be stronger for it."

"Did you make the appointment for the out-patient clinic?"

"Of course I did."

"For when?"

"Tomorrow," he says, his eyes on the floor.

"You better be telling the truth, Nigel. Because I swear, if I ever find out that you're not

serious about your recovery, I'll walk away. No matter how much it hurts me, I'll walk away."

He grabs my hands with both of his. "I will change, I swear. I'll make you proud of me again, Star."

"I'm going up to lie down for a bit then change. Please don't follow me. I just need a bit of time on my own," I say, as I disengage from his grasp and start climbing the stairs.

"Your Nan called," he calls after me.

I stop and turn to look at him. His face is turned up, making him boyish.

"She asked how you were feeling. I told her you were lying down."

"Thanks."

"Your mother called too. She wants you to call her back."

I nod and start to turn away.

"You didn't tell her, did you?"

I shake my head. "What do you take me for, Nigel. The last person in the world I'm going to tell is my mother."

"Sorry. Sorry, of course you didn't. I'm just so confused, Star."

"Join the club,' I say, and run upstairs.

Twelve

Star

I lay down on our unmade bed and close my eyes. I didn't make it this morning so it has remained unmade. I think of Nigel opening my legs last night, and my stomach churns at the thought of giving my body to a complete stranger. I clench my hands and take a deep breath.

Then I dig my phone out of my bag and call my nan. I keep up the fiction that I'm not feeling well and she agrees to go see my dad alone tomorrow. In fact, she suggests that I take the whole weekend off. I thank her, then call my mother.

"Hi, Mum," I say quietly. I can hear the sound of a TV in the background.

"Nigel said you were not feeling very well. What's wrong with you?"

"Probably one of those flu things."

"Well, that's what you get for going to hospital every single day. Oh, for heaven's sake anyone would think that man was dying the way you keep running to his bedside."

"What did you want, Mum?"

"Can't I just call my daughter without wanting anything?" she huffs.

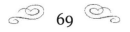

"Yeah, sure. How are you?"

"I'm fine."

"And David?" I ask, referring to the man she married two years ago.

"Yeah, he's fine too … um … I was wondering if I could borrow a couple of hundred pounds. I'll give it back at the end of the month. You know how it is. Ha, ha, of course, you don't with Nigel being so rich and everything."

I swallow hard. "I'll transfer the money Monday morning."

"Um … I would prefer if you could do an internet transfer this afternoon, sweetheart."

"Fine, I'll do it straightaway."

I look at my watch. It's getting late. "I've got to go, Mum. I'll speak to you soon."

I end the call, transfer the money out of my account into hers, and go into the bathroom. I stand in front of the mirror and stare at myself. How strange that I look exactly the same. None of the momentous upheavals going on inside me shows on my face. I turn on the shower, undress, and step inside the cubicle. The hot water doesn't wash away the feeling of grime and dirt.

I wrap a towel around me and go sit in front of my dresser. Wet blonde curls hang down to my shoulders. My mind is blank as I blow out my hair until it lies in soft waves around my face. I take off the towel and stare critically at my naked body in the mirror. No man other than my husband has seen me nude.

My body is not perfect. My breasts are too small and my thighs are thick and round. Nigel likes them, but what if the Russian finds them a turn off? Will all this be for nothing then? Will he send me away and expect the debt to be paid in another way?

A chill runs through me.

In a panic, I pull open a drawer and look through my lipsticks. I locate a deep red color. I hardly ever wear anything this rich. Nigel prefers me in peachy colors. I apply it to my lips and the change to my appearance is immediate. My mouth looks big and inviting. I swipe two layers of mascara. That makes an even bigger improvement.

I go towards my wardrobe and glance at my clothes anxiously. I own nothing sexy. I pull my black dress out. It is not revealing, but it is sophisticated. Perhaps a billionaire will think it is old-fashioned.

I slip into my dressing gown and go downstairs. I am barefoot so I make no noise as I go down the stairs and cross the hallway into the living room. Nigel is sitting on the sofa with his head in his hands. I feel my heart tug. It's a disease. I have to keep reminding myself of that fact.

"Nigel?"

His head jerks up.

"What if I go there and he decides he doesn't want me? What happens then?"

"Then the debt gets paid anyway."

71

"But I thought we had to sign a contract first."

"He's already signed and couriered his contract over to us. He can't back out anymore."

"Oh! You didn't tell me he sent the contract over."

He makes a vague movement towards the writing table. "It's there. I'm not worried about his stupid contract, Star. My heart's breaking. You're going off to be with another man. You're mine. My baby. You don't know what it's like to be sitting here while you get ready to go to him. Knowing it's my fault. My stupidity. My greed. My carelessness. What was I thinking? God! What a fucking fool I've been."

My heart feels like an ice splinter in my chest. I take a deep breath. I want to run to him, wrap my hands around him and comfort him, but I don't. I don't want to make it easy for him. I don't want to be the enabler who tells him that I'll always be here to pay his debts off with my body.

"What's the time now?" I ask.

He looks at his watch and flinches. "Half-five."

"I guess I better finish getting ready," I say turning away.

"You're wearing red lipstick," he calls.

I lift my chin and turn around. "And what of it?"

"Nothing. You don't wear it for me."

"You don't like red lipstick."

His forehead burrows. "I love it. I just didn't want other men to see you wearing it. I would have loved you to wear it for me when we were alone at home. Remember when you used to cook and I would make the cocktails. We'd eat and drink and I'd make love to you in front of the fire ... Sometimes you'd get so drunk I would have to carry you upstairs."

The old magic of him weaves itself around me. "Maybe I'll wear it when we are alone again," I say softly.

He smiles sadly. "Yes, I'd like that very much."

I stare at him. He walks towards me and wraps his arms around me. I stand stiffly in his embrace. He pulls back and looks at me. "I love you, Star," he whispers fiercely.

Suddenly, I can take it no more, and I break away from his hold and race up the stairs.

Nobody knows what I have with Nigel. Nobody outside our relationship can understand. I rush to the mirror and scrub away the red lipstick. I scrub so hard my lips feel raw. Then I clean off the mascara. There are two twin spots of color on my face.

I won't make it easy for the Russian.

I'll make him regret the day he thought he could ruin my relationship with my husband. Yes, my husband has a disease, but people like him make it worse. He had no business letting Nigel run up such a big debt.

A thought enters my head. Yes, I will show Nikolai whatever his last name is the unvarnished version of me. Let's see how much he still wants Nigel's unglamorous wife. I will arrive not as a whore who has been chosen to be the dish of the day, but as the hired help. Maybe, he will find me so unpalatable, he will reject me.

Then I will return and Nigel and I will work through this sorry mess together. There is so much work that needs to be done. So much trust needs to be restored, but if we both truly care for each other we'll make it work.

The knots in my stomach begin to loosen and I pull out a pair of baggy blue jeans and an oversized patterned shirt. I match it with a pair of worn trainers I use for gardening I find in a bottom drawer. Then, I spray my hair with water, so that it becomes a curly mess again. Haphazardly, I scrape my hair back and snap a band around it. Even if I say so myself, I look pretty unappealing.

I smile with satisfaction.

Let's see how he feels when he sees this package standing in front of him. I stuff some cash in my bag together with a strip of my contraceptives, my toothbrush, my cellphone and its charger, and I go back downstairs.

Nigel is hanging around the hallway and his eyes widen when he sees me. He strides towards me and grabs my upper-arms with both his hands.

"I swear on the lives of our unborn children, that as long as I live I will never gamble again."

"Don't swear on our children," I scold automatically.

"May I rot in hell if I break this promise to you."

I stare into his eyes and I see nothing but determination to beat this disease. "I believe you," I whisper.

"Thank you. I'll never let you down again, Star. Never. You're my wife and my life."

"Is it time?"

"The car is waiting outside."

I take a deep breath.

"Can I kiss you goodbye?"

I swallow. What has this world come to when my own husband has to ask if he can kiss me? I nod.

He bends his face and takes my lips. The kiss is gentle and sweet and I feel myself start to cling to him. I don't want to leave him. He breaks the kiss and looks into my eyes. "They think they can break us. They can never. You are mine. You will always be mine."

"Take care of yourself, Nigel," I say, then I walk swiftly to the front door.

"I'll call you," he says as I open the door.

My throat is so tight I am unable to answer him. I pull the door shut behind me. There is a black limo waiting on the street. As I take a shuddering breath, a man in a chauffeur's uniform steps out of the car and walks to the passenger door. He opens it and stands next to it. He doesn't look at me. Just stands there respectfully.

A weird sensation overtakes my body.

Nothing will be the same again. I turn back and look at my closed front door. For a second I want to open it and run back into Nigel's arms, back into my enchanted house, where I have felt so safe, so loved, and protected. Then I steel myself, and walk down the pathway to the waiting car.

Thirteen

Star

https://www.youtube.com/watch?v=ETxmCCs
MoD0
(Money, Money)

The chauffeur nods and waits while I slide into the seat. Soft classical music is playing and the car smells of expensive perfume. The door closes, and the man walks around to his side of the car.

I turn my head to look at the windows of my house. At the living room window, I see Nigel standing there staring at me. There is something so lost and forlorn about the defeated droop to his shoulders that I bleed inside.

The driver gets into his seat and the car starts to move. I stare out of the window seeing nothing. All I can think of is Nigel standing at the window. As the car leaves Earls Court and takes the M4 out of London, I start to pay attention. We make steady progress until the car smoothly joins the M25. There is more traffic here, but less than twenty minutes later we take the slip road out of the motorway. After a little while, I see signposts for Virginia Water, Surrey.

I've been there once. One of Nigel's friends lives on the Wentworth estate.

We pass the estate and keep on the main road until there is a sign for Windlesham. Less than a mile later we turn off into a tree-lined road. There are large houses on either side of it. The road takes another turn and we come upon two large stone pillars with lions on the top. The name of the house is craved into stone. I take my cellphone out and text Rosa.

Knightsbrook Manor,

Windlesham

Rosa's reply is instant: **Jesus, I know that place. It's a fucking palace.**

The car comes to a stop in front of the tall black gates. Video cameras swivel in our direction. The driver does nothing and after a few seconds the gates swing open noiselessly. The car starts up again.

The driveway is long and curves though land dotted by glorious, old trees. The trunks are so thick it will take two or maybe three of me to embrace them.

We travel at least one kilometer before I see the stately mansion set on elevated ground. The last rays of summer sun fall on it, giving the white stones a beautiful reddish glow. The effect is one of unbelievable majesty and splendor.

My stomach is now doing cartwheels. A strange mix of fear and anticipation. Who the hell lives in a place like this and gets into the kind of arrangement that includes an unseen woman? Why would such a man need or even want to hurt a small fry like Nigel?

We follow the road as it turns around in a semi-circle up to the frontage of the house. Wide, stone steps lead up to enormous double doors adorned on each side by beautiful topiary. I find myself awestruck by the extraordinary beauty and majesty of the house.

The car comes to a halt, and I touch my stomach nervously. It is fluttering with anxiety and tension. The driver comes around to my side and opens my door. I slide out and thank him.

"You are expected," he says formally with a solemn nod.

I begin to climb the steps. Before I reach the top, a large broad man with a head the size of a football, and almost no neck, comes out of the doors, and stands with his arms folded. His unfriendly, wary eyes make me feel uncomfortable.

I reach the entrance, and he looks at my purse and says, "Do you mind? It's just protocol."

I hand him my purse silently and he rifles through it quickly. Satisfied there is nothing there that could be a danger, he returns it to me, and steps back to allow me to enter.

Inside, I stop and stare in amazement.

The hallway is bigger than my whole house and the kind of wealth on display is astounding. It is like I have entered onto a film set in another period, a time gone by when Lords and Ladies rode in carriages and ruled the land.

Pillars soar up to a Sistine Chapel type scene with half-nude muscular men and Rubenesque women; winged cherubs, and a horned demon or two. The floor, an intricate pattern of stone tiles, has been polished to such a high shine I can practically see my own reflection. The wide central staircase is made of white marble with intricately wrought balustrades. It has a red runner carpet on it that looks so pristine it makes me wonder about how many times a day it is cleaned. The walls are full of tall paintings, and higher up there are stained glass windows with elaborate designs. This is not a home. No one could curl up with a good book and a cup of hot chocolate here.

Mr. Muscle clears his throat pointedly to get my attention.

When I turn my dazed gaze towards him, he jerks his head sideways at me, to indicate that I should follow him. I nod and he starts swiftly marching towards a pair of duck-egg blue double doors. Our steps echo in the vast space.

He opens the doors and we enter an elegant, many-windowed drawing room. It has fine carpets, antique furniture, and stunning period designer wallpaper. It smells of lavender polish. My eyes glance around the numerous beautiful paintings adorning the walls.

"Take a seat," Mr. Muscle barks from the side of me, and I jump. His tone is that of a Sergeant major instructing one of his recruits. I think it would be safe to assume from his walk and his voice that he must be some type of ex-military guy. I take a seat on the brocade covered settee closest to me. He leaves the room without another word. His footsteps die away in the hallway outside.

Alone in the vast room, I gaze at the paintings. Unlike other fine houses that display the ancestors of the current owners, all the paintings are modern works of art. One painting, the main one, positioned above the fireplace, and artfully lit up, catches my attention.

I rise from my chair as if in a trance and walk towards it. It is of a child, a well-dressed, blond boy sitting on a chair. There is something strange about his face. I walk closer to him. His face is dirt streaked, his enormous green eyes dare me to pity him.

I glance at the name of the painter embossed into a piece of metal on the gilded frame. It is a Russian name I do not recognize. Why would a man who owns all this splendor have a painting of such pain? My curiosity for the Russian increases. Instinctively I sense I've just had a glimpse of a complicated personality.

I'm so engrossed by the painting I do not hear the footsteps heading towards the door.

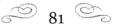 81

Suddenly the door opens. My stomach tightens. I do not turn around instantly. Instead, I take a deep breath.

"Hello, Star," a man's deep voice says. There is supreme indifference in his voice.

A vague recognition flashes inside me. I look at the face of the boy in the painting for another second, then I turn around, and my eyes widen in shock.

"You," I gasp.

Fourteen

Star

Three Weeks Previously

"**Y**ou are the most beautiful woman in this room, Star," Nigel says, looking into my eyes.

"Oh yeah? And that brunette I saw you looking at just now?" I tease.

"What brunette?" he asks innocently. The candlelight falls on his cheeks making him look even more irresistible than he normally does.

I lift my wine glass and take a small sip. "Look. I really don't mind if you look at a beautiful girl. I would look at a beautiful man too. There's no harm." I grin. "Looking at the flowers in other people's gardens is allowed. You just can't pick them."

"You would look at a beautiful man?" Nigel asks. He is still smiling, but there is a slight tension in his jaw.

I shrug. "Just the same way I would look at a beautiful piece of art. I wouldn't want to take it home with me."

"But if you're looking at a man, you must be thinking sexual thoughts about him," he insists. I can see that he is getting a bit annoyed.

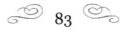

I look deep into his eyes. "I swear that from the day I met you I have never had a sexual thought about any other man. Not one. Ever."

He grins happily. "Good. That's the way it should be."

"Bet you can't say the same," I challenge. I know men are different than women. They have sexual thoughts all the time about random women they meet on the street. I once read in a magazine that men will pass a woman in the street and get a hard-on thinking about having sex with her. Incredible!

"Believe it or not, I haven't thought of another woman like that since you seduced me at that party."

"I didn't seduce you," I protest. "You came on to me."

"Only after you batted your eyelashes outrageously at me."

"I did not," I say with a laugh.

He reaches for my hand. "No, you didn't. That's why I liked you. You were so innocent you blushed when I came up to you." He pauses. "Look at you. You're blushing now."

A waitress comes to our table. "Would you like to have a look at our dessert menu?"

Nigel doesn't let go of my hand. "No, I'm having my wife for dessert," he says.

"Nigel," I gasp, and look up apologetically at the waitress.

She smiles politely. "How about some coffee then?"

 84

"Nothing for me and a black coffee for my wife," Nigel orders.

The waitress moves away.

"Why do you do that?" I scold. "It's embarrassing for me and her."

"Why should either of you be embarrassed? It's the truth. I'm having you for dessert."

"There is no hope for you," I say.

He grins and looks at his watch. "I have to make a quick call to New York. Can you amuse yourself for ten minutes?"

I smile. "I have to go to the Ladies, anyway."

"Good girl," he says, and leaves the table.

I stand up and start to walk in the opposite direction he went. As I get to the corridor that leads to the toilets I turn back to see if I can still see Nigel and suddenly I slam into a wall. My head snaps back and I nearly die.

It's not a wall.

It's a tall, broad man with raven black hair, an arrogant mouth, sensual lips, and a square jaw. His clothes are expensive and yet his shirt is unbuttoned casually. His throat is brown. His shoes are immaculate.

He is beautiful, not the way a male model is, but the way a sleek, shining panther stalking its prey is. His hooded silvery-gray eyes look down at me without any expression in their depths. There is something cruel and indifferent in his mesmerizing eyes.

His presence is so powerful that I feel a shiver go right through me. He stares down at me with those strangely impassive eyes. Eyes that should belong to a predator cat. I stare back unable to look away. Something alive and electric sizzles between us.

My lips part to apologize, but I am so shocked by him, no words come out. My tongue comes out to lick my dry lips, and his eyes drop to my mouth. My knees feel as if they will not support me. I realize then that his hands are curled around my upper-arms. What the hell am I doing? I should break away.

"Sorry, I wasn't looking where I was going," I whisper.

"No problem," he says, his voice deep and velvety, and supremely indifferent. He is foreign.

His hands leave my upper-arms. He steps away from my body and the strangest thing happens. My body misses him. The way it has never missed Nigel. The desire for him is so strong, my hands claw: I want to reach out and press my body into his. I want him inside me.

He nods distantly, and walks away.

For a few seconds, I can do nothing. Shaken to my core, I draw deep, even breaths. Then, I take a step towards the Ladies. In that briefest of encounters, I have learned something about myself. I am not as pure as I imagined. Nigel is not as safe as he would like to believe.

My resistance is nothing more than a house perched at the edge of the cliff top. One bad

storm and the raging sea will tear my house to smithereens.

Fifteen

Nikolai

https://www.youtube.com/watch?v=mWO
Tdt9Bovk
Me And Mrs Jones

She stares at me in shock, her beautiful eyes wide, her mouth parted, and a river of primitive possessiveness rushes through my veins. *I've got her. She's mine now.*

"Did you ... are you Nikolai?" she gasps.

"If he's not me, then he's one lucky bastard," I say.

Her mouth snaps shut and she squares her shoulders.

"Would you like a drink?" I ask.

"No thank you," she says stiffly.

I smile and walk to the liquor cabinet.

"Sorry, but can we please get on with this?" she shoots. Her eyes are combative. She wants to take control of a situation where she knows she has none.

"We already have. You are here under my roof, are you not?"

Her eyes regard me with hostility. "Why did you bring me here?"

"I wanted you," I say simply, watching her.

 88

Her dowdy appearance cannot disguise her unique beauty. Her long golden hair tightly pulled back only serves to highlight her flawless skin. Even in this most intimidating scenario her eyes sparkle like brilliantly cut blue diamonds as she calculates her situation.

"And if you want something you just reach out and take it." Her voice drips with scorn.

"That's the general idea, yes."

"Even if that person is already married?"

"That does complicate things a little, but where there is a will there is always a way."

"So you'd have a woman who doesn't want you," she asks derisively.

I place a short glass tumbler on the polished wood of the bar and look up at her. "Are you trying to imply that you don't want me?"

Her face floods with pretty color. She's as delightful as a butterfly. "Did you somehow get the impression that I do?" she asks.

"Yes, I got the impression you wanted to be in my bed."

Her eyes widen. "Is that why you went to all this trouble to get me here?"

I hide a smile. "Yes."

She shakes her head, her forehead creased in a frown. "I'm so sorry. There has been a terrible misunderstanding. I don't want to be in your bed. Not at all. I'm very much married. I love my husband with all my heart, and he is the only man I want."

Her words infuriate me, but I smile politely. "Prove it."

She frowns. "What do you mean?"

I lift a shoulder casually. "Show me how much you don't want me."

She folds her hands in front of her. "Tell me how to and I'll do it."

"Come over here and kiss me," said the spider to the fly.

She recoils, actually recoils as if I really am a spider. Her back becomes ramrod straight, and when she speaks her voice is hard and violent with anger. "I was given the impression that everything had to be consensual."

I nod. "That's a pretty accurate impression."

Her shoulders almost sag with the relief that pours through her system. She takes a deep breath and prepares for a battle that she has already lost. "So I evoke my right to say no to such a repulsive request."

I lift the crystal stopper off the decanter, and pour myself a glass of cognac. "Are you sure I couldn't interest you in a glass of something?"

She shakes her head.

I lift the glass to my lips and take a sip. "So: let's see if I've got this right. Basically: your spineless husband has taken nearly half a million of my money and can't pay it back. Out of the goodness of my heart I told him he could lend you to me for a month in exchange. It seemed like a good idea to him. You obviously agreed. I drew up a contract and he promptly sent you to me, but now that you are here, you have decided not to ... perform."

She swallows hard. It sounds bad put like that. "I'm just playing by the rules of the contract you wrote," she croaks.

"Perhaps I expected more ... fair play from you."

"You expected fair play from me after you concocted such a sordid and unfair arrangement?"

"We all have our illusions," I say mildly.

She looks at me warily. "We have an impasse. What now?"

I shrug. "I guess, you can go home."

Her eyes widen. "Really?"

"Of course. I never say what I don't mean."

For a second she looks dumbfounded, then she starts babbling. "Oh, thank you. Thank you very much. I ... I'm so sorry if I gave you the wrong impression at the restaurant. It was never my intention."

I take another sip. "No problem."

"Also I didn't mean it when I said kissing you would be repulsive."

"No?" The sound comes from deep inside my chest.

"No, of course not. I was just nervous. You're not repulsive at all. In fact, you're a very good looking man."

"That's good to know."

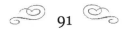

"Well." An unnatural laugh erupts from her mouth. "Well, I suppose, I better call a cab."

"No need. My driver can take you back," I tell her smoothly.

"Oh, that would be really kind of you. I'm really sorry that Nigel lost all that money in your club."

"Hmmm." Every time I hear his name come from her lips I want to smash something.

"Don't worry," she assures, her eyes huge, "he won't ever be back there again. I'll make sure of that. He's going to go into treatment. Gambling is an addiction, you know."

I watch her force herself to stop talking.

"Well, I guess, I better go look for your driver. I know the way out so I'll just … Once again, thank you. I'm really grateful to you." She starts moving towards the door. "Goodbye, Mr. Smirnov."

"Goodbye, Star. Don't forget to tell Nigel to be careful."

She stops in her tracks and turns around slowly. "What's that supposed to mean?"

I walk across the long drawing room to a window at the far end and gaze out of it. One of the gardeners is tending to the hedges in the distance. They do a good job those men. I make my voice sound disinterested. "Well, obviously, I'll have to sell his debt on, and there is no telling how the buyer of the debt will decide to collect."

"You bastard," she snarls. "You did this on purpose."

I turn around and raise an eyebrow. "Did what?"

Her eyes glitter with hatred. I stare at her, surprised. She is even more beautiful than I thought, and something feral jerks inside me. I can't wait to make her submit to me. Tame her. Make her beg.

Make her mine.

"You made me believe that you were going to let me go," she accuses.

My gaze is steady. "I'm not stopping you. You're free to leave."

"How can I leave if you are going to sell the debt to another criminal?" she cries.

"I told you, Star. To completely cancel the contract and wipe out the debt you only have to do one thing."

"What's that?" she demands.

"All you have to do is prove that you don't want me."

"Don't want you? Does it look like I want you?"

"Prove it by kissing me."

"I hate you."

"Be careful, Star."

"Why?"

"Because of what's on the other side of the coin."

"Love?" She laughs harshly. "To start with I could never ever love someone like you. But even that is beside the point because I already love someone. My husband!"

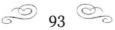 93

"That's okay, little butterfly. I don't want your love. All I need from you is your lust."

"Are you deaf? I don't want you."

"So grit your teeth and kiss me, and you can return to the man you claim to love so much."

"How about I detest you so much it would make me sick to kiss you."

"So leave and let Nigel take his chances with another moneylender. See if he will be kinder. Perhaps you can grace his bed instead?"

She stands there glaring at me, her chest heaving.

I put my glass down. "Well, what's it to be? A kiss? Leave Nigel to the wolves? Or submit sexually to me for a month?"

She stands there shaking with emotion. "What? Just one kiss?"

"One kiss."

Sixteen

Star

His eyes betraying nothing but indifference. *Yes, I'd like to use your body for a month, but it wouldn't bother me too much whether you stayed or went.*

But my hands are shaking with terror.

Not fear of him, but of my own unnatural desire for him. It's the kind of craving I've never known before. Until now I never suspected there could be such a need for another human being. A stranger.

Of course, I love Nigel. I love him deeply. My love for him feels as warm and comfortable as an old blanket. Makes me safe. I know I can trust that love to last until I am grey and wrinkled.

What I feel for this cold-eyed monster is raw and dangerous. Even from where I am standing I can feel the waves of sexual tension coming from him. Like heat from the Mediterranean sun. Heating up my blood. Making me feel hot and strange.

One kiss?

I'm already hanging on to the edge of the cliff by my fingernails. Barely able to sustain the pretense that I find him repulsive. If I kiss him I

will tumble away into the dark abyss waiting below, and everything will be lost. Everything. My plans. My lovely house. My garden. My birds. My yellow room. The stack of little romper suits with the shop tags still attached to them. I cannot sacrifice all that for this blind lust. I just cannot. The lust will die away, and I will be left with nothing.

I will have children with Nigel.

I will grow old with him.

I will not give that up for this worthless pleasure. Never.

I walk towards Nikolai and look him in the eye. "I will not kiss you. You are not my lover. You bought the use of my body for a month, and that's all you'll get from me."

"I accept," he says quietly.

My belly clenches with excitement. Have I just made my deal with the devil? I lift my chin proudly. "Now what?"

A slight movement twists those sensuous lips. I think of them on my body and I have to suppress a shiver of need.

"Now, we eat. I'm hungry."

"Well, I'm not hungry," I say, even though I've not eaten all day.

"Then you can watch me eat," he suggests coolly. His startling light eyes remain aloof and completely expressionless.

Unable to think of a single thing to say in reply I stare at his mouth.

"Perhaps you'd like to change first?"

 96

"I won't bother."

He takes his cell out of his suit pocket, touches a couple of buttons on it, and says, "Send Celine in." He drops his phone back into his pocket. "Celine will take you to your room, show you how everything works, and help you to choose an outfit."

"I said, I didn't want to change for dinner," I say tightly.

His eyes gleam with a glimpse of something savage, but his voice is pleasant. "I think you'll find that we will get on much better if whilst you are here you remember never to question, or deny my wishes."

There is a soft knock on the door.

"Come in," he calls, not taking his eyes off me.

I drag my gaze away. A woman about my age is standing at the doorway. She smiles deferentially at us.

"Show Miss Minton to her room, please," he says without taking his eyes off me.

Three impressions hit me at once. The weirdness of being called Miss Minton after five years of being Mrs. Harrington. The feeling of unease that someone you did not even know existed until a few hours ago knows so much about you. And the irritation that he wouldn't acknowledge my marital status.

"Of course, Mr. Smirnov," Celine says immediately.

I force my legs to move and start walking towards her. My gait is wooden and stiff. She smiles politely at me, and I realize that it would have been awkward if he had introduced me as a married woman when it must be obvious that I am here as some sort of temporary mistress. I leave the room without looking back.

"Since we haven't been formally introduced, I'm Celine Bradford, and I'll be your personal assistant during your stay here."

"Nice to meet you, Miss Bradford." We start walking up the grand marble staircase.

"Please, call me Celine," she says immediately.

"All right. Then you must call me, Star."

"I love your name."

"Thank you."

When we reach the top, she waves her palm out to the left of us. "It's just this way." The corridor is wide, with a carpet running down the middle of it. There are many doors leading off it. My room is the first one.

She opens it, and oh, my goodness me, it is like something out of a storybook. The wallpaper depicts climbing roses. One wall is taken up by a massive, dark-wood, four-poster with a dusky rose canopy. There is a gorgeous armoire with painted panels and a cream antique day bed. Tall doors lead off to a balcony.

Celine goes ahead of me and opens the armoire. It has a few items of clothing hanging inside it. She turns to me. "They are all in your

size. After you choose something, I'll help you with your hair." She smiles. "I'm actually a trained hairdresser."

"Oh! Have you worked here long?"

"No. I was hired last week to assist you."

My eyes widen with shock. Wow! He hired someone especially for me. And the confidence! He was so sure I'd come. "What are you supposed to do for me?" I ask softly.

"I can turn my hand to almost anything. I can help with your hair, press your clothes, bring you breakfast in bed, take instructions for special meals, run general errands like getting your favorite magazines, or driving into the village for anything you need. Whatever that makes your stay here more comfortable and pleasant, I guess."

"I see."

I walk over to a window and look out. My room is front facing and opens out to a balcony that stretches along the main part of the house. Elegant stone balustrades edge it. From where I am standing I can look down and see the cars on the gravel car park, the long winding driveway, and a view of the wonderful ancient trees dotting the grounds.

"Would you like to pick out a dress for tonight?" Celine asks, breaking into my thoughts.

I turn around, and she smiles brightly.

"I guess so," I say dully.

"Great," she says enthusiastically with another big smile. It is clear she is trying very hard to please me and I start to feel slightly sorry for her. She is just trying to do her job.

I walk towards her and decide that I will not make her life difficult. None of this is her fault.

Seventeen

Star

Standing next to Celine, I rifle through the small collection of outfits.

There are seven items, and I can tell even without looking at the labels that they are all uber expensive. It is also quickly apparent that they are all extremely sexy. A mix of plunging necklines, backless designs, daring slits.

There is a beautiful silver mini dress that Rosa would love, and a clinging, silk pantsuit I wouldn't be caught dead in, but there is also a long, black dress with a deep-plunge, wraparound halterneck.

"Great choice. Very classy," Celine approves.

I undress quickly.

"You won't be able to wear a bra with this.

I ditch my bra, and pull the daring dress up over me. Celine ties it at the back of my neck, then comes around the front to stand a couple of feet in front of me.

"It suits you perfectly," she says with a satisfied nod.

Then, she crouches down on the floor, and pulls out a shoe box from the bottom of the armoire. "How about these Jimmy Choos to go

101

with your dress, hmmm?" she asks, lifting up a beautiful pair of gold textured lamé sandals trimmed with sleek, black leather. The heels are at least four inches high.

"Okay," I approve.

She puts them on the ground, and I slip my feet one at a time under the cross-over straps while she fastens the ankle buckles. They fit perfectly. I don't ask her why they do. I just file it away as information that needs clarification.

She stands up and grins. "That was easy. Now, how would you like to wear your hair?"

I shrug. "Whatever you think is best."

"I would suggest something plain and Grecian."

"Fine."

I sit on the bed while Celine does my hair. She works quickly, fluffing it, braiding it, and adding a gold-leaf comb on one side.

She stands back and eyes me critically. "I think we'll keep the look plain. Maybe just red lipstick and black eyeliner?"

I shrug again.

I can't help feeling I've lost control of the situation. I feel like a doll, or one of those courtesans in the olden days. The way they used to be dressed by servants and made up before they were taken to the King to be deflowered. Celine opens packets of cosmetics and paints my eyes and lips.

"All done. Come and have a look," she invites.

I walk over to the mirror in a daze. My first reaction is to gasp. That's not me. I've never done my hair like that, and I can't remember the last time I painted my eyes like that or wore such a deep red on my lips. Worse, there is so much of me on display, as the neckline ends almost at my belly button. I take a step closer and I actually sway, as if I'm dizzy or drunk.

"I think you look beautiful," Celine says.

I catch her eyes in the mirror. "You don't think it's a bit slutty?"

Her eyes widen. "No, I don't. Not at all. You look incredible. I promise you, Mr. Smirnov will be very pleased."

"Will he?" I find myself whispering.

"Yes," she says firmly.

I frown.

"Would you like me to escort you to the dining room?"

"Where is it?"

"Next to the room where we met."

"In that case, I'll find it myself. Thank you for your help."

"Okay." She walks to a tasseled sash hanging next to the bed. "I'm in a room down the corridor. If you need me just pull on this. It will ring in my room."

I thank her again, she wishes me good night, and slips out of my room. I turn back towards my reflection. With a start of surprise, I realize that I have not thought of Nigel once since arriving. I quickly take my cell out of my purse and call him.

He answers on the first ring. "Oh, thank god, you called. I've been going out of my mind with worry. Are you all right?" His voice is distraught and urgent.

"Yes," I say walking towards the mirror.

"Where are you now?"

I stare at my dolled-up self in the mirror. "In the bedroom that's supposed to be mine during my stay here."

"Are you alone?"

"Yes."

"Where is he?"

"Downstairs, I think."

"Have you met him yet?"

"Yes, as soon as I arrived."

He exhales sharply. "Was he ... all right with you?"

"Yes."

"He didn't ... do anything to you, did he?"

I bite my lip. "No."

"Oh, Star. I can't believe that you're there. That my stupidity has caused this. I don't know if I can take much more. I've been pacing the floor ever since you left. I've never been alone in this house without you in the evening and it's horrible. I'm so fucking lonely." He makes a sobbing sound.

"It's okay, Nigel. If we get through this we'll be stronger for it," I say the platitude automatically, without believing it.

 104

"Promise?" he sniffs.

"Promise," I lie. There is a different creature in the mirror staring back at me. That is not Star. That is someone else who has been hiding inside me all these years. In my heart, I know, that nothing will be the same again.

"What are you going to do now?" he asks.

"I'm going down to dinner."

"With him?"

"Yes."

"And after that?"

I say nothing.

"Oh God," he chokes.

"Perhaps it might be better if we don't talk about that part of this arrangement again, Nigel."

"You're right. I'm being selfish. This must be so difficult for you. Will you call me later? Before you go to sleep."

"I'll try."

"Please, Star. Please. You must find a way to talk to me again tonight. I won't be able to sleep. I won't be able to do anything. I'm a total wreck."

"Okay, I will."

"I love you. I never knew just how much until this evening."

"Yeah, I love you too."

"Think of me, Star."

"All right then."

"Don't let him take you away from me. Think of me even when you are with him."

 105

I feel a surge of anger and I force it down. "I've got to go, Nigel."

"I love you," he cries desperately.

I don't answer him. Staring at my own reflection blankly, I hit the disconnect button. *What will be, will be.* I take a deep breath and walk out of my bedroom. As I come down the stairs I see a shadow fall on the bottom step. Nikolai Smirnov is standing there looking up at me. He has changed into a dark suit and a snow-white shirt.

Eighteen

Star

These violent delights have violent ends

-Shakespeare

His gaze locks on mine. In the cluster of lamplights by the stairs, his eyes glow like a wolf's. He doesn't move or say anything. Just looks at me. I feel it then. How completely isolated he is. Like those strange twisted, gnarled trees that grow on barren wastelands. They get their nourishment from deep within the earth so they have no need for anyone or anything.

Suddenly, I feel unsteady on my feet.

I grip the banister and carefully, continue on my journey down.

As I reach the third step from the bottom I come level with him. Something flickers in his hooded eyes. He has secrets. Rooms of them. Rooms I can never enter.

He reaches out a hand and touches the skin of my stomach. Desire snakes down my spine, the hair on my skin stands, and my whole body comes alive. I have to fight not to reveal how affected I am by that simple touch. I inhale deeper, and without meaning to I breathe him in, the scent of his cologne, the warmth of his skin. I already know what he will taste like on my tongue.

"I had a dream last night," he murmurs. "You were riding me. Up and down my cock. Your hair loose and bouncing."

My eyes widen with shock.

"And when you came you screamed my name."

"I don't think it's *your* name I'll be screaming," I say sarcastically, but my body responds differently. It aches for him.

He smiles slowly. So slowly, it's like watching ice melt. "Careful with your claws little pussycat. That sounded like a challenge. Was it?"

"Take it how you want," I reply defiantly.

His eyes flash as he wraps his hand around my waist. "Hmmm ... I've always liked a feisty lay, but let's eat first."

"I told you I'm not hungry."

"Nevertheless, I've ordered food for you. I assumed you hadn't eaten all day."

"Well, I'm not hungry," I repeat in a bored voice, even though I am surprised by how perceptive he is.

"We'll see," he says mildly, and lets his hand slip to the small of my back. He is barely touching me, but I can feel the warmth from his hand as he leads me to a vast, red room.

At one corner of the long dining table, two places have been set. Light from a candelabra makes a circle of soft glow. It looks romantic.

A man, he looks like he might be Greek, or Spanish, or even Middle-eastern, steps forward and pulls out a chair for me. I thank him and sink into it. He nods and fills my glass with champagne before quietly withdrawing from the room.

I turn towards Nikolai and find his eyes on me. The intensity of his gaze unnerves me. "Don't you get lonely living in this massive place by yourself?"

"I don't actually live here. Just some weekends."

"What a waste of money," I say scornfully.

"Would you rather I gambled it away?" he mocks arrogantly.

That veiled criticism of Nigel immediately gets my back up. I'm loyal to a fault. How dare he criticize my husband. If he carries on in this vein I'll end up hating him. "Addiction is a disease, Mr. Smirnov. Like cancer. Would you blame a person because they had cancer?"

His expression doesn't change. "Do you plan on calling me Mr. Smirnov when my cock is in your cunt?"

I glare at him furiously. "I find that term incredibly vulgar and distasteful."

His eyes fill with amusement. "Which one? Cock or cunt?"

"The latter," I say between clenched teeth.

He lifts his glass and looks at me curiously. "What term would you prefer?"

I drop my eyes. "Vagina."

He laughs.

I lift my head and stare at him. Suddenly he seems younger, carefree and different.

"A vagina is some cold intellectual's attempt to turn an incredibly mysterious and beautiful body part into just another organ. Like a kidney or a liver. A vagina, little butterfly, is not the proper receptacle for a cock. A vagina is dry. You can't spread it open and suck it. Or finger it as it drips for you. A vagina is what you find in a biology textbook."

He leans forward and I stare at him, mesmerized.

"Now, a cunt. That is a whole different ballgame. It is sweet and pretty and greedy. Very, very greedy. So if you are calling your cunt a vagina, it means you've never been fucked blind by a man."

I bristle with anger. "I have been fucked blind by a man, thank you very much."

"We'll soon find out, won't we?'

He takes a sip. "To your education."

I refuse to join in the toast.

There is slight noise in the corridor, and the door opens. The man from earlier comes in with two dishes. He puts a deep dish of soup in front of me.

"Leek and potato soup with crème fraîche," he murmurs politely.

I raise my eyes to Nikolai Smirnov. He is watching me. His eyes veiled. It cannot be a coincidence.

I slide my gaze over to the server. "I'm not hungry. I don't want it."

He has kept his face totally expressionless until now, but at my refusal an expression of surprise shows in his eyes. He veils it quickly, and reaches out to remove the plate.

"Leave it, Gregorios." The sound is like a whiplash in the vast room.

Gregorios freezes, then straightens, nods respectfully, and leaves the room without ever making eye contact with me again.

I wait until the man has gone before I say, "It's not a coincidence that you are serving my favorite soup, is it?"

"Of course not," he agrees blandly.

"How did you know?"

"My head of security."

Gregorios enters with a bread basket. He holds it out to me to make my selection, and I shake my head.

"Put a mixed seed roll on her plate," Nikolai says.

The man obeys and I clench my hands under the table. He goes over to Nikolai, serves him a bread roll, and leaves. Nikolai breaks his roll and the smell of freshly baked bread wafts over to me. My mouth starts watering. Nikolai butters his roll. I drag my gaze from the bread to his face.

"Did you have me investigated?"

"Naturally. You didn't imagine I would bring anyone into my life without knowing anything at all about them?"

I lean back against the chair, angry. "What else do you know about me?"

He bites into his roll. He has strong straight teeth. "I know you're on the pill."

My jaw drops. "How did you know that?"

He chews. "What would you rather believe? That my security guard saw the contraceptives in your purse, or someone went through your garbage for the last few weeks."

I stare at him in astonishment. "What? You paid someone to go through my trash?"

He picks up his spoon. "Why are you so surprised? Teams of people working for the Eastern European Mafia regularly go through the rubbish of Londoners. That is also why you shouldn't tear your bank statements into four pieces and leave them out for the trash man to take away."

I gasp with shock. He knew how much money I had in my account! My eyes narrow. "Your security man didn't find out about my favorite soup by snooping about in my black bin bags, did he?"

"No. You must have mentioned it in your emails, or your phone calls."

I stare at him in disbelief. "Someone has been listening to my calls and reading my private emails?"

He stops eating and laughs. He actually laughs. "You've obviously not taken Snowden's revelations very seriously. Someone is always watching and listening, Star. This time it happened to be one of my men."

"Watching?"

"I'm afraid my head of security tends to take his job very seriously."

"Stop pretending to be uninvolved in this disgusting invasion of my privacy. He does that because you expect him to," I shout angrily. I am so angry I feel like picking up the fancy deep dish of soup in front of me and pouring the contents over his smirking, self-satisfied, arrogant head. How dare he snoop about in my personal communications. The debt wasn't even mine to begin with. My breath comes fast.

"Do you have cameras in my home?" I demand.

"No."

"I should report you to the police."

He smiles. "And say what?"

"Tell them what you've done. It's illegal."

He picks up his glass of champagne. "Your husband gave me permission."

"I don't believe you."

"Are you calling me a liar?"

Nineteen

Star

His voice is polite and his eyes glitter, but I don't care. "Yes, I am," I reply. "I know Nigel wouldn't have given you permission to pry in my affairs."

He takes a sip of his champagne, returns the glass back to the snowy tablecloth, and raises his eyes to meet mine. "When one decides to play little housewife and bury her head in the sand, it is always a good idea not to throw around accusations like that. Your husband signed a contract where it clearly states that anyone taking a debt from us will be closely monitored. And that includes their family members and friends."

I collapse back against the chair and stare at my lap. My palms feel clammy. First Rosa and now him. Both have made me realize how naïve and stupid I have been. I trusted Nigel implicitly. He said he would always put my safety first, and I believed him.

"The soup is good. You should try it."

I look up. I wish I could do something outrageous to wipe that smug look off his face, but I dare not. I don't know how he would react. He is not Nigel. I've never known any man like him. He is like a cheetah, wild and full of coiled power and strength. "I'm not going to eat your damn soup," I declare angrily. I lift my glass to my lips and sip at the champagne. It is cold and delicious.

He puts his spoon down and wipes his mouth on his napkin, and Gregorios comes into the room. Is he somewhere where he can see what his master is doing? Silently, he clears away my untouched dish. He leaves and the silence in the room stretches. I stare resolutely out of one of the windows at the darkness falling over the grounds. This will be my only form of defiance. I won't even look at him. I'll behave as if he is not even in the room. Gregorios comes in and refills his glass.

My stomach rumbles. I am actually hungry. My eyes stray to the bread roll on the plate to my left.

Gregorios goes out and returns with the next course.

"Pomegranate molasses glazed lamb with crispy potato bites," he says as he puts the large white plate in front of me. The lamb is pink, the edges are brown, and it looks like a piece of art.

The smell makes my stomach growl. With a determined tilt to my chin, I brave a glance at Nikolai. He catches my gaze. There is amusement dancing in his eyes. That makes me even more furious and I pick up my glass and drain it. Bad mistake. The alcohol goes straight to my head. Gregorios refills my glass.

"Is that man watching us from another room?" I ask when Gregorios leaves the room.

"No, why do you ask?"

"He seemed to know exactly when you finished your soup."

He smiles. "Gregorios knows exactly how long it takes me to finish any meal. It's why I pay him so well."

There is nothing to say to that so I take another sip of champagne. My head has started to feel a bit funny. In my peripheral vision, I see him pick up his knife and fork. Lamb is my favorite, and the aroma is making me feel ill with hunger, but I refuse to lose this battle of wills. I pretend to look out of the window, while I am actually looking at him cutting into his meat. It must be very tender because he appears to exert no pressure at all. He puts it into his mouth. I imagine it melting on his tongue.

"It's very good. You should try it," he says, and I know he is laughing at me.

"I'm not hungry," I insist coldly.

"Shame your stomach doesn't agree with you. It keeps rumbling."

I flush to the roots of my hair. "I don't know what you're talking about."

"When you faint later, I'd rather it wasn't through hunger."

My head whirls around. "Faint?"

He grins. "From pleasure."

My mouth drops open.

He cuts a piece of meat and brings the fork to my lips. Saliva starts collecting in my mouth. I want to resist. I order myself to resist. I stare at him. His eyes are silver. I see the black flecks in them. The pupils are big. It's not my fault that I am finding him so difficult to resist. The champagne. I am so drunk my head swoons.

"You can't win this battle. Evolution has hardwired humans to consume almost anything when they are hungry. You might as well eat," he says softly.

The smell torments me. More water fills my mouth. I swallow it. Damn him. My stomach growls loudly, but I won't let him win. He rests the food on my bottom lip. I let my mouth part and the meat enters my mouth. What was I to do? The meet was already at my lips. Some of its juices had already hit my tongue.

He smiles. "That was not so hard, was it? I only made you do what you were desperate to do, anyway."

I chew slowly. The meat is tender and juicy. It could even be the most delicious thing I have ever eaten. My hands reach out for the knife and fork. Damn this man. I start to eat. I eat quickly. I'm starving. I butter the bread roll and bite into it. The whole time I never look at him. Never utter a word. When I finish the meal, I lay my knife and fork down.

When Nikolai finishes his food, Gregorios returns. I thank him as he clears away my plate.

He nods solemnly. Nothing in his expression betrays the fact that I have cleaned my plate.

"Was your room to your satisfaction?" Nikolai asks.

"Yes, it was fine."

"Good. Did you like Celine?"

I frown. "What difference does it make whether I like her or not?'

"If you didn't she will be replaced."

"I liked her," I whisper immediately, shocked by his coldness. Poor, eager to please Celine. All I have to do is say I didn't like her and she will lose her job for no other reason than a whim. I hope he carries on behaving this way. Then I can be certain that I will detest him by the time I leave.

Dessert is coconut chiffon cake layered with strawberry jam and served with pina colada ice cream. Well, his head of security certainly did a good job. I love coconut, strawberry jam, and pina colada. So, yay to that intrusive bastard. I lift my spoon to my lips and slip it in. Whoa ... dessert in the Smirnov household is indescribably delicious. Almost divine.

"Will I be staying here for the whole month?"

"No, you will only be here when I am. Wherever I go I will take you with me."

I stop eating. "I can't leave the country. I have to go and see my dad every day. He is in hospital."

"I know. You normally go before lunch. Ivan will take you."

"I can take a taxi."

His jaw tightens. "I must have neglected to inform you that during your stay with me you will be chauffeur-driven everywhere. It is for your own safety."

As soon as I spoon the last mouthful, Nikolai stands. "Come, we will have coffee and brandy in the South Room. It has a lovely view." In spite of all the food I have consumed I still feel a bit tipsy and I stumble as I stand. His hand shoots out instinctively and grabs my arm.

My eyes fly to his face, but it is as unreadable as ever. For a second, I feel that strange magnetic pull of his eyes. Then he takes his hand away. My arm tingles and I rub the place where his skin touched mine.

He leads me to an elegant salon.

There are dusky pink couches and armchairs. I perch at the end of a couch, and Gregorios brings in the coffee on a large tray. He hands me a cup of coffee, just the way I like it. It's unnerving when perfect strangers know so much about you.

Using a silver pair of tongs, he drops two cubes of sugar into my cup. Just the way I like it. Then he serves Nikolai and slips away unobtrusively.

"Are you always so thorough with finding out the background of the people you are coming into contact with?"

"No."

My forehead furrows. "Yet it appears you have been extremely thorough in finding out my likes and dislikes."

"I wasn't planning on sleeping with them. Anyway, it is the way I am. Obsessive. When I want something, whether it is a house, a painting, a business deal or a woman, I never stop until I have it or her in my possession."

I take a sip of my coffee. "Do you often take a man's wife in exchange for his debt?"

He downs his coffee in one gulp. "Never."

"Then why me?"

"Because I wanted you."

"What if I didn't want you?"

"Don't you?"

"I love my husband."

He stands up and walks over to a set of tall doors and stares at the rolling countryside outside. "Have I once asked for your love?"

I say nothing and he turns around to look at me. "Have I?"

I bite my bottom lip. "No."

"Good. Now that we have cleared up that little misunderstanding, have you finished your coffee?"

"No."

"Finish your coffee."

I take another sip and, leaning forward, put it on the beautiful walnut coffee table. His tone makes me nervous.

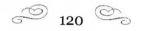

Twenty

Nikolai

The sweetest honey is loathsome in his own deliciousness.

Shakespeare

Outside it is getting dark. The daylight loving animals are settling down for the night. Like a nocturnal animal, my mind fills with anticipation.

It's time to hunt.

My back is to her, but I feel her gaze. She averts her eyes as I turn around. I walk slowly but purposefully in her direction. On my journey, I stop to flick some table lamps. Yellow light fills the room. My brain notes how nervously she shuffles in her seat.

I stop behind her. I am standing so close I can smell her. Flowers, mixed in with heady excitement and a touch of fear. I bend down until I am so close to her, my breath ghosts her neck. Her breathing becomes more pronounced. Steeling herself she turns to look at me. The look in my eyes causes her pupils to enlarge with sudden panic. She quickly drops her head. I run a finger along her pale cheek. She has beautiful skin. Smooth and cool.

"It's time, little butterfly."

"Time for what?" she whispers, her body trembling.

"Time to pay the debt."

She swallows the lump in her throat. "This is … difficult for me." She stumbles into silence, her cheeks taut with tension.

Awww … I've got a shy one. "Don't worry, I'll make it easy for you."

"I won't let you humiliate me," she vows. The defiance brings color up her creamy throat and into her face. I like that. I like it that she won't just roll over and play dead. Nevertheless, I can't be satisfied with anything except complete submission. I need that. From her I want absolute obedience. Total control.

"Take your clothes off."

"What?" Her face shoots up, shocked.

"Disrobe for me, beautiful Star."

"What, here?" she cries.

"Uh … huh"

"Can't we do this in a bedroom?"

"Don't worry, you'll be doing a lot of that there too," I mock.

She stares at me. Her face is flushed. The usual suspects: champagne, embarrassment, and pure sexual arousal.

"Well?"

Her teeth sink into her bottom lip. "I'd like to finish my coffee first."

123

I smile. "It's already cold."

"What if someone outside sees me?"

"They can consider it an unexpected perk of the job."

"You are a bastard."

I walk away from her and sit on an armchair. "Relax, little butterfly. There's no one out there, traipsing about in the dark, just hoping to get a glimpse of your delectable body."

"This is cruel."

I shrug. Cruel. She has no idea.

Her bright blue eyes accuse me, but she stands up.

"Get on the coffee table and face me," I instruct.

"Why?"

"Because I said so."

Her knuckles show white as she clenches her hands into fists. I watch the emotions play across her face. Her mouth is a straight line when she climbs on the low table, but she is a little wobbly on her feet, and that little unintended show of vulnerability makes my cock jump. I'm going to enjoy riding this sweet filly. She fiddles with the clasp at the back of her neck, and for a few second holds on to it, and stares at me with hostile eyes.

I raise a careless eyebrow. The gesture is calculated to annoy her. I like it when she is raging and glorious.

With a glare of fury, she lets the material fall. It slips down her breasts, skims her waist and belly, and gets caught at her hips. She pushes it down roughly. She is being deliberately unsexy.

She has no idea that it is her reluctance that is the major turn on. I've had willing pussy too often. She tries to kick off the material pooling at her ankles, and nearly loses her balance. Her arms flail as she straightens herself.

Weirdly, my heart jumps into my throat. The thought of her tumbling down and hurting herself fills me with a strange dread. It's been a long time since I cared about the wellbeing of another human being.

Her underwear is plain white. I should have expected it.

"Lose the underwear."

Her fingers slip beneath her panties' rim. The gesture is instinctively slow and sensuous. Worthy of a first-class stripper. She was completely wasted on that fool. Then, she remembers to be outraged, and pushes the cotton briefs unceremoniously down her legs. She stands before me naked, her palms covering the triangle between her legs.

I watch her intently. Saying nothing.

Slowly, her hands move away and hang by her sides. Her pussy is freshly shaved. The sight of her deliciously sexy body on full view makes my blood pound. God, I want to take her right now.

"You shave your pussy?"

She looks at me defiantly. "Nigel likes it."

She wants to anger me, but she has no idea how much fury pours into me. It almost makes me want to hire someone to smash every bone in his body. I keep my jaw straight and eyes cold.

"Figures," I murmur mildly.

"What's that supposed to mean?" she demands furiously.

"I think you know exactly what I mean."

"As a matter of fact I don't. You better spell it out.'

"Babies and little girls have no hair, Star."

"How dare you?" she rages. "It's a personal preference."

"It's my preference that you no longer shave while you are here. I want you to be natural."

"Fine," she says tightly.

My blood throbs with a mix of anger and lust. A dangerous combination. "Now sit down, open your legs, and show me your little cunt."

I see the flash of anger, and how much she wants to refuse, but she sits down, and parts her legs. At the sight of the pink slit I inhale sharply.

"Wider."

Her thighs move further apart, and I see how wet she is. That makes me smile. I stand and walk up to her.

"Lie on your back," I order.

"Why?" Her voice is shaky.

"Just do it." For a moment, she freezes like a deer in headlights. Then she swallows her anxiety, and lies back as naked as the day she was born.

I stand over her and look down at her naked body on the dark wood. White and all mine. In the yellow light her skin is creamy and flawless. I gaze at her chest, at the rose tipped peaks. There is a bruise at the side of her right breast. A love bite. The sick asshole left a love bite for me to find. Silly man. There will be nothing for him to find by the time I am finished with her.

Her full lips are pursed and her hands are lightly placed across her abdomen. In the silence of the room her deliberately slow, deep breathing betrays her attempt to remain calm and in control.

But she is not.

I am.

I trail my fingers slowly down her chest brushing across each breast. I feel her heartbeat rise as my fingers make their way down to her belly button and stomach. I let my hand drop lower and nudge apart her legs. She tightens her muscles against my hand.

"Poor vagina. It's been waiting for a real man's touch."

"Don't kid yourself," she snaps, but her voice is shaky.

"Pretend all you want, but we both know the truth, little butterfly."

Her breath hitches as I draw my finger between her pussy lips.

I stick my honeyed finger in my mouth and suck it slowly whilst I keep my eyes on her shocked expression. She tastes like ripe peaches washed in rainwater. So fucking sweet.

She scowls at her body's betrayal.

I sit on the table alongside her. Then I reach down and fist my hand in her hair. She gasps with surprise. After the passion, the anger will set in again, but now, now she is mine to play with. My fingers slip down her body. Pinching her nipples making her moan. Moving lower. Feather light touches. My hand parts her thighs. For a second she fights me. I can force my way in, but not tonight.

That is for another time.

I bend my head and swoop down on her nipple. I suck it until her thighs fall open. My finger enters her and her mouth opens at the sudden intrusion. I move my hand from her hair to clamp on her mouth. Her eyes widen, and she tries to eject my hand. I strengthen my grip and watch her glare intensify as she loses the battle. My finger moves in and out of her. I feel cruel. She makes me feel things I don't want to feel. I cannot allow her to have so much power over me.

I add a second finger. I pump them hard and furiously. I never let up as she writhes against me, twisting on the table top. She screams as she breaks apart. It is violent. As I knew it would be when I clamped my hand over her mouth. Her body jerks and clenches, and she gushes uncontrollably. Her fluid drenches my hand and spills on the table.

Her eyes stare at me with shock.

Twenty-one

Star

https://www.youtube.com/watch?v=6dOwHzC
HfgA
Died in your arms tonight

I think I am dying. It is the only way I can describe the sensation. Everything starts leaving me. There is nothing left in the world but me on that table with his hand sealing my mouth shut, my legs wide open, and the friction of his long fingers working me. Forceful, fast, possessive. Then even that goes and I disintegrate and become one with pure pleasure. Waves and waves of it.

But it doesn't last. I don't die. I come back. To voiceless sobbing and acute embarrassment. His fingers are still inside me, and I've squirted all over his fine furniture.

I look up into his cold eyes and I think they will mock me, but they don't. His eyes are more beautiful than anything I've ever seen in my life. I feel breathless. I am transfixed by his eyes. I feel as if I'm being sucked into them. The water is cold but it is impossible to resist. It pulls me deeper and deeper.

Slowly, he takes his hand away from my mouth and I inhale a shuddering breath. His head swoops down. To my shock, I feel him swirl his tongue in the folds of my sex. The strokes are luxurious, gentle, lazy, sure. My skin starts to feel like it is on fire.

He says something, but it is a guttural rumble to my ears.

He eats me out, taking his time, sucking, licking, biting, until another orgasm tears through me. I gasp for breath, panting like a stranded fish. He holds me through it all, watching me with those cold, cold eyes. I stare back helplessly.

I've never felt this way before.

Then he stands up, fully clothed, completely in control, and looks down on me. Naked, used, my legs wide open, my sex completely exposed. His eyes rove my body. I can't name the expression on his face. It looks like triumph, satisfaction, and just plain lust.

In this moment, there is nothing more I want than him inside me. There was an aching void inside me, and I wanted him to fill it.

"Get dressed and go to your room," he says, his voice harsh.

As I stare at him wide-eyed he turns around and walks out of the room with long strides, as if he can't bear to be with me for another second. For a while, I am too confused and stunned to move. Then I quickly get dressed, and slip out of the room. The hallway is deserted and silent.

I run up the sweeping stairs and go into my room. My phone is buzzing on the dresser. I pick it up. There are seventeen messages from Nigel. I stare at them. Each one is more desperate than the earlier one.

Call me
Please call me.
I'm really worried here. Where are you?
Star. I'm going to call the police if you don't call me soon.
Fucking hell. Call me.
Star. I'm going mad here.
Oh God. I can't do this for a month.
Star. Call me. Please. I'm dying here.
Are you there?
Call me as soon as you see this.

There are more messages, but I don't click into them. I dial his number, and he picks up on the first ring.

"Star," he cries desperately.

"Yeah," I say guiltily. I never thought of him once while I was with Nikolai. Not once.

"Are you all right?"

I take a deep breath. "Yes, yes, I'm fine."

"Where have you been? I've been going crazy here."

"I was having dinner. I told you."

"Dinner? You've been MIA for more than two hours."

"Have I?" My head feels fuzzy. I can't think.

"For fucks sake, Star. What's the matter with you? You are acting like you don't care."

"I do care. Very much. Otherwise I wouldn't be here." My voice sounds strange. I wanted the other man inside me.

"Star, I love you. I can't do this anymore. I want you to come back."

I feel that flash of anger. "Yeah, and what happens to my dad?"

To my horror he starts sobbing softly.

"Please don't cry, Nigel. Please."

"I'm sorry. I think I'm just stressed and worried. You sound like you don't give a shit about us anymore."

"Of course not."

"Do you love me, Star?"

"Yes."

"Are you sure?"

"Absolutely." I feel good saying it. That at least is true. I feel guilty that I enjoyed everything Nikolai did to me and that I wanted more, but that is just a physical thing. I love Nigel. I love him very much.

"Has he done anything to you yet?"

"Yes."

There is a shocked pause. "You mean he didn't wait for tonight?"

I feel a flash of irritation. "No, Nigel. He didn't wait. Just like you didn't wait for the night to come when you were first dating me."

"You didn't enjoy it, did you?"

I've never heard him sound so unsure of himself. "Look, Nigel. I don't want to talk about it, okay. For this to work we can't talk about what I do with him."

"You did enjoy it then," he pounces.

"I didn't say that. I said, I just didn't want to talk about it. It feels too weird. This is just the arrangement you made."

Suddenly the door flies open. I whirl around and see Nikolai standing at the doorway. His face is a mask of such rage I actually take a step back as if struck. I stare at him with my jaw hanging loose. There is a white band around his mouth.

I know I shouldn't, I have no reason to feel it, but I suddenly feel as if I've done something very wrong. Nigel is saying something, but I don't hear it. All I see is Nikolai's blazing eyes. He strides towards me and wrenches the phone from my nerveless fingers. He holds it to his ear and listens to Nigel for a couple of seconds then he opens his mouth and I recoil at the utter contempt in his voice.

"Don't you dare call her again while she is in *my* house. If I catch you sniffing around her again, I'll break every bone in your miserable body." His voice is so low and deadly I can hardly believe it is the same man who fed me a piece of lamb.

Before Nigel can say anything, he flings the phone towards the wall. It smashes on impact and falls down in pieces.

"Oh, my god," I wail in horror. "My dad. The hospital needs to be able to contact me. I need my phone."

I rush to the wall and crawling around start picking up the pieces. I try to put them together but my hands are shaking so much I can't.

"It's broken." I look at him with hatred. "You broke my phone. How dare you? How could you do that? First you humiliate me then you break my property. You didn't have the right to do that. I hate you. You're nothing but a big bully," I scream, and tears start running down my face. "I've got no phone now. You arrogant asshole."

He stares at me, crouched on the floor, tears running down my face.

A muscle in his jaw ticks furiously. Something flashes into his eyes. Suddenly he looks confused or hurt. But how can that be? Then his jaw tightens.

"You'll have a new phone in an hour." He turns on his heel and walks out.

I fall on the floor and sob. I wouldn't normally have reacted so badly, but the incredible emotions of the day must have finally caught up with me.

Twenty-two

Nikolai

"**Y**ou're nothing but a big bully."

The words reverberate around in my brain like an echo. I thought I had killed that motherfucker, but it is not dead. The past can never die. It lies down quietly in a dark well of sorrow, and when you least expect, it jumps out at you. After all these years. The scars have outwardly healed, but the ugliness underneath remains as vivid as yesterday. I turn away from her quickly. I don't want her to see. Not her. I'm already too exposed. Too vulnerable.

My hand shakes as I close the door behind me. I hear her crying and I want to go to her, but I won't. It's not safe for me.

The past. There is no escaping it.

It's not dead.

It's still calling ...

Twenty-six Years Ago ...

"Boys can you come down, please," our housekeeper, Duscha, calls.

I turn instantly to my younger brother, Pavel. It is a late autumn afternoon, and we are both in our study room doing our homework. His head is bent over his picture book and his expression is one of intent concentration. It is possible he didn't even hear Duscha, but any excuse to stop studying works for me.

"Come on. Let's go see what she wants," I say, jumping up.

My brother looks up from his book. His eyes are green like Mama's, and his fair hair is long and curly. It makes him look more like a girl than a boy, but Mama can't bear to cut it because it is so beautiful.

"Nikolai. Pavel," Duscha hollers up again.

We race down one flight of stairs, then another. My legs are stronger and longer than Pavel's so I get there faster, but I skid to a stop at the end of the hallway. Duscha is standing next to a man and woman I don't recognize.

"Come here, little ones," Duscha calls gently.

We do as we are told, but warily. There is no smile on Duscha's usually cheerful, round face. My gaze slides over to the strangers standing next to her.

The man is wearing a hat and a long, black coat. His face is still and pale. The woman is dressed in a navy suit. She is so perfectly groomed there is not a hair out of place. Mama has the same pair of sturdy shoes as hers, but unlike Mama she has cold blue eyes.

Duscha nods and says, "Come my little darlings."

137

I take my brother's hand and we walk towards her, stopping close to her. She crouches, opens her arms out to Pavel, and envelops him in a hug, but keeps her gaze on me.

"Nikolai, these people work with your father and mother. They have ... they have something to tell you both." Her lower lip is trembling and she looks nervous and sad.

The man steps forward and removes his hat. "It is my duty to inform you that your parents were involved in a road accident. They are both dead." His delivery is robotic and devoid of any emotion.

I feel Duscha reach out and squeeze my hand tightly. I turn to look at my brother. He is only six and I can see that he doesn't understand. He stares at me with large, frightened eyes. My hands clench into fists. It is impossible that my parents are dead. I refuse to believe them. I know instinctively not to trust these people.

"They are not dead. I just spoke to them last night," I say fiercely.

"I know it's difficult to accept, but they are dead," the woman confirms.

I break free from Duscha's grip. "No. I don't believe you."

"Nevertheless, you must come with us," the woman says.

Dushca stands.

I try to grab my brother and run back upstairs, but the man catches me by the arm, and pulls me away from Pavel. Pavel starts crying.

"Leave us alone," I scream, and kick wildly at the man's shins.

He does not let go. He just looks angry and irritated. "It's no use resisting. Your parents are gone and you must come with us."

"Why? Why must we go with you?" I ask defiantly. I remember Mama told me when I was only Pavel's age that if anything ever happened to my parents, then I must take my brother (he was only a baby then) and go to my grandmother's house. She made me learn the address by heart, then she showed me how to lift the loose floorboard in her bedroom and access the blue box hidden underneath. Inside was money and our papers. "If anybody at all comes here and tries to take you, or your brother away, you must immediately call Uncle Oksana. He will know what to do," she said. I nodded and she made me memorize his number.

"You must come with us now," the man barks, holding me sideways so that my kicks and flailing were useless.

"I want to call my uncle," I say as ferociously as I can.

"There is no time for that now. You can call him later," the woman says. Her face cracks into a smile. It just makes her look like a crocodile.

"I want to call him now," I insist stubbornly. "Mama wanted me to."

The woman looks at the man and raises her eyebrows.

"Duscha, help us," I say, but she just sobs helplessly. When I see her crying so pitifully, I suddenly become very frightened. Our parents are not here, and these horrible people are going to take us away, and Duscha, always smiling, happy, Duscha, is crying like her heart is breaking. "Please, Duscha. Please, help us. Do something."

Duscha falls to her knees, clasps her hands in a prayer position, and looks up at them. "Please don't take the boys, they need to go to school. Let the boy call his uncle. I can take care of them here until he gets here," she begs, her voice shaking with fear.

"These two children have been designated as children of the enemies of the people, and by resisting their removal you are acting against the state's wishes. Instead of worrying about them you should start making preparations to leave immediately as this house and everything in it now belongs to the government." The woman's voice is sharp and Duscha flinches as if she has been struck.

"I don't want to go," I yell.

"Look how they are dressed," Duscha cries desperately. "Please, have some pity. It's freezing cold outside. At least let me get some warm clothes for them," Duscha pleads.

"There is no time. They must come with us now," the man repeats stonily.

Duscha takes off her warm woolen shawl and, with tears running down her face, wraps it around Pavel's shoulder. Pavel uses that opportunity to fling his hands and legs around her body and cling tightly to her.

The man looks at the woman. "Hurry up and get him. We're wasting time here."

The woman takes two steps forward and roughly pries Pavel away from Duscha. She rips the shawl off his body, throws it to the ground, and she drags my screaming brother towards the front door.

I try to fight the man holding me with all my might, but he is big and too strong. Without warning, he lifts his hand and punches me on the side of the head. The blow is so hard, my head swims. I actually see stars. For a second I even go deaf. My body becomes limp, and he drags me down the steps.

There is a long, black car parked outside.

I know instinctively that we must never get into the car. With every ounce of energy I have, I start struggling and screaming as loudly as I can for the neighbors. But the street remains deserted. Not one curtain twitches. Not one person opens their door to investigate what is happening in the Smirnov household.

Why the children are screaming?

Why there is a big black car parked outside?

Why two strangers are dragging the children away?

"Help, help. We are being kidnapped," I yell.

Suddenly, I feel a sharp pain on my upper arm. When I jerk my head towards the pain I see a needle sticking out of my arm.

The world goes black very quickly.

Twenty-three

Star

Before the hour is up I hear the sound of a motorbike roaring to the front. Minutes later there is a quiet knock, and when I open it Celine is standing outside.

She looks at me strangely. I know my eyes are swollen and red.

"Your new phone has arrived. A woman who can teach you how to use it is also here."

I follow her downstairs where a young Italian girl smiles at me and proceeds to show me how to use the phone. It is very different from mine and I have never heard of the brand before, but she is a good teacher, the interface is easy, and soon I am using it confidently.

"That's it. If you have any problems don't hesitate to call me," she says standing up.

"I'm sorry you had to come out at this time of the night."

She grins broadly. "I wish more people would call me out at this time of the night. I'm getting paid almost a week's wages for this, so believe me when I tell you, it is no hardship at all."

At my blank expression, she explains that she works for a high-end phone shop in Bond

143

street. Her boss called her while she was getting ready for bed and sent a courier to pick her up and take her to the shop where he gave her the phone. Her task was to deliver it and teach me how to use it.

The big guy that Nikolai had called Semyon is waiting for her in the hallway. After she leaves I go upstairs. In my room, I go into my bathroom, lock the door, and text Nigel.

Me: **I'm going to bed now, Nigel. Please do NOT text or call me unless I text you whenever I can. I don't want Nikolai to hurt you. I love you. No matter what. I'll text you tomorrow.**
Nigel: **Are you all right?**
Me: **Yes, I'm fine.**
Nigel: **I heard a loud bang. Did he hit you?**
Me**: No.**
Nigel: **So what was the noise?**
Me: **He broke my phone.**
Nigel**: WTF!!!!**
Me**: It's all right. It's all sorted now.**
Nigel: **Whose phone are you using?**
Me: **He got me another one.**
Nigel: **He must be nuts.**
Me: **Just don't call or text me. I'll contact you when the coast is clear.**
Nigel**: Now I'm really worried about you. What if he hurts you?**
Me: **He won't.**

144

Nigel: **How do you know that?**

Me: **The only person who can hurt me is you.**

Nigel: **We'll get through this. I promise.**

Me: **I'm tired. I'm going to bed. I'll call you tomorrow.**

Nigel: **I'll be waiting for your text tomorrow. I love you so much it hurts.**

I close my eyes and then I say what I always say: **Me too.**

His reply appears on the screen and it just makes me so sad I want to cry: **Goodnight my darling. I'll dream of you.**

I crawl into bed. The sheets are silky soft against my skin. It takes me a long time to fall asleep and when I do, I don't dream of Nigel. I toss and turn with nightmares of a man with silver eyes full of pain.

Twenty-four

Nikolai

1990

*W*hen I wake up it is nearly night, my brother is huddled against me, and the car is travelling on a lonely road. I try to stretch, but can't move my hands. I look down and see that they are tied with ropes.

The man and woman are sitting in the front.

"Where are we going?" I ask.

The woman turns her head around. "If you don't shut up, I'll have to tape both your mouths," she warns.

No one speaks again. My brother holds me close to him as we drive through swathes of countryside until we come upon a high wall. It is studded with sharp pieces of broken glass and the top of it is strung with barbed wire. The car stops at a set of big, black gates. The man gets out and rings a bell. After a while, an elderly man comes to unlock the big padlocks on the gates.

We drive through and stop in front of a huge, gray building. I'll never forget the sight of that building. It is so big and imposing. All the windows have bars. It looks like a prison. We are pulled out of the car and forced up the stone steps.

A skeletal man with a thin, long face opens the thick black door. He does not look at Pavel or me. Merely nods gravely and opens the door wider. The stench that greets us is hard to define. I have never smelt it before. It seems to be coming from the dank walls and the stone floor. I can even smell it on the thin man. It smells like stale urine, and boiling cabbages, but something else too. Something that makes me afraid.

It is colder inside the house than it was outside. There is a huge bust of Lenin to the left of us. Ahead is a long, dark corridor. There are posters on the walls showing children praising Stalin with the caption: *Thank You, Dear Comrade Stalin, for a Happy Childhood.*

We follow him down the corridor.

An elderly woman is furiously mopping the floor. Her mop is gray and the water in the bucket is also gray with a few soap suds floating on top. She does not look at us.

We pass empty classrooms on either side of us. There are no sounds of children from within the house. Further down the corridor a boy, much older than me, passes us. He has dark eyes and he stares at me with a sneer.

We reach a door and the tall man knocks politely. Someone calls 'enter' and the man pushes open the door and steps back. A bald, fat man stands from behind a big desk with many papers on it.

"Have you brought more littlest enemies of the people for me to plant in my garden?" he asks cheerfully. He would have made a good clown or buffoon, but there is something sinister in his bulging brown eyes. They slide over me like oil, but when they move to Pavel they become sticky and stay. He smiles and licks his lips. "And who do we have here?"

"The older one is Nikolai and the little one is Pavel," the man who brought us says. There is a note in his voice that wasn't there before. Scorn and derision. He doesn't respect the fat man.

"I am Konstantin Razumovsky, and I am the director of this institution," the fat man announces proudly. "We opened in 1918 and we have had many successes to be proud of here. More than 7000 children have come through our doors and many of them are now fine, upstanding graduates with their own children."

"I need to phone my uncle," I say loudly.

The director smiles. "Phone calls must be earned with good behavior. If you are good you will be allowed to use the phone." He lets his eyes travel down to the ropes around my wrist. "Are you going to be a good little boy for me?"

"Yes," I say immediately. I have already understood that I must do everything in my power to earn that phone call to Uncle Oksana. I might be able to, but little Pavel cannot climb

*those glass embedded walls. They will cut him
to ribbons.*

*The Director's smile widens as he regards
us benevolently.* "Good. You will like it here,
there are many boys of your age."

*We are passed on to another man called
Igor. He has a thin, unsmiling face and he takes
us to a dank room where my ropes are cut and
we are ordered to strip and change into
shapeless clothes made of thick, coarse
material. He opens a cupboard and extracts
two pairs of striped pajamas and two
toothbrushes. They don't look new. The bristles
are curved.*

"The toilets are over there," *he says,
waving down a dank corridor,* "but they are all
not functioning at the moment. You'll have to
use the latrines outside. Do you need to use
them?"

Both Pavel and I nod.

*With a long-suffering sigh, he leads us
outside and waits for us while we use the toilets.
The toilets are freezing cold. We use them as
quickly as we can and join Igor.*

*Shivering with cold, we follow him
upstairs to a long room full of cots. The smell of
urine is much stronger here. There are shelves
on the walls and there are neat little piles of
clothes, soap and toothbrushes on them. No
toys, books, photos of family, or any kind of
personal possessions.*

Igor tries to give us cots in different parts of the room, but I insist that I want to stay with my brother. Something flashes in his eyes. A secret smile. As if he knows something I don't.

"I'm hungry," Pavel says in a soft voice.

"You've missed supper time. You'll have to wait until the morning for breakfast. It'll be lights out in twenty minutes, so you boys might as well stay here."

As soon as he goes away, Pavel turns to me, his eyes filling with tears. "Are Mama and Papa really dead?"

"I don't think so."

"So why have they brought us here?"

"I don't know. I think it's a mistake. I need to call Uncle Oksana. He will come and take us back," I mutter.

"Are we really the littlest enemies?"

I grab both his hands. "No, we're not. We didn't do anything wrong and neither did Papa and Mama. It's all a mistake. A terrible mistake," I say fiercely.

He nods and I let go of his small hands.

"I'm afraid," he whispers, his beautiful eyes filling with tears.

"Don't be afraid. I'm here. I won't let anything happen to you."

"Do I have to sleep alone?"

"No. I'll sleep with you."

He frowns. "But you don't like sleeping with me."

"I'll sleep with you tonight."

 150

"Are you sure?"

"Yeah."

"Thank you." His small hand goes around my back. "Who will sleep with Lyubov tonight?" he asks.

That is the moment I get really scared. In my head Papa is saying, "Now walk to the shop together. Hold Pavel's hand. Don't ever let go. You are in charge of your little brother." Pavel is still too small. How am I going to protect him in this vast place?

"Will Lyubov be alone?" Pavel asks again.

"No," I say softly. "Duscha will take him with her."

His lips wobble. "That's good. I wouldn't want him to be alone. You don't think she'll put him in the washing machine, do you?"

"Why would she do that?"

"She's always threatening to."

"She doesn't really mean it. She only says that when you don't pick your toys up, or eat your food."

For a while he is silent.

"Where do you think Mama and Papa are?"

I look at him seriously. "I'm going to tell you a secret, but you can never tell anyone, okay?"

"Okay," he whispers, his eyes huge.

I lean close to his ear and say, "I think they've gone to America to find a home for us."

"How do you know?" he whispers back in my ear.

"Because I heard them talking. They said they were going to find a home, and then we were all going to move to America. We can all go to a drive-in, eat burgers and fries, and drink Coca Cola."

"Really?" His eyes are shining.

"Really. But you can't tell anyone."

He shakes his head solemnly. "No. I won't. Wolves can tear away my heart, but I won't tell anyone."

I smile. "That's what Mama says."

"And I agree with her."

"It's going to be fine. I'll take care of you."

"I want Mama," he says, and begins to cry.

"Shhh ..." I say, and holding his small body close to me, rock him the way I have seen Mama and Duscha do to him when he has a fever.

We huddle together on the cot in that cold room and stare at the blank gray walls. Both of us are in a state of profound shock. We can hardly believe we have somehow gone from our warm study room, a little bored with doing homework and the smells of Duscha preparing a hearty stew, to one of the most dreaded and hostile places imaginable for a child in Russia.

A dyetskii dom (A children's home)

Twenty-five

Star

I wake up early and check my new phone. No calls or messages. I go into the beautiful marble bathroom and take a shower. Wrapped up in a fluffy robe, I sit on my bed, and call Nan. She asks how I am and I tell her that I am better, and that I will be going to see my dad tomorrow.

"Yes, that would be good. He was asking about you yesterday."

"I'll see him tomorrow," I repeat.

"What are you and Nigel up to today?"

I close my eyes. This part is even more painful. "Not much. We'll probably stay in today."

"Probably best. You stay indoors until you feel completely better."

"Yeah, I will."

"If you want I'll make you some soup and your grandad can take it around to you."

"No, don't do that. I'm almost better."

"Are you sure, Love? Cause it's no trouble."

"No need. Rosa said she'll bring something around."

"All right then."

"I'll call you tomorrow."

I hang up with a sigh, and call Rosa.

"About bloody time," she says. "How's it going?"

"I don't know."

"What does that mean?"

"I guess I'm just confused about everything."

"Well, I'd be confused too if I ended up in the bed of one of the richest men in the world. I can't believe you told me his name was Nikolai Something or other, when he is Nikolai Smirnov, a fully paid up member of the Russian billionaire club."

"So you know about him?"

"Of course, I know about him. Everybody in my line knows about him. He dates fashion models and he's broken a heart or two."

Instantly, there is an odd lurch in my stomach. I'm not model material. I'm average height and I'm not skinny.

"He is a dish, isn't he?"

"Mmm."

"Mmm? Come on? He's miles better looking than Nigel."

"You can't compare them," I say uncomfortably.

"Hang on. I'm just going to butter this toast. Facetime me in two minutes. I want all the details."

"I can't facetime you."

"Why not?"

"I'm not sure this phone has that function."

"You got a new phone? You didn't have it when I saw you yesterday," she asks surprised.

"Nikolai broke my phone so got me a new one."

There is a couple of seconds of stunned silence. "He broke your phone? I'm getting a bad vibe here. Want to give me more details before I make them up in my head and totally freak out?"

"When he came into the room last night, I was talking to Nigel. He got so mad he told Nigel to not contact me again while I was living in his house or he'd break every bone in his body. Then he threw my phone on the wall. He was like a beast, Rosa."

"Oh my. Where has this man been hiding all these years? I don't think that is beastly at all. I think he was quite right to behave in that way. If I was him I would have done the same."

"What?"

"Of course. As far as he is concerned Nigel has passed you over to him for a month in exchange for writing off a massive debt. Imagine if that debtor then tried to take back part of that one month. I'd go mad."

"But Nigel is devastated."

"Good. I would have loved to have seen his face while the Russian was tearing into him."

"Rosa," I admonish.

"Hang on, I'm just going to finish buttering this piece of toast." I hear the sound of her knife scraping the toast. "Don't Rosa me. Nigel

deserved that. How dare he think that he can use you to pay off a debt?"

"I told you I offered."

"And I told you, bullshit."

I refuse to engage and go silent.

"I know you don't want to believe me, but I don't feel even a tiny bit sorry for Nigel. He's so up his own ass. In fact, I'm glad he's been forced to wake up to the smell of coffee and realize that someone else is drinking his stash. He thought he was so clever. He could have it all. Send you to pay his debt and still keep you keen on the phone. Well, he made a big fucking mistake this time."

There is nothing to say to that.

"So, what kind of phone have you got now?"

"It's a Vertu."

"Really? What kind of Vertu is it?"

"I don't know." I take the phone away from my ear and look at it before putting it back to my ear. "It's quite sleek with a mother of pearl inlay and it comes with a matching white alligator skin clutch-style case."

She squeals.

"What?"

"That phone is worth nearly £18,000!"

"What?"

"Yes, that little stone select key is a Princess Cut diamond! And those face pieces, they're all sapphires."

"Oh, my god!"

"Sweet Jesus. This guy doesn't mess about, does he?"

"Why would he give me such an expensive phone?" I whisper.

I hear her take a big chomp of her toast. "I have no idea, but you know what? I am liking this guy more and more. So, come on, tell me about the sex."

I have an image of him with his fingers inside me while my naked body writhes and gushes all over his antique table. I feel hot all over and something inside me tightens. Damn him. I can't tell anyone about him. I'd be too embarrassed.

"Listen. I've got to go down for breakfast, but I'll call you later."

"Okay. Call me later. Star?"

"Yeah."

"What shall I tell Cindy?"

"I'll call her later and tell her."

"Great. Have fun, babe."

"You too."

I hang up and go over to the armoire where I select a sleeveless blue dress. It is simple and sweet. I rummage around in the boxes at the bottom of the cupboard and find a pair of white ballet pumps. I run a silver comb through my hair, plait it into a long braid down my back, and go downstairs.

The hallway is deserted so I walk to the room where I had been first taken to. It is empty too. As I stroll along the corridor towards the dining room, I pass a door that is open. It is a sunny room with a piano in it. Celine is sitting at a table with her laptop open.

She looks up and grins. "Good morning. Did you sleep well?"

"Yes, thank you."

She stands up. "Good. Mr. Smirnov has gone out riding, but he is expecting to have breakfast with you."

"Oh."

She glances at her watch. "He will be back in less than an hour. Would you like a quick tour of the house before you eat?"

I shrug. "Sure."

She closes her laptop.

"Celine, do you know if I can get my hands on a laptop?"

She starts walking towards me. "Of course. What brand and model would you like?"

"I'm used to a MacBook Air."

"What software would you like installed in it?"

"Just Word."

She smiles. "I will have it delivered by lunchtime. In the meantime you are welcome to use mine."

I smile back at her. "It's not urgent. I can wait until lunchtime."

Celine has taken the time to learn the history of the place and she is full of interesting bits of information.

There are five-hundred meters of corridor in the house.

The big ballroom was used as a hospital during the war.

As we climb a set of wide, shallow stone stairs in the West wing, she tells me the children of the first Earl who built the house used to ride their ponies up those stairs into their playrooms on the first floor. Their playroom was the entire floor.

She opens a door and we enter the long almost empty room. It has many mullioned windows, a bare wooden floor, and white walls. It is markedly different from the splendor and grandeur of the rest of the house. The thing that keeps it different is an old rocking horse. There is something indescribably sad about the space. I couldn't even imagine that this place was once filled with children's toys and their sound of their feet and laughter.

"This is the only undecorated room in the house," Celine says moving towards one of the windows and looking out of it.

"Why is that?"

She shrugs and turns to face me. "I was told Mr. Smirnov didn't want it decorated. He wanted to keep it in its original form."

A shiver goes through me. "I see."

Twenty-six

Nikolai

1990

*I*n minutes the other children start to file in followed by Igor. Some of them glance at us, but most of them keep their eyes firmly on the floor. No one says anything. A boy with brown hair and sad eyes comes to stand near my cot.

"You will sleep over there," Igor says, and points to another empty cot.

Without a word of protest the boy moves to the other cot.

In minutes, everybody, including Pavel and me, have changed into our pajamas and climbed into our beds. The lights go off and the door closes. In the sad silence, Igor's footsteps echo as he walks down the corridor.

I turn to face Pavel.

His big bright eyes are gleaming in the faint moonlight coming in through the windows. I put my finger on my lips to indicate that he should remain silent. When I can hear that all the other children are sleeping soundly, I climb into bed with Pavel. I notice that he is sucking his thumb, something he has not done since he was a baby, but I say nothing. I cover *him with both our blankets and stroke his hair until he falls asleep.*

I am too cold and anxious to fall asleep, but it turns out to be a good thing, because it means I get time to take action when I see the roving flashlights through the slit underneath the door. Slipping out of Pavel's hug, I quickly climb into my own bed, and stay very still. The door opens.

The flashlight comes toward our cots. Whoever they are, they seem to know exactly where we are. A flashlight shines onto my face. I shield my eyes and sit upright. I know there are more than one, but it is impossible to see their faces. My heart is pounding so fast I can hear it galloping like a horse.

"Get up and follow us," a voice says.

The flashlight moves away from my face and shines on Pavel's. He is fast asleep, his blond hair falling over his forehead.

"No. Not him. He's a baby," I whisper urgently, and jump out of bed.

The flashlight trains on my face again. I stare into it defiantly.

"Come now," the voice says.

There are three of them. I follow them out of the chamber of sleeping children. We go down the stairs to one of the classrooms. Someone lights a storm lantern. In its light I start to make out their faces. They are all older than me. One of them is the sneering boy who passed us down the hallway.

"So your parents were plotting against the state?" he says. He has a strange accent.

"No, they weren't. My parents are doctors," I jab back angrily.

"Were," one of the boys sniggers.

"They're not dead."

"They're dead, otherwise you wouldn't be here."

I decide not to antagonize them. I fix my attention on the boy who passed me. It looks like he is their leader. "What do you want?"

"We wanted to warn you."

"About what?"

He holds out a pair of scissors. It looks old. "Take this and cut your brother's hair. Then give it back to us."

I look at them suspiciously. "Why do you want me to do that?"

One of the boys laughs.

"Shut up," the leader tells his friends harshly. Then he turns to me. "Your brother's too pretty and there are men here who like that."

The hair on my body stands. I reach out and take the scissors from him. My hands are shaking. "Thank you."

"My name is Sergei Koshkina. This is my gang. We are called the nightwalkers. You can join us if you want."

"What does your gang do?"

"We look out for each other. There are bullies here. The director uses them to keep the

162

discipline. You have to watch out for them. They don't bother us. They won't bother you if you join us."

"Why do you want me to join you?"

The boy smiles. "Because you came in ropes. Every one of us here did."

I smile back. He is a kindred spirit. "My name is Nikolai Smirnov."

"Meet back here tomorrow night."

One of the boys offers me a biscuit. I take it and thank him. Clutching the scissors, I hurry back to the bed chamber. I shake Pavel awake. He rubs his eyes and makes a groaning sound. I clap my hand over his mouth until he opens his eyes and looks into mine.

I put my finger over my mouth and he nods.

I make him sit up and give him the biscuit. While he is eating it, I hack off as much of his hair as I can. To my horror, he doesn't look bad. His eyes look even bigger and his little face looks angelic. I run my hands under my shoes and smear the dirt on his face.

"What are you doing?" he asks with such perfect innocence I become terrified all over again.

Twenty-seven

Star

In less than an hour we cover the most important parts of the main house.

"You can explore the rest at your own leisure," Celine says, closing the door of the pool room. "Now let me take you to the breakfast room. Mr. Smirnov should already be there."

The breakfast room is east facing. There are three sets of doors and they are all open. The view is amazing, but the only thing I see is Nikolai sitting at the table reading a newspaper. He is dressed in an oyster-gray suit, a light-gray shirt, and a white tie. He looks aloof and unreachable. I can't equate this immaculately groomed man with either the sexually experienced one who took me on the coffee table or the furious beast who shattered my phone.

I take a deep breath and step into the room. He raises his stunningly silver eyes from the story he is reading, and lets them sweep down my body. He folds the newspaper and places it on the table.

With impressive timing, Gregorios comes in. Silently, he moves towards the chair next to Nikolai. He pulls it out and waits for me. I walk towards it and he seats me smoothly.

"Good morning," Nikolai greets.

"Good morning," I reply awkwardly. I put my phone on the table. "Thank you for my new phone."

He nods.

"You didn't need to get something so expensive."

He frowns and seems annoyed. "Don't be coy."

My back becomes rigid. "I wasn't being coy. There was absolutely no need to buy something that expensive. A replacement phone would have done the trick nicely. I don't need expensive toys."

A smile curves his lips. "Ah, but I want to spoil my little butterfly. Shower her with beautiful things."

"Why?"

He shrugs. "It's probably a control thing. I like knowing that everything you wear, eat and own has been provided by me."

Gregorios takes a step forward. I have been so involved with Nikolai I actually forgot he is standing just behind me.

"What would you like for breakfast?" Nikolai asks.

"What's on the menu?"

"Anything you desire?" His eyes gleam.

I find that I can't hold his gaze without blushing. I avert my head in confusion. "Then I'll have an English breakfast, please," I tell the hovering Gregorios.

"*Syrniki* for me," Nikolai says. "And bring me another coffee."

As silently as he entered Gregorios leaves with our orders.

Nikolai looks at me with a considering expression. "With all the possibilities you ordered an English breakfast."

"That's right, and you ordered a Russian dish while in England."

He chuckles. "Touché."

For some weird reason I feel pleased that I made him laugh.

"So you've had your tour of the house. Did you like it?"

I nod. "It's a beautiful house. You're very lucky."

His lips twist. "Luck? I made my own luck little butterfly."

I look at him intrigued. "You made all this money in one lifetime?"

"Yes."

"How?"

"I was willing to do what other men weren't."

"What do you mean?"

His eyes flash. "Exactly what you are thinking."

"Like when you took me from Nigel?"

"Exactly. Another man would have hesitated. He might have allowed his conscience to trouble him, or turned it into a question of morality. Me? I considered nothing. I wanted

you and I plucked you right out of your husband's careless hands."

"Would nothing have stopped you?"

He looks deep into my eyes. "What do you think innocent little Star?"

I stare at him. I've never met a person who is so open about their immorality. "What about if you had to kill someone?"

He lifts one shoulder carelessly. "Everyone has to die at some time. So what if it is a day, a month, or ... even twenty years earlier? In the scheme of earth's history, billions of years, what does it matter?"

I frown. "You've killed a human being before?"

He smiles. A tiger's smile. "If I had, and I'm not saying I have, I certainly wouldn't be confessing the deed to you."

Breakfast arrives. My dish seems ordinary compared to his.

"What are you eating? Are they pancakes?" I ask curiously as Gregorios leaves the room.

"These are Russian dumplings. They are made from cottage cheese, flour, eggs, and eaten with jam or sour cream. Want to try?"

I lick my bottom lip. He fed me yesterday and even the idea brings to the fore all kinds of things I don't want to feel. "No. I'll try it another day."

"As you wish," he says, and reaches for the cream,

"How old were you when you met Nigel?" he asks casually.

I shift in my seat. I don't want to tell him. I pretend to chew the eggs for a bit longer. "We were both very young," I say finally.

He smiles mockingly. "Nigel is a year older than me. He couldn't possibly have been very young. How old were you?"

"Sixteen," I say as casually as I can.

His eyes remain carefully veiled, but his eyebrows rise. "The pervert."

"He's not a pervert," I defend hotly. "And I resent the accusation. This is the second time you alluded to it. As a matter of fact I was very mature for my age. I didn't look young at all."

"You look barely legal now."

"I was an early developer," I insist aggressively.

"Yeah? The first time he met you how were you dressed?"

I feel myself cringe. "None of your damn business."

"I thought so."

"What the hell do you mean by that?"

"Do you want to bet I know what you were wearing?"

"I could lie."

"You're not a liar."

Unable to meet his knowing gaze I scowl down at my plate.

"I'll bet the dress you're wearing. If you win you keep your dress on. If you lose you lose the dress."

"That's a very one-sided bet," I say.

He laughs darkly. "Those are the kinds of bets I like."

"I don't want to discuss my personal life with you anymore," I say, cutting into my sausage.

"How strange that you would protect such a pervert. If there's one thing I hate, it is men that interfere with children."

Anger rises in my stomach. I concentrate on laying the knife down calmly, as if he has not infuriated me so much I want to stab him with it. "Stop calling him that," I say quietly.

"Why not? It's the truth."

"It's not the truth. I was not a child."

"You were wearing your school uniform."

I swallow hard. I can't look him in the eye. How could he possibly have guessed that? When Nigel arrived at the party I had not gone up to change yet. Both Sara, Nigel's niece, whose birthday it was, and I, were still in our uniforms eating ice lollies in the kitchen. He had come in and something in the way he looked at me while I was sucking my lolly made me blush.

Irritated that he guessed right I glare at him. "But I didn't look like a child. If you think you can make me feel revulsion for Nigel by calling him vile names you can stop right now because it won't work. My father tried that and it had absolutely no effect on me."

"So your father agrees with me," he pounces.

I take a deep breath. God, give me strength. "While my father's first instinct as a parent was to protect me he doesn't think that anymore. He has since realized that Nigel is a good man." I cross my fingers under the table.

"Hmmm ... I'll have to revise my opinion of you."

I frown. "What opinion?"

"You *are* capable of lying."

I sip at my coffee. "Why would you think that I wasn't? Everybody lies. I've told some massive corkers in my time."

"When was the last time you lied?"

The last time was when I told him I didn't want him. I shrug. "I can't remember now."

"Hmm ..." He lapses into silence and only turns his attention to me again when he finishes his food. "Do you plan to see your father today?"

"No, I'll go tomorrow. My grandmother is visiting him today." I smile cynically. "I had to lie to her. She thinks I'm not very well and I'm at home with Nigel."

As usual the mention of Nigel makes his face darken. "I'll be away most of the day but you are welcome to explore the grounds, ride, swim, find a book in the library or catch a movie in the cinema room. Do anything you want. I'll be back for dinner."

I nod.

To be honest the idea of not spending the day with him is a relief. The time we spend together seems fraught with confusing emotions and barely suppressed hostility.

He stands and walks over to me. Immediately my heart starts pounding.

"What?" I ask nervously.

"Before I go, stand up and take your underwear off."

My eyes widen. "What?" I exclaim, even though I can already feel my body responding to the sexual demand.

"You heard."

"Why? You are going away." My voice sounds breathless.

"Because I like to think of you walking around my property; your cunt swollen and wet between your legs."

Twenty-eight

Star

For a few seconds I stare rebelliously at him. Then it occurs to me that if I don't obey he might decide to take matters into his own hands, and then he will see how right his assessment has been. I can feel how wet I am. I take my panties off. Bunching them up in my fist, I drop them into his outstretched palm.

"I expect to find you bare when I return," he says before he walks out.

****

It's a strange sensation to walk around without my underwear. I've never done it, especially not while wearing such a short dress. It is at once liberating and slightly worrying. What if a sudden breeze picks up my skirt or I have an accident? Everyone will see my bits.

Since the weather is so lovely I decide to take a walk in the grounds. I veer off the path and walk on the carefully manicured carpet of grass towards a pretty red-brick and stone building. I walk up the steps and try the wooden door. It opens.

To my surprise I'm standing in a small chapel filled with light coming in from the stained-glass windows. It is very beautiful and spiritual, and I have a moment of disquiet. I shouldn't have entered a place of worship without my panties, but then I laugh at myself. How silly of me.

God created us all naked.

It is cool and peaceful as I walk to the front. There is a plain wooden cross on the back wall. I kneel on the ground and close my eyes. I pray for my father's health. Then I pray that Nigel will be cured of his addiction. Finally, I say a little prayer for me. I pray that I will stay strong. That I will not be consumed by my own carnal and base desires. For a few minutes afterward, I sit on one of the pews in quiet contemplation. Then I cross myself and leave that quiet sanctuary.

I follow the path towards the stables. There is no one around so I enter the building. Oh my, what impossibly majestic creatures! The only horses I've come into close contact with until then were the thick farm horses giving children rides on the beach.

These horses stand tall and are so sleek their necks shine even in the dim light of the stables. I walk up to one of them, and she looks at me without moving. Gently, I raise my hand and when she does not react I lay my hand on her glossy neck. She looks at me quietly. You can see her intelligence in her eyes.

I walk further in and become transfixed by a huge white horse in one of the back stalls. He is absolutely stunning, and I have this weird sensation. Almost as if I've discovered a mythical creature. I start walking towards him and he makes a jerky gesture with his head and paws the ground. I don't know much about horses but his actions are definitely not welcoming, so I stop and cautiously head towards another horse. She is such a sweet thing and so friendly I wish I had brought her a lump of sugar or an apple.

As I am standing there stroking her silky neck, whispering nonsense, and admiring her beauty, a husky puppy comes bounding up to me. The gorgeous little thing jumps excitedly around my feet. I bend down and scoop him up in my hands. He licks my face enthusiastically, making me laugh.

I catch sight of a man entering the stable and approaching me. He is dressed in khaki trousers, a checked shirt and mucky boots.

"Come here, Storm," he calls, and the bundle of fur leaps out of my hands and makes a mad dash over to him. He picks it up and looks at me with a smile. "Sorry, Miss Minton. I hope he didn't ruin your clothes. He's still a puppy and a bit full of himself. If he's not careful he's going to get kicked in the head by one of the horses."

I brush at the fur on my clothes. "Not at all. I love dogs and I enjoyed his company." I walk up to him. "Please, call me Star," I say, extending my hand.

He takes it in a rough, firm grasp. "Ray."

I tilt my head towards the horses. "Do you think I could learn to ride one of the horses?"

"I don't see why not. I'll have to ask Mr. Smirnov first, of course."

"He said I could."

"In that case. I have just the horse for you, a docile mare. Come on, I'll introduce you to Miss One Penny."

He is right. Miss One Penny is as placid as you could possibly want. She has the kindest warmest brown eyes, and I fall in love with her instantly.

"When do you want to start?"

"I don't know," I reply, rubbing Miss One Penny's face. "I don't have any riding gear. I'll have to ask Celine."

"Just let Celine know when you want to start. I'm always around anyway."

"Thanks. The white horse is really beautiful, but he seems very hostile. Does anyone ride him?"

"He's very highly strung. Only Mr. Smirnov can ride him. His name is Belyy Smert."

"Does that mean something?"

"Yeah." He chuckles. "White Death."

"Wow. That's a really wild name."

"That's only because you haven't seen him in action. He rides like the wind."

It's already twelve by then, and I head back to the house where Celine is waiting for me. I see that she has already got a laptop waiting for me.

We have lunch together and I must say I really start to enjoy her company. She is friendly and extremely eager to help me in any way she can. I ask her for some riding clothes and she instantly agrees to go to London that afternoon to buy them for me.

"Oh good. Maybe, I can start riding tomorrow," I say excitedly.

"I don't think you are here tomorrow. If I'm not mistaken you will be in London."

"Oh, okay. When am I back?" I ask feeling a bit stupid.

"I'm not sure. I can ask Mr. Smirnov's secretary, but perhaps it might be better if you find out directly from Mr. Smirnov."

I smile faintly. "Yes, I'll do that." I stuff a bit of chicken into my mouth, and wonder what Celine must think of my presence here. How odd it must seem to her that I do not even seem to know where I will be from day to day.

I feel another spurt of anger that Nigel has put me in this position, but I take a deep breath and tell myself that I'm in one of the most beautiful places on earth. There is so much for me to do, learn, explore and enjoy. I will treat this month as a holiday and take advantage of everything it has to offer. These are things that I could never dream of experiencing otherwise.

After lunch I carry my new laptop to the Chinoiserie room in the West wing of the house. I earmarked it earlier as the room that I will feel most comfortable to work in.

There is a small Victorian writing table there that reminds me of the one I have at home. It is in one corner of the room, half-hidden by a Japanese lacquer screen, and when I get behind the desk I feel quite secluded and safe. If I turn my head, I can look into the garden where there is a rose arbor close by. As I lay my laptop down and look out, and see pheasants roaming the grounds, a trio of Muntjac deer wander into my sight and start grazing. I watch them, a smile of pure pleasure on my face. What a paradise this man owns.

How lucky to be able to live here forever.

I sit down and open my laptop. Celine has already installed Word into it so I sign into my Dropbox account and access my manuscript. For the next few hours I hardly look up. My fingers fly over the keyboard as I dive back into that other world that I live in. Hours pass without me noticing. A knock on the door interrupts me. Celine comes in to say Nikolai cannot make dinner.

"That's fine," I tell her, but I am strangely disappointed.

The rest of the evening passes slowly. Celine hands me a bag with my riding gear. I phone Nigel. I bathe. I stand outside on my balcony and watch the sun set. I eat. I have

coffee. I find a book in the library and take it up to read in bed.

****

In the early hours of the morning I am startled awake at feeling a large body come into the bed and know instantly it is not Nigel. In the darkness I feel no shame, and my body opens out to welcome him.

He takes me roughly and I welcome that too.

It is *nothing* like sex with Nigel.

Sex with Nigel is warm and slow and delicious. Like being curled up on the sofa feeling warm and safe while watching a storm lash outside. Sex with Nikolai is like standing in the middle of a storm, naked, while lighting flashes all around me, my skin tingling with electricity and my heart pounding with fear and excitement.

Twenty-nine

Nikolai

All day long I tried to forget her. I told myself I didn't need to rush back for a bit of pussy. Then, like a cheap strung-out addict, I climb into my car in the early morning hours, and speed to her body, my cock hard as stone. Fuck, I even run up the stairs.

She sleeps with only a thin sheet to cover her. I walk up to her and look down on her. It's like looking at a fucking angel. Something I dreamed up.

I lift the sheet. Her nightgown has ridden up. I lay my hand on her thigh and push the nightgown upwards.

She is bare underneath. One good thing. She knows how to take instructions.

She wakes up then. In the dark she opens her legs in invitation. My body becomes electric with anticipation. I unzip my trousers and take my rigid cock out. Getting on the bed, I plunge it into her sweet cunt. She cries out. The sound is feral and uncontrolled, exciting me.

I don't use a condom and she doesn't ask for one either.

I need to be bare inside her. I just want to fill her pussy with my cum. It must be the same

for her. As soon as her wet, warm pussy sheaths me, the pent-up rage and frustration gnawing away inside me eases away. She feels incredible. So much tighter than I imagined.

I find a steady rhythm and lose myself in it. I fuck her deeply, each thrust measured, allowing me to revel in the intense pleasure of her sex.

When she lets out her scream of pleasure and comes hard around my cock, I thrust into her faster and harder, again and again, until my own release approaches.

I take her twice. The second time I am rough. She claws my back and grunts at every thrust.

When I pull out of her, she looks up at me with wide eyes. In the dim light, her eyes gleam and her hair shines like spun gold. I don't like blonde hair on a woman, but I want to bury my face in hers. I want to smell her hair.

It won't smell of biscuits, I tell myself, but I can't bring myself to do it. Through the fog, the memories come.

I leave her bed, grab my trousers, and get out of her bedroom.

1990

We wake while it is still dark, and wait our turn to use the outside toilets. Afterwards, we wash in the unheated water. Together with all the other forgotten children we file into a massive dark, dank room with row upon row of long wooden tables and benches. It is so Dickensian it reminds me of the movie *Olivera Tvista* (Oliver Twist).

We join the line of silent children moving in an orderly fashion to the counter where there are two middle-aged, uniformed women wearing blue scarves around their heads. Their hard, unsmiling eyes refuse to make contact with either Pavel or me when it is our turn. They slop thick buckwheat porridge into our trays like robots.

Both Pavel and I are starving and we scarf down the cold food quickly. I look around for Sergei and his gang, but I don't see them. After breakfast Pavel and I are separated.

He is taken to a classroom for children his age, and I am forced to join a room filled with eleven and twelve year olds. All of them look defeated and resigned to their fate. There is a girl sitting in the corner, on her own, rocking away, oblivious to us all.

The teacher wears thick glasses that make his eyes appear twice the size of normal people's eyes. He stands stiffly, several arm lengths away from his charges. There is a thick strap of leather hanging beside the blackboard. It is well worn and there is no doubt what it is used for.

We have History, followed by Math, followed by Geography, followed by Literature. Every change of routine is announced by the ringing of the bell. We don't change classrooms or teachers. We simply open new books to suit the next lesson.

As soon as recess is announced I dash out to look for Pavel. He smiles at me, and I feel relief. Unlike the children in my class who look like they have been beaten into dull acceptance, the smaller children in his class look terrified. I know I will see the same terror in my brother's eyes too if we stay here for much longer. I have to find a way to call my uncle.

"Just wait here for me," I tell him and run to the Director's office. There is no answer when I knock. Looking around me, I try the door, but it is locked. The door looks too secure to be broken in.

Lunch is watery cabbage stew. There are a few bits of vegetables floating in it. Then it is back to more lessons. We are given a short fifteen-minute break at four when we are allowed onto a concrete playground. It is bitterly cold and the kids don't seem to do much except huddle around in groups, shivering and waiting for one of the staff to allow us back in.

Here is where I see the bullies Sergei had told me about. They are older than me. One looks like he might even be sixteen or seventeen. He has dark hair and a livid scar on his face. I see them glance at me. One of them smiles. It is not a good smile. I turn away quickly and try to shield Pavel from their eyes.

After more lessons it is playtime. We go into a big room and play with a few broken toys. Two children beat an orange ball dispiritedly. Strangely there are glass cases full of donated toys still in their packaging. It is the old Russian mentality of saving for a rainy day. No child was allowed to have its personal toy. The toys belonged to the "collective".

Afterwards we are sent to wash. There is no hot water so no one wants to wash properly. After pretending to wash we file into the cold chapel for half-an-hour of prayers. The teachers walk up and down the aisle to make sure that no one talks or rises from their kneeling position.

Dinner is the same as lunch. Thin cabbage stew with a few disintegrating vegetables suspended in it, but this time there is a small piece of dry black bread to go with it.

I eat quickly and, telling Pavel to wait for me, run to the director's room. It is still locked, but as I walk back along the corridor, I meet the director coming towards me.

"Good afternoon," I greet immediately.

"Good afternoon," he returns the greeting, and carries on walking towards his office.

"Director Razumovsky, I need to make a phone call to my uncle."

He whirls around slowly, a bizarrely graceful movement for such a fat, round man. "Yes, you do, don't you?"

"Can I make it now? Please."

"It depends on ..."

"On what?"

"Whether you plan to be a good boy."

I frown. "I am good."

"Come into my room and we'll see how good you can be."

I follow him to his room and wait for him to unlock his door. We enter the room and he locks the door. Already something feels wrong. I can see his phone on the desk.

He pulls a chair to the middle of the room. "Sit down," he says with a smile.

"Thank you," I say politely and sit.

He goes behind his desk and from one of the drawers he pulls out a white handkerchief. He pulls another chair out to face me and sits in front of me. "So you need to make a phone call?"

"Yes. It is very urgent that I do, Director Razumovsky." My voice is low and respectful.

He strokes his handkerchief. "It is actually against the rules of this dyetskii dom to allow the children to use the phone as and when they please."

"This is very important. My brother and I do not belong here. I have to call my uncle so he can explain that to you. He needs to come and pick us up. He has money. He will pay you for the phone call."

His eyes gleam. "Very well. I will break the rules for you this time, but what will you do for me in return?"

It is the Russian way, bribe the doctor, bribe the nurse, bribe the director of dyetskii dom. I stare at him. "What do you want me to do?"

"Nothing too difficult," he says, and starts unbuttoning his fly. There is a fixed smile on his face.

Thirty

Star

The first thought in my head when I wake up is the shocking way I gave myself to Nikolai last night. Completely. Without any inhibitions. As if I was desperate for him. My fingernails raking his back, my hips pushing up, forcing him deeper and deeper into me. If Nigel could have seen me. How greedy I was. He would be so shocked.

I close my eyes at the memory.

We didn't even use a condom. Worse still, I don't regret it. I wanted to feel him bare inside me. I still do. Even now, just thinking about him makes me throb with desire.

My hand strays between my legs.

My flesh is distended and puffy. Ever since I arrived here I have been like this, and I cannot understand why. Why he has this effect on me. I don't even like or respect him. He exploited Nigel's weakness and blackmailed him so he could get what he wanted. That is despicable behavior.

Besides, he makes it abundantly clear that he only wants me for one thing. Not even the smallest hint of tenderness has he shown to me. He uses my body callously, then he leaves me as if I am dirt. Something unclean that he has to have, but hates himself for the weakness.

And it is a weakness. I felt it last night. This undeniable need in him for my body. He could not wait to get inside me. When he climaxed the release wasn't one from someone who had been waiting two weeks, but years and years. He became utterly rigid. Then dropped his face in the crook of my neck and remained panting for a long time, while he tried to recover.

My fingers slide over the whorls of my flesh. I think of his tongue sliding between my folds and groan. I move my fingers in a circular movement until I fall over the edge with a gasp. The orgasm is short and strangely unsatisfactory.

I get out of bed and go to the bathroom. After my shower I quickly call my nan to confirm that I will be going to see my dad at lunchtime. I know Nigel is probably in the underground on his way to work so I just leave him a text message. Then I get dressed in the same outfit I wore yesterday and go downstairs.

Celine is waiting for me.

Even though it is still early, 7.30 a.m., she tells me that Nikolai has already left for London.

"I thought I was going to London too," I say confused.

"I told Mr. Smirnov that you had mentioned wanting to learn to ride this morning, so he said you might as well stay until it is time for you to go see your father, and you could go to his London residence after seeing your dad."

"Oh!" I exclaim, surprised that all these plans were being made for me without consulting me first.

Celine nods. "I've spoken to Ray and he is ready to teach you whenever you want this morning."

I change into my new jodhpurs, polo T-shirt, and riding boots and I'm off to learn to ride a horse. I can barely contain my excitement as I walk over to the stables. Ray is already there and he waves when he sees me. "Mornin', Star."

Miss One Penny is so placid and Ray is so confident and clear in his instructions that I quickly learn to mount and dismount. In no time at all I find myself sitting on the horse while she calmly walks around the paddock.

An hour after my lesson I shower and get ready to go see my father. Taking my laptop with me I go out to the car. The same driver that came to pick me up from my house shows up.

This time Celine comes out and introduces us. His name is Oleg. He seems shy and can barely meet my eyes. The three of us travel together to London. Celine gets out at Knightsbridge since she has some errands to run. Oleg takes me to the hospital.

****

"Hello, Dad," I call cheerfully as I enter his room.

He peers at me from his bed. "Your nan said you were ill. Are you sure you're better now?"

"Dad. Take a look at me. Does it look like I'm still ill?"

He frowns at me. "No, actually, you look better than you have for years. What's up with you?"

It is my turn to frown. "What do you mean?"

"Well, you've got color in your cheeks and you don't look stressed."

I kiss him on his cheek. "I used to look stressed?"

He tilts his head to look at me. "I'm glad to see you well, Star. I've been worried about you."

I shake my head. "I can't believe we're having this conversation when you're the one just out of intensive care with a perforated bowel, a horizontal cut on your abdomen, and enough antibiotics in your body to down a horse."

"Eh, don't forget the attractive colostomy bag I'm sporting too."

I smile. It's good to see that he hasn't lost his sense of humor. "Well, hopefully that will be coming off pretty soon."

"The thing about a colostomy bag is it makes you realize that your body is actually one great big colostomy bag."

I laugh. "Stop trying to gross me out, Dad."

My phone pings, and I see there is a message from Nigel. I feel a shaft of irritation.

Me: **Weren't you supposed to wait for me to text or call?**

Nigel: **You're with your dad, aren't you?**

Me: **Please don't take any more chances.**

Nigel: **I have good news. I went to a Gamblers Anonymous. It was good. I'm going to do this Star. I'm going to beat this addiction.**

Me: **I'm so proud of you.**

Nigel: **I want to make you proud of me again.**

Me: **Let me text you when I finish with Dad.**

Nigel: **Missing you like crazy.**

I put my phone back into my purse and smile at Dad. "That was just Nigel."

"Hmmm," he says sourly.

Lunch arrives and I watch my dad pick listlessly at his tasteless food. He is supposed to be on a very strict diet for weeks. Thank god, he will be moving in with my nan. She'll keep him on the straight and narrow.

Afterwards we chat about the plants flowering in my garden. Both dad and I are keen gardeners and we always share information. I taught him that pansies can be forced to flower at the same time as sunflowers. He taught me to

190

bury a tin filled with a little beer around my dahlias. The slugs are attracted to the smell. They crawl in and drown.

I hate lying to my dad but know I have to tell him some believable story about why I will not be reachable at my home number for the next month, so tell him that I'm at a writing retreat in Surrey. Before he can ask any awkward questions, I start telling him about my horse riding session that morning. It works. We start talking about that until it is time for me to leave.

Oleg is waiting for me downstairs. He walks me to the parked car and drives me to Nikolai's London residence. Obviously he lives in a mansion right in the middle of Mayfair.

I guess there is no other way to describe his home other than to say it is exactly what someone would expect from a Russian billionaire. Lofty ceilings, granite floors, leather walls, marble pillars, intricate moldings, all designer inspired and executed from head to toe.

His housekeeper, Yana, comes out to the hallway to greet me. She is polite but stiff. She offers a tour, but I decline, so she takes me upstairs to my room. The room is cream and gold. It looks totally pristine. As if no one has ever lived in it.

She offers me something to eat and I ask her if I can have a ham and tomato sandwich in my room. Her expression of surprise is fleeting. "You can have anything you want," she clarifies.

"I know, but that's all I want right now. And a pot of tea if it's not too much trouble."

She nods and leaves me. A few minutes later a young girl knocks on the door and comes in with a tray of finger sandwiches and a pot of tea.

I eat quickly. Settling myself on the big cream bed, I open my laptop and enter my make-believe world.

Thirty-one

Star

The door opens and I jump. Without even saving my work I hurriedly shut my computer and look up. It is a force of habit. I actually feel guilty when I write. As if I'm wasting my time, or indulging myself. I never felt like that until that time I gave my work to Nigel to read.

Not even Rosa knows about that one time. I never told her because it hurt me so much I locked it away somewhere deep inside me and just pretended it never happened. After that I learned to write in secret.

What did he say that hurt me so bad?

Well, he kissed me gently on the forehead and said, "You know I love you and I want only the best for you, right?"

My heart was breaking as I nodded.

"I'm going to be really honest because I don't want you to go down the wrong path. Is that okay?"

Dumbly I nodded.

"I'm afraid to say it's very childish, my darling."

"It's a children's book," I whispered.

"I get that, but it's just badly written. I don't want you to get hurt and rejected by other people. Maybe you can try again when you are much older and you have more maturity. Then your voice and delivery style won't be so irritating."

I couldn't say a word.

"Look, why don't I take you to dinner? We'll go somewhere really nice, hmmm? How about Nama? You like their fermented mocha cheesecake, don't you?"

I nodded and forced a smile.

He smiled back and kissed me again. After that time, we never spoke about my writing again.

Now I glance up towards the door. Nikolai is standing there. There is a frown on his face. He walks towards me and I stand nervously.

"What are you doing?" he asks.

"Nothing," I say instantly.

"Are you writing to Nigel?"

"What? No. I'm not."

His eyes narrow. "So what were you doing?"

I shake my head. "I was just messing about."

"Messing about?"

"It means just wasting my time."

"Show me."

"No," I screech, alarmed.

His eyes narrow. "What are you hiding, little butterfly?"

"I'm just writing a little story."

"A story?"

"Like a book?" I try to explain.

His whole face relaxes. "You're writing a book?"

"Well, not exactly a book. Okay, yeah. It's a book. But I'm not very good and I'm not expecting to publish it, or anything. I'm just writing for fun. It's just a meaningless jumble. Just random thoughts. I'm not thinking—"

"Star?"

"What?"

"Show me," he says gently.

I take a deep breath. I can't show him. "No. It's not very good."

"Have you showed anybody?"

I bite my lip. "Yes."

"Nigel?"

"Yes."

"And he didn't like it?"

I shake my head. My god, the hurt is still there. Tears start prickling the backs of my eyes and I look down and swallow hard.

He walks over to me and puts a finger under my chin. I am so shocked by the tenderness of his gesture that my eyes widen. "What kind of book is it?"

I swallow the stone in my throat. "It's just a kids' book."

"What is it about?"

"This group of four kids who set up a private detective agency and together with their

195

dog go around solving crimes in their neighborhood."

"I want to read it."

"Why?" My voice is just a whisper.

"Just trust me and let me read it."

I hesitate.

"One chapter. If I don't like it, you've lost nothing."

"But ..."

"You can't trust the judgment of one person. So what if Nigel doesn't like it? Do you know what they told JK Rowling when they gave her a measly advance of £2,000?"

I shake my head, mesmerized that we were talking at this level.

"They told her not to give up her day job." He raises his eyebrows. "They are one of the biggest publishers in the world, and what did they know?"

I chew my bottom lip. "One chapter?"

He nods seriously. "One chapter."

"I'll get it printed off tomorrow and give it to you then."

"You'll be dead with anxiety by then. Just pass me the laptop. I'll read from there."

"But it won't feel right."

He walks away from me and settles down on one of the pristine cream couches. "I'm ready when you are."

I carry on looking at him for a few seconds more, then I make my decision. I open my very first book, when the four kids first met, and take it to him. Our fingers don't touch.

He bends his head and starts reading, and I take a step back. Not knowing what to do with myself I walk to the bed and perch on it, but I can't sit still, so I stand up and walk to the window.

I tell myself that it doesn't matter if he doesn't like it. He most probably won't, because it's not written for a billionaire. It's meant for children. I look down at the garden, and don't see a thing until I hear a sound behind me. I whirl around, my face expressionless, determined that I won't let him hurt me.

"Well?" I gasp.

Thirty-two

Star

He smiles slowly. "It's wonderful."

My eyes widen. "Are you serious?"

"I never say anything I don't mean."

I can't stop grinning. "It's actually meant for children."

"I know. It is delightfully carefree, fun, and engaging."

I keep grinning like a Cheshire cat on steroids. "Really?"

"Have you finished the whole book?"

"Finished? I'm on to my fifth adventure."

He raises his eyebrow. "You've written five books?"

"Yup."

"Why don't you find a publisher?"

"I haven't really thought about it. I didn't think it was good enough and I was just writing because I love writing. It's an escape for me. When I write I live in another world, where I can make whatever I want happen."

He smiles. "If you draft out a query letter to a literary agency I'll get Sophia, my secretary, to do all the legwork for you. She can find the appropriate agencies and send out your sample chapter, CV or whatever they require."

"Really?"

He shrugs. "Why not? There's no point keeping it locked up in your laptop."

I grin again. "Okay."

"Good."

"Thank you, Nikolai. It's very kind of you."

His face closes over again, as if he has just remembered that we are not supposed to be friends. He nods curtly. "Be ready for eight. We're going out to dinner."

When he walks out I launch myself onto bed and laugh with sheer joy. Somebody actually likes *my* writing!

****

At 7.30 p.m., I open the cream cupboard in my room and I find glamorous clothes in my size. It's almost like a Beauty and the Beast scenario, and it makes me smile.

I choose a white fitted dress with a slit at the back and team my outfit with a pair of skin-colored court shoes. I leave my hair pinned on one side with a clip and tumbling loose down my back. A slick of nude lip gloss and a layer of mascara later I am ready. I put my phone on silent mode and go downstairs. Semyon is standing in the entryway. He walks to a door, opens it for me, and stands back. He doesn't smile and neither do I.

I enter an immaculate ultra-modern sitting room. Nikolai is standing at a window looking

 199

out. At the sound of my entrance he turns around and looks at me. Instantly I feel that intense magnetic pull between us.

He turns around fully and comes towards me, stopping a foot away. "Very, very sexy," he says softly.

I feel myself blush. He is wearing a black suit, white shirt and a silver and black striped tie.

"You look pretty hot yourself," I say daringly.

His eyebrows rise in surprise. "Would you like a drink?"

"I'll have a gin and tonic, thank you."

He inclines his head. "Have a seat," he says as he saunters away.

I let go of the breath I'm holding. Whenever he is near I feel nervous and hot and bothered.

"Is Celine staying here?" I ask.

"No, she is next door with the rest of my staff."

"You bought the property next door to house your staff?" I ask incredulously.

He looks up from mixing my drink. "Why wouldn't I? It makes perfect sense. There's no travel time, and I have access to them anytime I need."

I sit. "Yes, I suppose when money is not the object you can do such things."

"Yes, money oils everything."

"I suppose you have many charities that you support?"

He smiles at me. "No."

"Why not? You're a billionaire. Think how much good you can do in the world."

He walks towards me with my drink. "Stop being naïve, Star. How do you think one becomes a billionaire in the first place?"

I scowl as I take my drink from him.

"I'm a billionaire because I made millions of people all around the world poorer. Through immoral and illegal means, I acquired resources for a fraction of the price they should have been. What should have belonged to the people I took for myself."

I stare at him, shocked.

"You seem surprised. Why?"

"That you so casually admit to immoral and illegal practices."

"All billionaires are ugly human beings, Star. When you see a billionaire receiving an award, or being applauded for his admirable philanthropy, don't be fooled. His efforts have nothing to do with charity. Billionaires are hungry people. Always wanting more and more. But after one becomes a billionaire there's only ultimate power and control left to conquer."

He takes a sip of his drink.

"I'm many things, but I'm not a hypocrite, so I won't do it."

****

He takes me to Clos Maggiore. I've heard of it but never been. It is very famous and bookings have to be made months in advance. We are shown to the coveted main room.

It is so beautiful and romantic it actually takes my breath away. It has a charming fireplace right in the middle, but what makes it so fabulous is the ceiling, which is a canopy of blossoming white flowers that seems to envelop all the diners. There are only a few tables so there is a lot of privacy. You almost feel as if you are in a magical garden.

Nikolai is charming and attentive. The wine is delicious, and in no time the sheer magic of the place snakes around me, making me feel as if I am out on a real date. Once our hands accidentally touch, I see that flash of fierce desire in Nikolai's eyes, but a waiter comes with our starters and the moment is gone.

I have truffle infused pappardelle, which is so soft and light it melts in my mouth. I look up at Nikolai. His eyes are on his food and his eyelashes make a shadow on his cheek. I watch him and feel a strange sensation in my stomach. I want to reach out and touch him. I want him to be mine. I blink in surprise. Where the hell did that come from?

He looks up. "What is it?"

I shake my head and make myself smile naturally. It must be the wine. Or the intimacy of this place. Of course I don't want him to be

mine. It's a crazy idea. To start with he can't be. And even more important, I'm married. I have Nigel. He is my life. This is just an interlude. We are passing ships. Nothing more.

"This is delicious," I say.

"Wait till you taste the beef," he replies.

He is right. The beef is amazing, and the duck fat chips are perfectly golden and crisp on the outside and fluffy on the inside.

Dessert is brought out. It is something that couples are supposed to share. I can't look away from his eyes as the burnt honey ice cream and Armagnac jelly coats my tongue.

In a strange lust-induced daze I get into the car. Our bodies don't touch and we don't look at each other, but I can feel the heat that comes from his body.

When I look down at his crotch I see how hard he is.

Thirty-three

Nikolai

https://www.youtube.com/watch?v=Q1fG OG3XXIQ
Poison

I follow her up to her bedroom. The maids have been around to turn down the bed and light the bedside lamps.

She stops in the middle of the room and half-turns to look at me. Even if I didn't know what an invitation looked like I couldn't miss that one. I look at her mouth slightly open, her cheeks flushed, and I want to hold her tight and kiss her so bad it fucking hurts, but that scenario is not in the cards.

Not for me.

I walk up to her and I hear her inhale sharply. My fingers graze the silky skin at the back of her neck as I grasp the top of her zip. The sound is loud in the silence of the room. She bends her head.

A waiting gesture. Quiet. Profound.

I let the dress fall around her ankles. Underneath she is not wearing her bra or panties. Perfect.

I loosen my tie and pull it off. The sound of silk dragging on silk is like a secret whisper. Her body tenses. I catch her right wrist, then her left, and holding them together behind her body I bind her arms with my tie, pulling it tight into her flesh.

I turn her around. Her eyes look up at me. There is no fear in them. Just pure submission. I let my eyes travel down to her breasts. The nipples hard and jutting.

She watches me as I discard my jacket and start unbuttoning my shirt. Her eyes widen at the tattoos on my chest and shoulders. I pull my shirt out of my trousers and fling it away. I take my shoes and socks off and step out of my trousers.

Her eyes drop down to my cock.

It is so hard it is jutting out of my briefs. I take them off and stand before her, naked. She exhales. Like someone who finds water at the end of a long journey across a desert.

Without being instructed she drops to her knees, slightly unsteady without her arms to balance her, and opens her mouth. Impatiently, I feed my cock into her warm, wet mouth, stretching it to its limit.

Ahhh ...

The inside of her mouth is soft, and she sucks me so gently it's addictive, but I can't have that. I'm already too involved. This has to be sex. Rough sex. Throw away sex. Just-a-woman-sucking-cock sex.

 205

I grab her hair and thrust my cock into her throat. My cock is big and she glances up at me, her eyes startled and wide, her throat making swallowing movements.

"I want to fill your belly with my cum," I growl.

She doesn't protest, just lets me fuck her mouth, long, slow, wet thrusts. It doesn't take long, before I'm spurting deep into her throat.

I look down at her. My semi-hard cock is still embedded in her mouth.

"Suck it," I say.

She suckles obediently and almost instantly I'm hard again. I pull out of her mouth and go open the bedside cabinet's drawer. I take out a bag and throw it on the bed. Then I sit on the bed with my back resting against the pillows. She doesn't move, just looks at me curiously.

"Come here," I order.

I watch her get up with difficulty, and come to the bed. I curl my hand around the base of my cock.

"Sit on my dick," I command.

She flushes a deep red. Clumsily, she climbs on the bed and knee-walks towards me. She lifts one leg over me and almost falls over. I grab her and help her to remain upright. She raises herself over me and sinks her wet pussy onto my cock.

Her head falls back and she moans with the sensation of my cock filling her up. Her tits thrust forward. I lean forward and bite a nipple.

 206

She hisses with the pain and looks at me. Slowly, she starts to fuck me. I lean back and enjoy the sight of her.

It's erotic to see her bound and helpless, but it makes her rhythm erratic. She stays too long before moving upwards, or pushes down too quickly, and gasps with pain.

"Pay attention," I growl.

She bites her lower lip and I can see her trying hard to get her groove. Her face is red, but she finally finds her rhythm, her stomach muscles tensing and flexing with effort. I start to enjoy the sensation of her tight pussy riding my cock. I push my hips up as she plunges down and she moans with pleasure as her little pussy catches my full erection. I can see by her face that she is about to come. She starts to grind herself on me.

I reach out and stop her.

She looks at me with frustration.

"You can't cum ... yet," I say and, grabbing her by her waist, move her up and down my shaft.

A grunt of distress escapes her mouth. "I have to," she squeals as an orgasm overtakes her and she comes hard on my cock, her juices run down my balls, and her pussy twitches and squeezes me.

She sits on me, impaled, bound, and panting hard.

I take her chin in my hand and pump my hips a few times, grinding her sensitive clit

against my pubic bone. She jumps. The movement drives me insane.

"I thought I told you not to cum," I say lazily.

"I couldn't help it," she mutters.

"This is your last warning. If you come again, I'll have to punish you."

Her eyes widen.

"Now ride my cock."

For a few seconds she is too stunned to respond. She just sits there with my cock fully buried inside her tight flesh, then she starts to move. Rising and sinking. I reach out my hand and slowly start to play with her clit.

"Don't," she begs.

I move my finger slowly, in circles. "No cumming until I say so."

She groans in an effort to hold back the climax, but this one's big, and it tears like a hurricane through her. Without her arms to support her she falls forward, her face landing on my chest, her muffled gasps of pleasure arousing me even more than the clenching of her pussy. Even then she doesn't stop. Her hips roll wildly as she rides me even harder.

When the last of the waves are gone and her body sags against mine, I lift her and sit her upright again. I reach forward and suck her nipple.

"That's two without permission," I say.

"Are you going to punish me?" she asks in a small voice.

 208

"What do you think?"

"What are you going to do to me?"

I put my hand into the bag and take out a pair of nipple and clit clamps, all connected by a heavy metal chain.

"Oh," she gasps.

I hold the nipple clamps open and hesitate. She looks at them anxiously and leans back.

"Come forward," I say.

Slowly she sways toward me. I hold them inches away from her breasts before suddenly letting them bite into her nipples. She jumps and whimpers in pain. Her body automatically rears back. I grasp the chain that hangs down and tug on it gently and she instantly comes forward. I pull her until she is so close to my mouth I can bite her mouth if I want to.

"Do you want me to take them off?" I ask.

She shakes her head.

I pick the other clamp and hold it open. "Are you ready?"

She nods.

I push her back and clamp her clit. Tears appear in her eyes, but fuck, she looks so perfectly sexy and erotic. I nearly cum.

I tug on the clamp. "Get to work."

She starts to rise off my cock, the chain swinging back and forth, the weight of it making her body tremble.

"Higher," I order.

She rises to the very tip of my cock.

"Now come down hard."

209

She slams down and moans at the sensation.

"Faster," I order. "It's my turn to cum."

She bounces on my cock, her tight pussy pulling and clenching at my shaft. Her pussy feels incredible and I have to hold myself back from climaxing. I like watching her. I enjoy the sight of her trying her hardest to give me pleasure. I'm getting off on the feeling of control.

Sweat glows on her skin. To my surprise I recognize the expression on her face. She is about to climax again and she is trying her damndest to hold it back. Her pussy starts clenching along my shaft.

I wait until she is at the very edge of pleasure then I reach forward and release one of the nipple clamps.

She freezes and her mouth opens in a soundless cry of pain, but it is too late, the climax is already upon her. Excitedly I watch her face, her hair, her body. She is like a fantasy come true. Perfect in every way. I wait as long as I can, just reveling in her beauty, as mind-blowing pleasure comes to claim her.

Hot blood rushes to my cock. I reach out and take the other clamp off. She screams. My hips thrust mindlessly into her, spurting hot seed into her body. I climax hard, harder than I've ever done. Breathing heavily, I look at her.

Her eyes are glazed, there are tears on her cheeks. I gently stroke her collarbone.

My cock should have been soft, but it's still hard. My gaze goes down to the last clamp. I look up and she is staring at me, her head is shaking from side to side, but her pussy is involuntarily clenching with excitement at the thought of it coming off.

"Come here," I say gently.

She rises unsteadily off my cock, her thigh muscles quivering. I grab her around her waist, lift her body, and bring her to chest level. My semen drips out of her onto my stomach and chest.

I can feel my breathing become heavier. Having her bound and completely submissive is powerfully erotic and exhilarating. I need this, I need to see her like this. Some part of me doesn't want this to end. I want to keep her like this, on the edge of madness.

I watch her carefully, the way her nipples are swollen, the shallow breaths she takes through her mouth. She is expecting pain, but she doesn't know there is a flood of pleasure waiting for her.

"You came again, didn't you?" I say softly.

She bites her lip and nods.

"Is a punishment in order?"

She doesn't say anything and I let the silence stretch. Finally, she nods.

"What sort of punishment would suit your crime?"

"Maybe you can take the last clamp off?" she whispers hesitantly. Her eyes are huge, her pupils nearly filling out her irises. She is so excited and aroused she is dripping and making a puddle on my chest. I insert my finger into her and she gasps.

"Do you like that?"

She nods.

I smile slowly and she shifts back nervously. She doesn't trust me.

I laugh.

Then when she is least expecting it, I grab the clamp and yank it off. Before she can scream I place my mouth on her clit and suck it hard, so the blood rushing to it will slow down, it will not feel as if her clit is being burnt off. Her pussy trembles as I suck her clit and finger fuck her.

Suddenly she cums. So fucking hard, her mouth opens in a silent scream and her body convulses so frenziedly she almost jerks out of my grip. She gushes all over my mouth, throat and chest, while I continue to suck her and work my fingers in her. Her orgasm just goes on and on.

In the end, she falls backwards and lies on my body, her silky hair spread over my cock. Her legs are wide open, her clit is swollen to twice its normal size, her pussy looks red and well used. A muscle is throbbing in it. I allow her to lie on me and recover for a few more minutes.

When she begins to shiver, I lift her and put her on the bed. Then I rise up. Standing over her, I turn her on her side and undo my tie. She sucks in a deep breath as her hands fall limply to

 212

the bed. There are red marks on her skin. I want to touch them, stroke them, kiss them, but I don't.

She turns back on her back and looks up at me. Her face is tear stained. She seems stunned, exposed, vulnerable. Something snaps inside me. I place my palm on her cheek and she rubs her face against my hand like a cat. The perfectly submissive action makes my cock hard again. I withdraw my hand.

"Who do you belong to?" I snarl.

"You," she whispers, as a single tear escapes out of one of her eyes and rolls down her temple.

I turn around and walk away from her.

Thirty-four

Star

I don't sleep for hours after he leaves me.

I lay on the bed, my nipples and clit throbbing, and stare blankly at the ceiling. What is happening to me? I've never been like this.

I think of Nigel. I think of our wedding. How proud I was of him. I remember our honeymoon. But none of it was ever like this. Sure we tried handcuffs and other toys, but most of the time I just wanted to giggle. At no time was it like this.

I sit up. My sex is so swollen I can't close my thighs properly. I walk into the bathroom and look at myself in the mirror. My mascara is clumpy and I just look slutty and horrible. I hear my phone ping. My dad looked so well today that I am pretty sure it's not the hospital, nevertheless I hurry awkwardly to it.

It is Nigel.

I can beat this if I know you are there for me. Don't let go, Star. Don't let anything change. I love you.

I feel so confused I can't bring myself to answer him. Nikolai's shirt is lying on the floor

214

and I pick it up and snuggle my face against it. The silky material feels cool against my heated skin.

He's nothing to you, Star.

I let the shirt drop to the ground, walk to the bed, and lie down in the dark. There are a couple more pings, but I don't get up to look at the phone. I just stay very still until I fall asleep.

****

When I go down the next morning Nikolai is nowhere to be found, but Celine is in the dining room. She jumps up with a big smile.

"Good morning," she greets cheerfully.

"Morning."

"Is everything all right with your room?"

I smile. "Yes. Thank you."

"Good. Can I order you something for breakfast?"

I stare at her for a few seconds. "Can I have a Russian breakfast today?"

"Sure. What would you like?"

"I think I'll have the Russian dumpling that's eaten either with sour cream or jam. I don't remember the name?"

"I know what you mean. I will tell the Chef. Be back in a sec," she calls and leaves the room.

I go and stand by the window. It is going to be a lovely day. Already the sun is high and bright and the air is hot. I hear her come in and turn around. "Where is Nikolai?"

215

"Mr. Smirnov had an early meeting."

I nod.

"Sophia, his secretary, has a list of literary agencies. She has already gone through it and picked out all the agencies that represent authors who write in the same genre as you. Mr. Smirnov thought that you could spend the morning crafting a letter for Sophia to send."

I smile. "Gosh. You are both very efficient. It would have taken me weeks to do that."

She looks pleased. "I try my best."

"Thank you. I really appreciate it."

"You're welcome. If there is anything you would like me to do just ask."

"I think I'm good."

"Would you like to do some shopping after you see your father today?"

"No, I'll just come back here and write."

"Mr. Smirnov was saying that you can go back to Surrey this evening if you want to continue with your horse-riding lessons."

"Will he not be going?"

"I don't think so, but I'm not a hundred percent sure. I'll check with Sophia and let you know."

I feel an odd heaviness settling in my chest. It's better this way. The more time I spend with him the worse it is going to be. "No. It's okay. Don't worry about asking Sophia. I would like to go back to Surrey."

"Fine, I'll arrange that for you," she says with a happy smile.

****

After I hammer out a query letter, I tackle writing a CV of sorts. It unfortunately has to be very short on account of the fact that I have never worked a day in my life, and my talents are non-existent to say the least. It will have to do. I email everything to Celine. While I am deciding if I should go out to the garden for a while, Nigel texts me. I lock my bedroom door and call him back.

"Hey," he says, and I clutch the phone hard. His voice is familiar and warm. He loves me. When all this is over he will be there for me.

"Hi," I say softly.

"How are you?"

"Fine."

"Miss me?" he asks. His voice is wheedling. He needs to hear me say it, but I can't. Not after what I did last night with another man.

"Where are you?" I ask.

"At home."

"Why aren't you at work?"

"I didn't feel good. I'm seriously thinking of leaving my job. I need to get away from all those old familiar things that remind me of my old addiction. I need new places, new faces, and new experiences if I am to beat this."

"I'm glad to hear that you are taking your recovery process so seriously."

"Damn right I'm serious about this. Look what I've done, Star. I've nearly destroyed us. I made a mistake, but I've changed. I wish you could see me now. Two days in and I already feel so good and empowered."

"Imagine what you'll be like by the time I see you."

"I can't wait one month to see you, Star."

I lean against the bathroom door. "One month is not a long time."

"Fuck, if only you were in London and not in Surrey."

"I'm not in Surrey." I bite my tongue as soon as I say it.

"Where are you then?"

"London."

"What?"

"Yeah, I'm in Mayfair."

"Star. You've got to come and see me."

"No. Nikolai will be furious."

"For god's sake, *I'm* your husband."

"No. I can't come to you. It'll be a mess."

"Can't you just make an excuse and come over? Tell him you're going shopping or something?

"I can't go anywhere alone. I have to take the driver everywhere. He'll find out."

"What a control freak. Hang on, I have an idea. Why don't you call Rosa and ask her if we can use her flat for half-an-hour? You keep a key to her flat here don't you?"

"Yes, but—"

"Come on, Star. I just want to see you. It'll give me the strength to be strong. You're my rock. I need this. Please, Star. I may never get another chance to see you again for a month."

"Rosa's not going to like it."

"She's not that fucking selfish and petty, is she?"

I sigh.

"Please, Star. I just want to see you. Five minutes."

"I'll have to call Rosa first."

"I'll be waiting here."

I hang up and wince. I know it's a bad idea, but I can't say no to Nigel. Besides, it will be good for me to remind myself that Nigel is my husband. The one that I owe my allegiance and loyalty to. The one I'm doing all this for.

I call Rosa and at first she says no. She doesn't want Nigel in her apartment and it would make her vomit to think of him naked anywhere on her furniture.

I assure her that neither Nigel or me will be getting naked in her apartment and she reluctantly agrees. I call Nigel back and tell him where Rosa's key is. We agree to meet right after I have seen my dad.

Thirty-five

Star

When I come down after seeing my dad I get into the car and, as casually as I can, tell Oleg that I need to go and see a friend. He nods politely and I give him Rosa's address.

"Wait here for me, please," I instruct, and quickly walk up the path to her building's entrance.

I'm so nervous my hands are shaking as I ring on the doorbell. Nigel buzzes me up immediately.

By the time I get to the fourth floor he is waiting for me outside the lift. He looks well, very well. There is no trace of sadness or regret in his face. I'm not sure how I feel about that.

He smiles at me and I smile back at him. With complete confidence, he curls his arm around my back possessively, and leads me into her apartment. Inside, he wraps his arms around me and tries to kiss me, but I evade him.

"Don't," I mutter, and walk away from him.

"What's the matter?"

"Nothing. I just need a bit of time."

He looks at me strangely. "Okay."

"So how are you?"

He shrugs. "Without you, I'm nothing, Star."

"It sure doesn't look like it," I mutter under my breath.

He walks up to me and touches my hair, his eyes pained. "Star? Why did you say that? I'm putting on a happy face because I don't want to spoil the little time we have together."

I look up deep into his eyes. He is not lying. *But you never could tell when he was lying, could you?* I ignore that voice of reason and let myself believe him. I love him. I know I love him. Of course, I love him. What I have with Nikolai is just lust. Sex. It will burn itself out. I know that. This is the real thing.

He bends his head and lets his lips gently brush mine. I stiffen.

"I want to make love to you, Star," he says.

"No," I gasp.

"Why not?"

"I can't," I gasp.

"Why not?"

"I'm not a whore, Nigel. I can't go from his bed to yours. Just like that," I cry.

"Jesus, Star. I'm your fucking husband."

I cover my face with my hands. "I know. I know, but I just can't do it. Not here. Not in Rosa's apartment."

"She'll never know. Come on."

"I promised her we wouldn't do it here."

"What a fucking selfish lesbian bitch! Why should she care if we fuck?"

I take a step back. "Stop being horrible about her, Nigel. Please," I cry angrily. It seems easier to fight about Rosa than deal with what is really going on.

He seems to take a hold of himself and forces a smile. "I didn't come here to fight with you about Rosa, Star. I just want to talk to you. Why don't we sit down and talk, hmmm?"

"I can't. The driver is waiting downstairs."

"Fuck's sake, Star. He's a driver. That's his fucking lot in life. He waits around all day for people."

I look at him astonished as if I have never seen him before. This arrogance. Where did it come from? Was it always there?

"I'm sorry. I'm sorry. I'm just hurt and angry and I'm lashing out on all the wrong people. Of course, you have to go. It's okay. I'm glad I got to see you, and see for myself that you are well."

"Yeah, I'm well."

He pauses. "He doesn't do anything kinky to you, does he?"

I flush to the roots of my hair. "No," I croak.

"I'll kill him if he hurts a hair on your head," he thunders.

My head starts to hurt. "I got to go."

"Won't you even kiss me before you go?"

I walk up to him and press my lips against his. I don't know what I expect, but I feel nothing. He wraps his arms around me and deepens the kiss. His tongue seeks entry, hooks my tongue into his mouth and sucks it ardently. My mind stays alert. It tells me it's getting late. He slips his other hand down and tries to lift up my skirt.

I pull away angrily. "I told you not to do that."

"What are you doing? Saving yourself for him?" he sneers.

My eyes widen. "How dare you?"

He runs his hand through his hair distractedly. 'I'm sorry. I'm sorry. I don't know why I said that. I can't handle this. You're my woman and ..." He drops his hand in a defeated gesture. "Never mind. What's the fucking point?"

"I wish I'd never come."

"I'm sorry, darling. All I ever seem to do is apologize."

"We're both stressed. Don't worry about it."

"Your mother keeps calling."

"I'll call her today. I'm telling everybody I'm on a writing retreat for a month. So if you can keep to the same story it should all be well."

"Right. That's a good idea." He looks at me beseechingly. "I'm counting the days when you will come back home."

I drop my eyes. "Yeah, me too."

"I can't wait for us to start our new life. We'll do different things. I'll be home more. We'll have a new life together. A better life."

He doesn't understand. I liked my old life, very much, but I found out it was a lie. "Okay."

"I love you."

"Me too. I've got to go."

He walks me to the lift. "I'll hang around here for a few minutes before I come down."

I smile. "Talk to you later."

The lift doors open. I go in and turn around to face him. He looks at me intently as if he will never see me again. The doors close on him and I exhale and lean against the metal wall. I don't allow myself to think. I just repeat in my head.

I love my husband. I love my husband. I love my husband.

Like a mantra, and like a mantra it stuns my mind, so I stop thinking.

I become blank.

Thirty-six

Star

https://www.youtube.com/watch?v=7HKo
qNJtMTQ
Skyfall

"**F**inished meeting your friend?" Oleg asks over his shoulder.

I catch a glimpse of his face in the rearview mirror. "Yes, thank you. We can go back now," I tell him. I suddenly feel very tired. I let my body lean back into the seat and close my eyes. I decide at that moment that I won't meet Nigel again during this month. It stressed me out and it didn't make me or him feel good. Right now I even feel as if I've done something shameful.

My phone pings. It is Nigel telling me he is sorry. I feel too exhausted to answer. I delete the message and stare out of the window until we reach Nikolai's house.

"Will you need me again today?" Oleg asks with a smile.

"Probably not. It'll likely be tomorrow."

"Just let me know," he says, before getting out of the car to open my door for me.

I walk to the house and press the buzzer. Yana opens the door.

"Hello, Miss Minton," she greets formally.

I hear footsteps coming from behind her and instantly my body stiffens and reacts so much that Yana cannot help but notice. She looks behind her then takes a respectful step backwards.

"May I speak to you in the library?" Nikolai asks.

Nervous energy cuts through me like a bolt of electricity. "Of course," I say as casually as I can.

Without another word, he turns and walks away. His tall body stiff and purposeful. I swallow my anxiety and follow him into the library.

"Close the door," he says, stopping in the middle of the room.

I shut the door quietly and turn around.

He looks at me and his face is entirely without expression. I mean nothing. Nothing. A shiver goes through me. I lift my chin. I won't let him scare me. I haven't done anything wrong.

"Where have you been?" His voice is pleasant.

"Nowhere," I say defiantly. I shouldn't feel guilty. I went to see my husband.

"I'll ask you one more time. Where have you been?"

"And I'll tell you one more time. Nowhere."

He walks over to me and catches me by the throat. I feel fear flash through me at the cold expression in his eyes. I swallow hard but I don't blink or back down.

"Did you give your body to him?"

My eyes widen with shock.

"Did you?" he asks again, his hand tightening around my throat.

"No, no I didn't," I choke out.

His hand eases the pressure on my throat but his eyes are narrowed and hard. "Why did you go to him then?"

Hot tears fill my eyes even though I try to hold them back.

"Tears, Star? I thought you were better than that."

"How did you know?"

"I have to be stupid not to. Rosa is at work and you sneak off to her apartment for fifteen minutes."

"I just wanted to see him again," I say miserably.

"I forbade any contact between you and him."

"No. That's not true," I deny hotly. "You instructed me not to call him. I didn't. I've not broken any of your stupid rules."

"But you *do* call and text him. All the fucking time."

"Well then, what do you want from me? He's my husband and he's ill and unhappy. I can't just leave him alone for one month. I need to know that he's okay," I cry defensively.

"He's neither ill nor unhappy. He's a psychopath who is playing you."

"I love him and I want to go back to him." It's far from the truth but that's what comes out of my mouth.

His lips twist cynically. "Why? Does he make you scream uncontrollably when you cum? Do you make those little kitten noises and rub your hot cunt on his dick to make yourself cum because you are so fucking desperate to cum?"

More tears run down my cheeks. "Fuck off you cold, ugly bastard."

"Answer the question," he orders coldly.

"None of your fucking business," I scream.

He smiles. An ugly movement of his lips. "If you didn't have sex. What did you do?"

I can't look him in the eye. I can't tell him that Nigel kissed me. My eyes slide away.

Very gently he lays his finger on my lower lip and inserts it into my mouth.

"Suck my finger," he orders.

I want to resist but I just can't. My body *wants* to do it.

"Look into my eyes."

I force myself to meet his eyes. Twin fires are burning in them.

"This mouth belongs to me. If you dare let any other man touch it, I will kill him. Do you hear me?"

I nod helplessly.

"Good." He pulls his finger out.

I am frightened of him, but I am wet between my legs. He lets go of my throat and steps away from me.

"Strip," he orders.

I don't even attempt to disobey. My hands are shaking as they fumble with the buttons of my shirt. His eyes never leave me. I shrug out of my shirt and let it fall to the floor. His phone vibrates in his jacket. He completely ignores it. I unzip my skirt, push it down my hips, and let it fall down my legs. I take off my bra. My heart is beating really fast. I let my bra drop. His eyes are like lasers. My hands cover my breasts.

"Like Eve. You learned shame?"

"Don't do this," I beg.

"Strip."

The word is like a bullet in the silence.

Casting my eyes down I take off my last article of clothing.

"Look at me."

I raise my eyes.

He watches me closely. Without lust. Without longing. As if I'm a piece of furniture he has bought and he is checking for scratches.

"I'm sorry, okay. I won't go and see him anymore," I blurt out.

"Sorry? Who do you think I am? Your priest? You do something you know is wrong and you go to confession to ask for forgiveness so you can do it all over again tomorrow with a clear conscience." There is raw anger in his voice.

 229

"All right. You've humiliated me now, okay. What else do you want from me?"

He undoes his belt and unzips his trousers. "I want you to suck me off, Princess."

My mouth opens in shock. "I'm not a whore."

"You're not a whore? Why are your eyes dilated then?"

"They're not," I deny.

"Princess, you can fight me all you want and pretend until the cows come home, but your mouth is watering for my cock."

I bite my lower lip. I hate him. I hate that he makes me feel the things I feel. When I am with him I feel like an animal. So cheap, and base, and ugly.

"It's your own fault, anyway. Look how hard you've made me," he says and takes his cock out.

I stare at it. It is throbbing for me. As if I am hypnotized I go forward and kneel in front of him. I take his cock in my hands. As soon as my fingers touch him I feel his body tremble.

As I open my mouth he rakes the fingers of both his hands into my hair and grabs my head. "That's right, Princess. Get me off. Make me forget that you went to see another man."

Pre-cum smears on my tongue as he pushes his cock into my mouth.

I swallow it with relief, close my eyes and moan. The taste of him to obliterate the taste of my husband. How can I admit how much I hated my own husband's touch?

I start sucking him deeply. He grips my hair tighter and pushes all the way down to my throat. I look up at him from beneath my eyelashes.

"Fuck you, Star," he growls. "Fuck you!"

I lick the underside of his cock and alternate with a sucking motion.

Greedily I milk the thick drops of cum that slide down my throat. The angry veins underneath his cock throb and pulsate on my tongue.

I stroke the bit of his cock that I cannot get into my mouth. Sucking his cock feels good. I swallow it as deep and as hard as I can.

"Play with yourself, Star. Show me how dirty you can be. Open your thighs wide and play with yourself."

I slide my hand between my legs and start to play with myself. I am so wet and swollen. I'm afraid I will climax before him. It's never happened to me before, but I'm going to climax while sucking cock. I slow my trembling hand down.

"Don't slow down," he orders. "I want you to cum while my cock is in your mouth."

I speed up and almost immediately a monster of an orgasm rips through me. I lose control of my muscles. My mouth opens in a strangled scream and my hands instinctively go around his thighs. As I come back down I gently suck on his cock as if it is a pacifier. It is my pacifier. I could go to sleep with his cock in my mouth.

He looks down on me. A possessive, cruel, expression on his face.

Then he starts fucking my mouth. Hard and rough. His cock choking me. I don't protest. No, to the contrary. I enjoy watching him lose control.

He is like a beast, a bull that is let out of its pen. He thrusts deep into my throat, and with a roar starts to climax. Not the way he usually does, but with a kind of pent-up fury. In a frenzy. I swallow the hot spurts eagerly. Finally, my orgasm is over. He stops bucking his hips. His chest rises and falls as he takes deep breaths. I look up at him and he is looking down at me. There is an odd expression on his face.

"Go take a shower," he tells me. His voice is hard and cold again.

I pull my mouth away from his cock, stand, and get dressed. Without looking back at him I go upstairs to my room and into my bathroom.

I switch on the shower and stand under the waterfall. Drops of water rush around me. I feel the first sob come so quietly. It is lost in the roar of the water. The second sob shakes my shoulder. I don't know why I'm crying, but it feels as if my heart is breaking.

I feel trapped. I'm married to Nigel and in an unexplainable sexual bind with Nikolai. I made a promise to Nigel. All said and done Nigel loves me. Nikolai, on the other hand, almost hates me. To him I am a thing.

In a month's time he will change me for someone else.

I cry because I am hurt. I cry because I don't understand what is happening to me. Why I am so addicted to Nikolai's body. This wild lust swirling around inside me confuses me and frightens me. It feels foreign. The shower door behind me opens suddenly.

I whirl around.

Nikolai is standing there. He comes in wearing all his clothes, even his shoes. He holds me against his chest and I sob. I really sob. When my sobs subside. He gets on his knees. Into the exact same position he had put me in. He parts my thighs.

Raking my fingers into his hair I pull him towards my crotch. Exactly as he had done to me. I grind my clit against his tongue and face until I climax. When it's over I collapse backwards against the warm tiles.

The air is filled with steam but his eyes glitter like sad stars.

Thirty-seven

Nikolai

I stare at the director in shock. I know about men like him. Mama warned me about them when I was Pavel's age.

He smiles at me before gently taking his penis out. It is small, fat and white. He strokes it lovingly and it grows. A sigh escapes his thin lips. I stay frozen in my chair. He spreads the white handkerchief on his lap and carefully, tenderly, as if it is the most precious thing in the world, lays his penis on top.

"Just put your hand on me," he coaxes in a thick voice. "You can make your phone call after that."

I stare at the white worm and consider my options. He makes my skin crawl. I don't want to touch him but I need to make that phone call.

"Don't you want to call your uncle to come and take you and your brother away?" he asks.

I nod.

"So come on over and kneel down in front of me."

I stand and take the two steps that put me right in front of him.

"Go on. Get on your knees. The sooner you do this the quicker you can call your uncle."

I kneel in front of him.

He licks his lips "Do you think I have a nice cock?"

I look at it. It is smaller than mine, and definitely much smaller than my father's. As a matter of fact, it's hardly bigger than Pavel's. I nod slowly.

"Would you like to touch it?" he encourages softly.

I reach out my hand and touch it. The skin is smooth and warm.

"There. That wasn't so hard, was it? Why don't you put it in your mouth?"

I look up at him. "Why?"

"You can suck it. Just like a lollipop. It tastes very good."

He is the director. I am just one boy. An orphan. Mama and Papa don't even know where we are. Nobody cares about me. Nobody will believe my story. I will not get my phone call if I do not do as he asks. I will get punished. The strap will be used on me. Far easier to do what he asks. Then I will get my phone call and Pavel and I can leave this horrible place.

I look at the director's penis. It doesn't look like a lollipop, but it looks clean. Maybe it won't taste too bad.

I once heard my mother tell my father, "I worry about Nikolai. He will either be a great man or a convict. He is too hard-headed, too inflexible. He doesn't know how to live and let live. To compromise."

How right you were Mama.

I'm doing this for all the other boys. I bend my head to take his soft white penis in my mouth. I'll hurt him so bad he'll never be able to do this to anyone else ever again. As I open my mouth in preparation to bite down as hard as I can, the blow to my head is sudden, completely unexpected, and so extremely hard that my head jerks as if it is about to come off my neck. My teeth feel like they are vibrating.

I fall to the ground.

My eyes cannot focus properly. Everything is a blur. The director stands up. The handkerchief floats to the floor near my head. It is so white. So beautifully ironed. Then it all goes black.

****

I'm blasted awake by pain. Blows, kicks and punches are raining down on me. My head, my face, my body, my legs. They arrive so quickly from so many places. It is impossible to defend myself against them. All I can do is curl up tightly and pray that it will end soon.

"Stop," a voice orders. Even battered, and in agony, I recognize the voice.

The blows stop.

I don't move. My whole body is on fire with pain.

 236

A pair of shoes come into my vision. "Now get up, and get out of my office."

Excruciating pain everywhere. I sit up slowly. Tears are running down my face. Every inch of me screams in pain as I try to stand. I end up groveling on the floor.

"Not such a brave man, are you?" he taunts.

I lift my head and look out of eyes that are blurred with the blood running into them and look around me. There are five boys. I recognize them instantly. The bullies. There is blood-lust in their eyes. They are strung up. They want to finish the job.

I stand up slowly, gritting my teeth with the pain, and limp out of that office. I know I have to find Pavel. I have to protect him. There are monsters in this place. The other kids are already in bed and I walk through the deserted building.

I find Pavel in his bed. He is shivering with terror. When he sees me he starts sobbing uncontrollably.

"Niko, Niko, what have they done to you?"

"It's nothing. I'll be all right. It looks worse than it is," I say through swollen lips. I can hardly see or talk. I need to lie down. I feel weak. I slowly lower myself on my bed. I reach for my blanket and tear a long strip out of it. I tie one end to his wrist and the other to mine.

"What are you doing?" Pavel asks.

"Don't take this string off no matter what happens. If anybody tries to take you, you wake me up, all right?" I say sternly.

He nods.

I lie down.

"I'm scared," Pavel says.

"Nothing will happen to you while I am here," I say.

Nobody comes for Pavel that night, but Sergei comes for me.

"I can't go," I whisper.

He shakes his head. "What did you do?"

"I tried to bite him."

He looks unimpressed. "That was a stupid thing to do. You're fucking lucky they did not shoot you up with chemicals and send you to the mental asylum or the lying down rooms. The kids there never leave their beds. They are tied up and spend all day staring at the ceilings."

****

That night the pain is awful. The bruises and wounds on my body heal over the next few weeks. I join Sergei's gang and get the gang's tattoo which protects me. There is no more talk of making a phone call. The only way Pavel and I are leaving this place is if we find a way to escape. The group of boys who beat me up look at me with sneering expressions, but they don't bother me again.

238

I watch Pavel like a hawk during the day and not a single night goes by that I forget to join myself to him with the strip of blanket. I keep him safe day and night, but as the days become weeks, and weeks become months, my brother's bright blue eyes dim. He becomes sadder and sadder.

I cannot understand it. He is like a plant that is wilting away right before my eyes. He shows no interest in anything anymore. Not even when I outline our escape plan to him.

Thirty-eight

Star

When I go outside to the car, Oleg is not there. There is another man wearing a chauffeur uniform who opens the door for me.

"Where is Oleg?"

He makes a downward movement with his mouth. "Gone."

I frown. "Gone?"

"Yeah. I've taken his place."

"Oh! Why?"

Something flickers in his eyes. "Because you gave him the slip yesterday."

My mouth drops open. "He's been fired?"

"Uh ... huh."

"But that's not fair," I blurt out to the complete stranger.

His lips twist with contempt. "Life's not fair. I've got to warn you that I'm not allowed to let you out of my sight. Even if you want to go to the bathroom I'll have to go in first and check that there are no windows through which you can climb out."

My face flushes with fury and embarrassment. How dare Nikolai treat me like this. I turn around and go back into the house. I stride to the study where Celine told me he was working. I wrench open the door and Nikolai looks up from his paper. He seems completely unperturbed.

"How could you be so heartless? How could you fire Oleg? He's such a good guy. It was not his fault that I went to see Nigel. I want him to be reinstated. I want him to be my driver."

Nikolai

She stands there spitting furiously. I love watching her when she is angry. It is in such stark contrast to when she was bound and helpless. I pick up my coffee cup and bring it to my lips.

"You must have misunderstood your position here. You have no rights other than to service me, little butterfly," I murmur mildly.

She becomes rigid as if I have struck her. I watch her swallow hard, she is about to say something else, when she decides not to. She drops her fair head in defeat.

The smooth curve of her neck is delicate and swanlike. My hands itch to encircle it but I haven't forgotten what she did yesterday. How dare she be so blindly loyal to him. A smarmy creep like him? I watch her over the rim of my cup and I feel anger boiling in my veins again. I realize I am clenching the handle of my coffee cup so hard it is in danger of breaking off. I lay it carefully on the saucer.

Suddenly the anger changes. Fuck him. I've got her now. And I'll have my fill of her. I'll fuck her until there is nothing in her head but me. To hear her scream my name.

"As a matter of fact, I think I'd like to have you again," I say softly.

She looks up at me, her eyes glittering with resentment and hate. We stare at each other but she can't hold my stare. She drops her gaze.

"I'll see you in my bedroom then," she says tightly, and turns away.

"No. Not there."

She swings around with surprise. "Where?"

I stand and sweep my hand over the things on my table. They crash to the floor. The coffee cup smashes. Semyon comes running in. I don't take my eyes off her face.

"Get out," I say.

Semyon closes the door quietly on his way out.

She walks towards me stiffly. I fit my hands around her slender waist, lift her onto the table and lay her on her back. She looks up at me, breathing hard. I pull her skirt up. She is beautifully bare and already soaking wet. Lifting her right leg I kiss the inside of her knee. She inhales sharply. I suck the thin skin, staring at her.

"Play with yourself," I murmur.

She bites her lower lip. That always drives me crazy. I can feel my cock hard and hot in my pants.

Slowly, her hand trails tantalizingly down her stomach towards her pussy. I watch hungrily as her fingers slide between the pink folds. At first hesitantly, then she goes for it. Rubbing herself. Her hips jerking. The smell of her arousal fills my nostrils driving me crazy. All I want to do is get inside her.

Just when I know she is at the very edge, and her body is already bowing with the coming onslaught, I grab her hand and hold it away from her throbbing flesh. She looks up at me, her eyes wide and begging.

I smile.

"Why won't you let me come?"

I bend my head and swipe my tongue on her open pussy. She shudders and pushes her groin towards my mouth. I hold back.

"Do you want me to suck you?"

"Yes," she gasps.

"How much do you want it?"

"A lot."

"Exactly how bad?"

"Bad. Really bad."

I swirl my tongue within the sweet flesh, making her moan. I dip my tongue into her hole and she shudders. I lick her a while, enjoying the taste, teasing her, and making her clench with frustration.

"Go on, make yourself cum," I order.

Her fingers move. When she is about to cum I stop her again. I refuse to let her come for ages, until her teeth are clenched, and she is almost in tears.

Then I instruct her to put her elbows under her knees and open wide. With her pussy completely exposed to me I unbuckle my pants and plunge my cock into that tight little cunt in one swift movement. She grunts with the sensation.

I pound into her until her orgasm washes over her. So hard she gasps for breath. I cum with her. Coating the walls of her pussy with fresh cum. My cum. I'll wash that spineless fool out of her. Not even the memory of him will remain by the time I am finished.

Thirty-nine

Star

For the next four days I don't see Nikolai. I write, I ride, I swim, I walk the wonderful grounds and I try unsuccessfully to befriend Belyy Smert, but he steadfastly refuses all my overtures.

Every day at lunchtime I go to visit my father and I chat with Rosa over the phone. Every morning and night I call Nigel and we talk. We seem to have come to a strange sort of truce. We behave more like friends. He tells me about his progress at Gamblers Anonymous and I tell him about my riding efforts. The unspoken understanding is that everything will go back to normal between us when this month is over. He must guess that things can never truly be the same, but I don't think he realizes how different they will be. How much I've changed.

During the night I find it hard to sleep, so I read until the early morning hours. I've already read two old classics and now I'm almost finished with Their Eyes Were Watching God.

Time passes quickly and I keep myself busy, but inside I know I am waiting. Waiting for Nikolai's return.

I push open my doors and walk out onto the balcony.

The air is lovely and warm and the inky night sky is alive with stars. Sometimes I can't believe how beautiful this little parcel of land is. I take a deep breath and become aware of another person on the balcony. I turn my head and see Nikolai leaning against the wall smoking a cigarette. The tip glows red but it is too dark to see his features.

I didn't even know he was back.

I watch him flick away his cigarette and come towards me. His gait prowling. My mouth is suddenly so dry. I have to swallow a few times to get the saliva going. He towers over me for a few seconds, looking down at me. Unsmiling. Unwelcoming. Remote.

Wordlessly his hand slides under my skirt and up my thighs. His fingers scratch under the rim of my panties. Since he's not been around, I've started wearing underwear again. He pulls them down roughly with a grunt of displeasure.

He unzips his trousers.

In the dark the thick tip of his cock gleams with pre-cum. I begin to throb for him. His hand curls itself under my thigh. He lifts it and, opening me up for him, slams into me. My eyes roll back with pure pleasure.

He fucks me hard. Really hard.

My back scrapes against the wall behind me. It never crosses my mind that I can ever have an orgasm by such a brutal coupling, but without warning I feel myself starting to crest.

Go over. And fall ...

The sound that comes out of me is a screech. Like a cat yowling, screaming his name. Filling the still air. Shocking me. He thrusts even harder and allows himself to climax too.

He stays inside me for a few more seconds, our breaths mingling. Then he pulls out of me. I feel his cream spill out of me and drip down my thighs.

He steps back. "Get on your bed and wait for me on your hands and knees. I haven't had enough of you yet," he says.

Silently, I pull myself away from the wall and go into my room. I position myself on the bed as he instructed, and wait for him.

I don't have long to wait. He takes me like a bull. There is so much need and urgency. I think I will break in two, but I don't.

I just reach for the stars and this time I touch them.

Nikolai

I look at her under me, satiated, and well fucked, her mouth swollen from all that cock sucking I made her do, and I want to fuck her all over again. It's weird. The law of diminishing returns says that the more I fuck her the less I

should want her. In this case, the more I fuck her the more I want her.

She's like a fucking Class A drug.

I pull away from her delicious body.

"Nikolai," she whispers.

I turn my head and look down at her.

"Who is that blonde boy in the painting downstairs?"

I stop breathing.

1992
Russia

Two goddamn years pass in that hellhole. Some of the bigger boys leave and new children are brought in. Sergei turns sixteen. In a year he will be gone. The other gang members want me to take over, but I refuse. My goal is not to be leader. My goal is to escape with my brother.

I can see that the longer we stay here the more he becomes a shadow of himself. His personality has completely changed. He sits alone for long periods without interaction. Yesterday when we talked in the dining room he'd suddenly looked at me and there was something desperate in his eyes.

"What is it, Pavel?"

"I wish I was strong and smart like you, Nikolai."

"You are strong, Pavel. And you're brave and kind."

"No. Not like you, Nikolai. One day you'll leave here and be free."

I frown. "I'm not going anywhere without you. We will leave together, Pavel, and very soon you'll see."

"'I'll never leave here, Nikolai." He dabs his eyes with the back of his hand. My heart aches to see my brother cry.

"Of course we will. We will leave together and we'll survive this world," I tell him.

I should have known then. I should have understood that faraway look in his eyes. He was not strong enough for this place. I should have taken him away from here.

I am in my class when Vasily, one of the teachers, sends for me. My heart starts to race. Somehow I know why I'm being summoned even before I step into his office.

Forty

Star

"**M**y brother," he says bitterly. Before I can ask him anything else he gets up, pulls on his pants, and walks towards the door.

"Nikolai, I'm sorry. I shouldn't have asked you."

He doesn't turn around. "No, you shouldn't have," he says coldly, before shutting the door quietly.

I close my eyes. Why on earth did I ask that? I'm so stupid. It's so blatantly obvious he doesn't want to share any information about his life with me. I don't see him again that night. I fall asleep feeling sad. Sad that everything I believed in is gone. Sad that I can never have anything more than sex with Nikolai.

****

I sleep badly and wake up even earlier than usual. It is only six o'clock, but it is already bright outside. I go out onto the balcony in the cool air as I do every morning and drink in the beauty of the grounds. Far in the distance I see something. I crane my neck forward and squint my eyes.

Nikolai is riding Belyy Smert.

The way they move takes my breath away. They fly over the green grass. They are perfect together. Both achingly beautiful but hostile and aloof. I watch them until they are hidden by the trees.

Nikolai doesn't stay for breakfast.

I can't help the disappointment that settles inside me. Every time it looks as if Nikolai's walls might be crumbling they repair themselves, right before my eyes, becoming stronger and more impenetrable.

I sigh deeply and tell myself it is better this way. Then I get into my riding gear and go for my riding lesson. Ray is pleased with my progress. I'm getting good. Obviously I can't gallop the way Nikolai was doing this morning, but I can confidently put Miss One Penny into a brisk trot.

An hour later I am back in the house. After a quick shower I have breakfast with Celine. Halfway through I almost die of shock. My phone pings and when I look at it curiously I see that there is an email from one of the agencies I sent my manuscript to in my inbox. Nervously, I stare at it.

"What is it?" Celine asks.

"It's one of the Literary agencies."

"Open it then"

I chew on my bottom lip worriedly. "I read on the net that if you get such a quick answer it's most likely a rejection."

She makes a small movement of her shoulders. "I don't think you should automatically assume that. Sophia did a very clever thing. She knew that all the other writers would be sending their applications in by second class post, so to make your submission stand out from everybody else she put it into handmade leather envelopes, and had it couriered to all of them. She thought, and I completely agree with her, that if you have the confidence to show that you think your work is important enough to deserve urgency, the agency will be sufficiently intrigued to give it priority too."

My eyes widen with astonishment. "Wow, she did all that. She doesn't even know me. I must send her a box of chocolates or something to say thank you properly."

"Are you going to look, or shall I?"

I hand the phone to her. "I think you better."

She takes it and taps on the email, her eyes moving across quickly as she reads the reply. She looks up from the screen. "What do you think they've sent?"

I stare at Celine. Surely, she wouldn't be keeping me on tenterhooks if they said no. "They said yes?" I ask uncertainly, hardly daring to believe such a thing.

She grins widely. "Yes, they said yes. They want to see the rest of the book."

"Give me that phone," I shout excitedly.

She hands me the phone and I read the precious words from someone called Daria Elizabeth Bowen from Peter Thiel's Literary Agency. Basically, she likes my first three chapters and wants me to send the rest of the manuscript as soon as possible.

'Oh, my god. Oh my god," I squeal happily, jumping out of my chair and doing a happy dance. Celine goes into the kitchen and comes back with a bottle of champagne. We open it and knock on wood so we don't jinx my luck. We toast to my success. We get a little tipsy together. I tell Celine that we must keep in touch even once my month is over. She gives me a funny look but doesn't try to pry.

After about three glasses (champagne glasses don't count as full glasses) Celine goes away to print out my manuscript and get it couriered over to the agency. I call Rosa.

"Yay! That is amazing news. I'm so happy for you. Put a bottle of champagne on ice and we'll drink it when the final verdict comes in."

"Too late, I've already drunk it," I say with a drunken giggle.

I only sober up when I have to speak to Nigel. I talk to him for about ten minutes but I don't tell him about the agency. I can't bring myself to. I'll tell him if the agency actually accepts my work. After lunch Nikolai calls. He has never called me before and I feel nervous and tongue-tied. Like some schoolkid talking to her crush.

"Sophia tells me one of the agencies asked for the rest of your book," he says.

"Yes," I say awkwardly.

"Do you want to celebrate it?"

"Yes," I croak.

"Dinner?"

"Okay."

"Do you have a restaurant you'd like to go to?"

"I'd like to go somewhere local."

"Local? The food is probably not very good."

"I think I'd like to go to a pub and have fish and chips or pie."

There is a silence. "All right. If that's what you want. I'll get Sophia to book something."

"I don't want to go to a place where we have to book. I just want to turn up, have a drink at the bar then eat in the restaurant."

"Really?"

"Yeah. It'll be fun. Maybe we can go somewhere we can bring Storm too."

"Storm?"

"The husky."

"You want to bring the dog?"

I giggle. "Yes. I'll ask around and find a place that allows dogs."

"Er ... right. If that's what you really want."

"It's what I really want."

"See you later."

"Bye, Nikolai. And thank you."

254

I hang up and smile with happiness that Nikolai and I didn't argue. It's funny, even though I just saw him last night I miss Nikolai. I miss his smile. I miss having him inside me. I miss his silver eyes raking over my body. I even miss his sarcastic sense of humor.

Before Nikolai arrives I get my first Thank-you-but-no-thank-you letter. Even though Peter Thiel's agency have asked for more chapters, the rejection is still somehow hurtful, and I am again glad I did not tell Nigel. Peter Thiel could still reject me.

I am dressed in jeans and a blue T-shirt when Nikolai comes through the door. He too is wearing blue jeans. They hug the tops of his muscular thighs and make him look rugged but really sexy too. He stops when he sees me and smiles.

"So, we're slumming it today, huh?" he says.

I smile back, my heart in my throat.

****

Storm, Nikolai and I end up at the Bricklayer's Arms. We have a pint of ale in the garden and Storm makes friends with a black lab. The man who owns her comes over to talk to us. He is a middle-aged Irishman and he just doesn't get it that Nikolai doesn't want to talk. Completely oblivious he talks for all of us. He tells us he lives around the corner from the pub.

I think he is hilarious and I have a wonderful time listening to his jokes. When it is time for us to leave Storm cries.

"Ach ... he's in love," he says with a wink.

He tells us he is thinking of having a barbeque at his place on Sunday afternoon. "Why don't the both of you bring your dog around then?"

He thinks we are couple. "Yeah maybe," Nikolai says.

"Here, put my number in yer phone and give me a call on Saturday," he says.

For a second Nikolai doesn't know what to do. He glances at me, then he takes his phone out and inputs the man's number.

When he is gone I tease Nikolai. "Are you going to his barbeque?"

"I'd rather cut my arm off and eat it," he says.

"So why did you take his number?"

He frowns. "I don't know why. I've never done something like that before."

We move to the restaurant. Just as Nikolai had warned, the food is not very good, but it is one of the best nights I've ever had in my life. Nikolai is so well read, so knowledgeable, that I just sit there staring at him in awe.

We finish the night in my bed. All the things I couldn't say with my mouth, I say with my body. Nikolai doesn't leave my bed until the early morning hours.

Forty-one

Star

I spend the next two days in London. The routine is the same. I wake up, have breakfast with Celine and then I go see my dad. I write for a while then I while away the hours and wait for the night to come. For Nikolai to come to me.

That day would have been the same if the Peter Thiel Agency had not called. Daria Elizabeth Bowen wants me to go in and meet them!

"Can you come today?"

"Sure," I say, stunned.

I dress in a yellow shirt and a pair of gray trousers. I put my hair up so it looks more formal, and Alexis drives me to their office at the Embankment. My hands are clammy with sweat. I ring on the doorbell and identify myself. Someone buzzes me in.

I push the door open and walk down a short corridor. I open another door with the sign that says Peter Thiel's Literary Agency. A woman in a bright red skirt and a dowdy green blouse walks up to me. Her short brown hair is full of grey roots. She extends her hand out to me. "Hey, I'm the one who read your book and just *loved* it."

I grin at her. "Hello, Ms. Bowen."

"Call me Daria. Everyone does."

"Okay."

"I didn't think you'd be so young."

"Oh," I exclaim worriedly.

She holds her hands up. "But it's good. It's all good. Youth is good 99.99% of the time."

I laugh.

"Come with me. We'll go get a cup of tea. Peter wants to meet you too, but he's just finishing up another meeting."

"Okay."

I follow her to a room with a long table and chairs around it. "This is our conference room. Have a seat."

I take a seat and look up at her.

"Isn't this exciting?" she asks.

"You cannot imagine how much," I tell her sincerely.

She smiles. "You deserve it. You wrote a really good book. Did you say that you have five more with the same characters already written?"

I nod.

She winks. "Tell that to Peter when he comes in. You'll make his year."

"I will?"

"Oh absolutely. He's planning to sell your book for loads of money."

My eyes widen. "What do you mean?"

"Well, I sold a cat book last week for £15,000, but Peter will get more for yours."

I can feel myself grinning from ear to ear. £15,000? I've never earned a penny in my life. "Really?"

"For sure."

Then Peter Thiel comes in and the mood changes. I'd already seen a picture of him on the Internet so I am not surprised when he comes in with a straw hat and a red bowtie. Appearances are deceiving, because he is shockingly sharp and clever and plays his cards very close to his chest. He welcomes me to the agency, congratulates me on having written a fine book, and beyond that I learn nothing more.

When I get into the car I see him standing at the first-floor window looking down. I wonder what he must think to see me getting into a big expensive car with tinted windows. Unsure whether to wave or not I am saved when he raises his hand first and waves.

****

Funnily enough I tell Rosa, Cindy, Celine, Sophia, Nan, Grandad, Mum, Nikolai, and even Andrei about being accepted by the agency, but I don't tell Nigel. I don't know why, but I decide to tell him only if the agency actually finds a publisher who wants to buy the book. After all, I've read on the net that some people find agents, but then can't find a publisher to take their book on.

 260

My father comes out of hospital and moves in with Nan. It is a great relief for the whole family and it feels like a big burden has lifted off my shoulders. No matter what happens now my dad is safe. The hospital bills are taken care of and he is on the mend.

I meet Rosa and Cindy for lunch and I realize as I am sitting with them that this month with Nikolai hasn't turned out to be the ordeal that I thought it would be. It's actually become my greatest adventure. I'm learning new things. New opportunities are coming my way, and the time away from Nigel is making me realize how small my life was before.

I had made my own existence so small and insignificant.

Basically I was Nigel's glorified housekeeper. I did nothing other than write, keep house, and garden. I hardly went out without him. I learned nothing new. I got my monthly allowance and I could spend that how I liked, but any big purchases I had to ask permission.

Even the thought that I would have my own money, money that I earned by myself, made me feel dizzy with excitement. Outside of the beyond amazing sex, Nikolai and I have settled into a cautious relationship. Sometimes he gives me the impression he wants more. Then at other times he pushes me away and makes it clear there is nothing between us but the sex.

There is just over two weeks left of our time together and a big part of me feels extraordinarily sad that my time will soon be over, but I understand that I can't have Nikolai.

He is too rich, too handsome, too mysterious, too unreachable, too sophisticated, too cold, too sexually experienced for me. I'm just an ordinary girl who happened to take his fancy one night in a restaurant, but I know it won't last. It can't last. I don't know much about how billionaires operate, but I imagine after a month, he will be bored with me and be on the look out for the next woman to fill his bed.

Anyway, I need to go back to my own life. To my real life. Not this fantasy adventure with a billionaire. My real life is with Nigel, my husband, the man I will bear children for and grow old with.

I need to mend the broken bits of our relationship and start again. Only this time I won't walk around with rose tinted glasses.

This time I'll keep my eyes open.

Forty-two

Star

https://www.youtube.com/watch?v=SQTH B4jM-KQ
Wild horses

"Hello, Miss Minton. This is Peter Thiel."

"Hello, Mr. Thiel," I say, too shocked that he has actually called my number.

"How are you?"

I clear my throat. "I'm fine."

"That's good. Well, the auction for your series is over."

"The auction?"

"Yes. There was enough interest in your book for me to hold a little mini-auction."

"Really?" I gasp.

"Are you sitting down?"

The first thought that crosses my mind is oh no, he received such lows sums, he's preparing me for the bad news. I won't be getting the £15,000 that the cat book got. Then I brighten up. What does it matter if it's just a small sum? The main thing is I will be published!

I'm not sitting down, but I just say yes so that he can get on with it.

"Right. This is just for the UK and English speaking markets worldwide, but not including the US. We'll do those separately."

I frown, not understanding where the conversation is going. I'm going to need to do some serious research. English speaking markets? What are those?

"Right. Are you ready for this?" he asks.

Why on earth is he prolonging this? "Yes," I say warily.

"Both Little Brown and Hachette offered £350,000 for the series of five with the option to buy the rest, but Hachette has the slightly better deal on royalties."

I blink. What did he just say? But the cat book sold for £15,000 and I'm supposed to get a bit more. "I'm sorry, I didn't catch what you said," I croak.

He calmly repeats himself and my jaw falls open. For a few seconds I can't say a word. "They want to pay £350,000 for my series?" I screech.

"That's right."

"Oh my god! I can't believe this. This is soooooo brilliant."

"This, Star, is just the beginning. I'm off to the London book fair in Earl's Court next week and we'll sell the foreign rights there. I think this series will do very well on the foreign language markets. Obviously, the American rights will be auctioned off in a similar way in two weeks' time. That should be a sizable chunk too. Probably a similar amount to that paid by the UK."

I walk to a couch and sit down, but I'm so exhilarated I can't even sit still.

"Why don't you pop into the office tomorrow and we can discuss all the details then?"

"I will."

"Book an appointment with Lisa."

"Mr. Thiel?"

"Yes."

"Thank you so much. I'm so glad I found your agency. You and Daria and all the girls have been amazing." My voice breaks. "You have no idea how awesome it is just to be published. Let alone all these crazy sums of money you're throwing around. I never imagined."

"Don't thank me, Star. It was a pleasure to read your book, and to represent you. Now, why don't you start making arrangements to go out and celebrate your windfall."

I laugh through my tears of joy. "Okay. Thank you again."

I hang up and stare out of the window into the garden. Tears are running unchecked from my eyes. I don't know why I'm crying. Then I call Rosa.

"Make it fast," she says. "I'm real busy."

"Rosa," I sob. "Peter sold my series."

"So why do you sound so cut up about it?"

"It's for really a lot of money."

"Oh yeah? How much?"

"£350,000 to start with."

"What?" she bursts out. "Jesus, Star. That is incredible."

"I know. Peter says the US publishers will probably offer a similar sum."

"Oh. My. God. You are rich!"

I laugh. "It *is* a lot, isn't it?"

"I'm so proud of you, Star. This is the best news I've heard for the last ten years."

"Thanks," I say shyly.

"Have you told Nigel?"

"No."

"Why not?"

"I'll tell him later. He'll be at work now and I don't want to disturb him."

'Does Nikolai know?"

"Not yet. I'll tell him after this call."

"Where is he anyway?" she asks.

"In his study."

"Go tell him the good news, then. I've really got to go, but I'll call you later. Congratulations, babe." She blows kisses before ending the call.

I stand up and pace the floor. I know what I must do, but some part of me doesn't want to do it. I know I have to. I walk to Nikolai's study and knock on the door.

"Come in," he calls.

I open the door and am confronted by a roomful of men in expensive suits. Every face turns to look at me.

 266

"Oh, sorry. I didn't realize you were busy," I apologize, backing away.

"Excuse me, gentlemen," Nikolai says, and stands.

"Don't worry, don't worry, I'll catch you later," I say quickly, and close the door.

I cover my mouth with my hand. Shit. I hope he's not mad at me for interrupting his meeting. It looked important. The door wrenches open behind me. I whirl around and Nikolai is standing there, his eyes narrowed.

"What is it?" he asks.

"Oh, it was nothing really. It can wait until you finish."

"If you found it important enough to come looking for me I want to know what it is."

I smile. "It's nothing bad."

His expression doesn't change. "What is it?"

"Well, Peter Thiel called."

"Uh ... huh."

"They sold my series."

His expression softens. "Yeah?"

"Guess how much?"

His lips twist. "I don't know. Surprise me?"

"This is just for the UK and English speaking worldwide market. It doesn't include America, or the foreign language translations."

He nods.

"£350,000."

He smiles, a genuine smile. "Well done, little butterfly. That's brilliant."

267

I bite my lip. "I … I wanted to thank you. If not for you I wouldn't have had the guts to send my work."

He shrugs away my thanks. "You would have eventually sent it anyway."

"Anyway, I was thinking I should use some of it to pay you back. It was not fair what Nigel did."

He starts frowning.

"I mean. I feel responsible. He's my husband after all."

He stares at me.

"Maybe we can work something out and I can return home sooner."

I see a flash of something in his eyes, it looks like hurt, but it's gone so quickly I must have imagined it. How can it be hurt anyway?

"All right," he says and his voice is even and neutral. "We'll work something out when we go out to celebrate tonight."

I feel a strange sense of emptiness in the pit of my stomach. Like how I felt when my pet rabbit died. Loss. This is it. This is the end of our time together. I force a smile. "Okay."

"Buy something pretty to wear tonight," he murmurs.

"Yeah?"

"Yeah. I'll get Sophia to sort an account in a nice boutique for you."

I smile softly up at him. I want to touch his face but I don't. He is not for me. Nigel is my

husband. I take a step back. "I'll never forget you, Nikolai."

He stares at me for a moment saying nothing. "No, I guess you won't," he says softly.

"Right, I guess you better get back to your meeting."

"Hmmm ..."

I take another step back and then I take two steps forward and, lifting myself on my tiptoes, kiss him on his cheek.

Then I turn around and run away from him, because I don't understand what is going on in my heart.

Forty-three

Star

I go back to my room and pace the floor. I know I should call Nigel. I should give him my good news, but for some weird reason I am reluctant. I never told him I sent my work and it feels like a betrayal. Or maybe I'm just afraid he will say something that will spoil my joy. Or I could just be afraid of how he will react to me earning money. Being financially independent.

For ages I hang around in my room unsure about how to break the news to him. Eventually, I decide that I won't tell him just yet. I will tell him once I have brokered something with Nikolai. Once I know exactly when I will be leaving for home. That will be better. More sensible. Anyway, I don't want to tell him on the phone. I need to see his face when I tell him.

I call Cindy and she squeals with delight. Then I call my nan. Granddad picks up the phone and I break the news to him.

"I didn't hear it right, Love. What did you say?"

I grin happily. "No, Granddad, you heard right."

"Three hundred thousand pounds?"

"No, three hundred and fifty thousand pounds," I correct cheekily.

"Pull the other one, little monkey," he says with a laugh

"I swear I'm not joking, Granddad."

"Crikey, lass. That's a whole heap of money." He holds the phone away and shouts for my nan.

When she comes on the phone it gets a lot more colorful and we end up laughing like crazy.

****

That afternoon, Andrei drives me to a very exclusive boutique in Notting Hill. As soon as I enter, a beautiful woman with glossy dark hair, and wearing a glamorous, two-tone dress, stands up and greets me. She must be in her thirties, or even older, but she is as well preserved as a Hollywood celebrity.

"Hello, you must be ... Star." Her voice is throaty and she is not English.

"Yes. That's me."

"And you're looking for a special outfit," she says with a smile, but her smile doesn't reach her eyes. She looks at me with a knowing, almost pitying expression.

"Yes," I say carefully.

"Come with me and I'll show you what we have in the way of very exclusive, one off designs. Some of them are practically off the catwalks." She walks me to the back of the shop.

271

"I have picked out something special that I think will suit you very well."

She takes me to a curtained off area where there are two dresses on the rack. "I think the red one would be perfect on you," she says.

I walk up to it and touch it. Something is bothering me. I don't like this woman, and I don't want to buy anything from her.

"You'll look beautiful in it. Niko likes his women in red."

Niko.

I don't get to call him that. I don't turn around. I know now what is bothering me. Either she was, or still is, his lover. He sent me to buy a dress from one of his lovers! What an unfeeling bastard. Somehow that hurts me. Really deeply. I don't know why it does, but it does. The air feels thick and poisoned and I feel as if I can't breathe. I turn around.

"I'm sorry, but I'm suddenly not feeling very well. I'll have to come back another day."

She frowns. "Oh?"

I start walking away from her. I can't even bear to look at her. He's been touching her, holding her, entering her body. I quicken my pace and open the door. Outside, Andrei looks at me funnily.

"Are you all right?"

"Yes. Can you take me back please?" I croak.

He walks to the car and opens the back-passenger door for me. I slip in and he shuts it and goes around the front. Less than five minutes later my phone rings.

"What's the matter?" Nikolai asks.

"Nothing. I must have eaten something that didn't agree with me."

There is silence on the other end.

"Where are you going now?"

"Back to the house."

"Do you need a doctor?"

"No. I'm fine. Really."

"Do you want Bella to send over some dresses for you?"

"No," I say quickly. "Don't bother her. I think I have something I can wear.

"All right. I'll see you at the house later this evening."

"Okay."

I lean back against the seat feeling strange. What is the matter with me? Why did I react so badly just because that woman and he were lovers in the past? Oh my god. What if they are still lovers? My stomach starts churning. I feel physically sick. I clutch my stomach and take deep breaths and the feeling goes away. I stare out of the window. Why don't I feel happy? I've just achieved my biggest dream.

As we get to Victoria, Rosa calls.

"How is the soon to be published author?" she asks.

"She's fine," I say, and my voice wobbles.

"What's the matter?" she demands immediately.

"I wanted to buy a dress, but the owner of the boutique was one of Nikolai's lovers so I got out of there fast, and now I don't have anything to wear tonight," I sob. I know that is not the reason I'm upset, and saying it like that makes me sound like a spoilt brat, but I don't want to face any unpleasant truths right now. I'm too afraid to look down into the abyss. I'm terrified of what I will see.

For a few seconds there is a shocked silence from Rosa's side. I have never behaved this way before. "Look," she says. "A really gorgeous black and gold Dior came in yesterday. It's for a fashion shoot next Monday. It'll be perfect for you. Want to borrow it?"

"Oh, my god, yes," I sob. By now tears are running down my face.

"I'll come around about six," she says.

"Okay."

"Have you got gold shoes?"

"I've got black."

"Sandals?"

"Mmmm."

"That'll do."

"Thanks, Rosa," I sniff.

"Hey. You know what?"

"What?"

"For the first time ever I know that everything is going to work out for you."

"Why do you say that?"

"Just trust me on this one. I can see things you can't. You don't have to do anything. Just let everything happen in its own time."

"What do you mean?"

"Go with the flow and you'll see what I mean. See you later."

Forty-four

Star

"**H**oly Mother of God!" Rosa says, her eyes as big as saucers, when I meet her in the hallway.

"And he bought the house next door for his staff," I whisper.

"Now why can't I find a man like that for me?" she says with a dramatic sigh.

"Come on, let's go upstairs."

I take her to my room and she lays the zipped up clothes carrier on the bed and looks around her. "So: this is how the super-rich live."

"The weird thing is all this doesn't attract me at all. I've never wanted this. I still don't. I want a nice house, a family, and a man who loves me to death."

"Well, why can't you have that and this?"

"I think when you have this much money you think you deserve more than one woman. There's so much choice. So many women throwing themselves at you. It must take a saint to say no."

"Oh, I don't know. I think I can totally rock being with a billionaire. So many people to boss around. Delicious."

I laugh. "God, you're bad enough at Christmas when you sit there with a mug of tea like a Queen and order Cindy and me around until we get your Christmas tree exactly the way you want it. And that thing with the lights."

"Yes, I do love my Christmas lights." She grins.

There is a knock on the door.

I run to it and open it. Yana is outside.

"Can I get your guest something to drink?" she asks.

I turn around to Rosa. "Want anything to drink?"

"Double vodka and orange juice. Go easy on the juice."

"And I'll have a Gin and Tonic please," I tell Yana.

She nods and withdraws.

"Come and look at your dress then," Rosa says, unzipping the gray plastic covering.

She pulls the dress out and I gasp.

"Oh, Rosa. It's gorgeous but I can't wear that. It's a mini."

"What do you mean? It's practically made for you."

I sit on the bed and look at her. "Rosa. That dress is practically made for you. You can carry off looking sexy while you're cleaning your toilet. I'm a mere mortal. I have thick thighs."

"You don't have thick thighs."

"I *know* I have thick thighs. Even Nigel says that."

"Nigel is an idiot."

"Regardless. I can't wear that."

"Yes, you can. The secret to looking sexy while cleaning your toilets is confidence. Now stop whining and get into this dress *now*," she says bossily.

She picks up the dress and turns it around so I can see the back. "Tell me this isn't the ultimate in luxury."

"Wow!" I say and walk up to it.

The dress is beautiful from the front. It is in two parts. The top is entirely beaded with gold crystals. It is classy with a high A-line neckline and a cute flirty short skirt, but the back is something else. It is sexy and luxurious. It leaves the wearer's back bare but for two strips of delicate gold lace that run down to the skirt.

Helga, one of the staff, knocks on the door and enters with our drinks.

"Thank god," Rosa says and takes a long sip.

She sits on the bed propped by pillows and crosses her ankles. "Go on then. Put it on."

There is no use trying to argue with Rosa when she gets like this, so I quickly undress and put the dress on.

"What do you think?" I ask uncertainly. I've never worn something this short since I was a kid.

"Hold your hair up," she orders.

I bunch my hair and hold it at the top of my head.

"Turn around."

I obey.

"Stunning. You'll blow his mind."

I walk over to the mirror and look at myself. The dress is beautiful, but honestly … I'm not sure I can carry it off.

Rosa appears in the mirror beside me. "Star, do you think I'd send you out of this house if I didn't think you could take on every woman who glances at Nikolai with greedy eyes?"

I shake my head.

"Exactly. Trust me. I do this for a living. I know what I am talking about."

"Rosa?"

"Mmmm."

"You said Nikolai dates models, didn't you?"

She nods. "Yeah, he likes models. So?"

"All his relationships don't last, do they?"

"No, they don't, but you know what I say. Even George Clooney got caught in the end."

I smile sadly. "Have you heard any stories about him?"

278

"I didn't pay much attention to them."

"Tell me, Rosa."

"There is nothing to tell," she insists with a laugh.

"I spent so many years with my head in the sand. I'm learning to be different. To ask questions. To find things out for myself. You're not protecting me by hiding stuff from me. I want to know where I stand." "Okay. Most of it was just salacious gossip. It's normal with him being so rich and handsome, but one thing did stick out though."

"What?"

"Apparently, the rumor is he won't go out with blonde women."

"I'm blonde."

"I know. Once he was dating this model, I even know her, and she changed her hair color to blonde so he just dropped her like a hot potato. She tried changing it back but he had already lost interest."

"Isn't it weird that he chose me?"

"Very weird, which is what makes me say don't rock the boat. Just go with the flow. You never know what's waiting on the other side."

"All this is neither here nor there, anyway, since I'm going back to Nigel. I've already told Nikolai that I'll be using some of my money to pay the debt back and—"

"You did what?" she explodes.

"Well, it seemed like the right thing to do ..."

279

She shakes her head. "This is exactly what is called rocking the boat.
If you could forget this bullshit loyalty you have to Nigel. He totally doesn't deserve it. If you weren't with Nigel wouldn't you like to be with Nikolai?"

"If I weren't with Nigel? I am with Nigel, Rosa."

"Forget it." She walks away from the mirror.

I turn around and look at her. "Are you angry with me, Rosa?"

She turns around and forces a smile. "No, I'm not. I just wish you could see what I can, but I guess you can't. It doesn't matter. What will be, will be. Now let's get your hair done."

"Celine will do it."

"Hell, I love your life at the moment," she says with a grin.

I ring for Celine and she comes to do my hair while Rosa and I chat. When Celine finishes, Rosa takes over and does my make-up. She twists open a strong red lipstick.

"Don't put too much," I warn.

"You know what I always say. Don't do the walk of shame, just do the walk," she says.

Finally, she snaps the lid of her gold eyeshadow and sighs with satisfaction. "Wanna see what you look like?"

I walk to the mirror. "God, I look so different," I say, turning to look at the back of the dress. "You don't think it's all too over the top?"

"That's the point whole. I want you to knock him off his feet."

I slip into my sandals and show Rosa to the door. We quickly hug and say goodbye.

"You have a fab time tonight," she says. I watch her walk, clicking down the stone steps in her high heels towards her car. "Don't forget to call me. I want to know everything," she shouts over her shoulder as she gets into her car. I wave as she drives off. From the corner of my eye I can see the black Bentley with Andrei inside inching forward. He stops in front of me and gets out to open the car door. His eyes slide over me in surprise but all he says is, "Good evening, Miss Minton."

Suddenly I feel nervous and a little awkward. I know that this is not a date and yet it feels like it. Actually, it feels like I am a Princess going out to meet my Prince.

Andrei holds open the door and I slide in.

Forty-five

Star

I get out of the car, surprised. I can see bouncers standing outside the understated entrance of some kind of club or restaurant. It is as if someone was trying hard to be ordinary. Everything about it is drab. There is an awning but even that is the dullest green you can think of. The name of the club is in black on gray.

Ziggurat.

One of the bouncers immediately leaves his position and comes towards me. It's a beautiful warm summer evening with an occasional gentle breeze and I stand there frozen.

"Good evening, Miss Minton. My name is Roman," he says when he gets close enough to me.

"Good evening, Roman. Where is Nikolai?"

"Mr. Smirnov is upstairs in his office and asked if you could wait for him."

"Oh." He makes me come here alone and now he won't even allow me to go up to his office. Instead he wants me to sit somewhere and wait for him.

"Please, come with me. You can sit and have a drink in one of our private rooms," he says.

"What is this place?"

He looks at me strangely. "It's a club."

What kind of club? I want to ask, but his face discourages any further conversation. Oh well, I'll find out soon enough.

I follow him inside. To my great astonishment the interior is nothing like the exterior. Inside it is grand and majestic. We walk through the beautiful marbled reception. Roman does not speak to the girls sitting there, both eye-wateringly beautiful, but they stare curiously at me.

A stunningly beautiful woman walks up to us. She smiles sweetly at me. "I absolutely adore your dress. Is it Dior?" she asks in a sexy Russian accent.

"It is," I answer, surprised that she could guess the label so accurately.

She smiles.

"You have a very good eye for fashion," I remark.

"I used to be a model. Fashion is my thing." She glances at the bouncer then back at me. "Can I get you a drink? A glass of champagne perhaps?"

"Thank you," I accept gratefully. I need to calm my nerves.

She turns and nods at a waitress hovering nearby carrying a tray of champagne glasses.

The waitress comes over to us and I snag a glass from her tray and take a sip.

"I hope you enjoy your night," the ex-model says with a polite smile before she walks away.

I watch her slender body swaying. I don't know why, maybe it is the fact that she used to be a model, or because she has wonderfully dark hair, but I suddenly think of Nikolai with her and a lump forms in my throat.

"Come, I will show you where you can wait," Roman says.

We go down a long corridor with deep plush carpet and walls lined with stunning Russian tapestries. I have to give it to Nikolai, he has absolutely wonderful taste. There is so much mystery to him I can't help but want to know more. We stop outside a room with tall antique doors. Roman opens one and with his open palm beckons me inside. The sound of laughter and voices fill my ears and I hesitate.

"You want me to wait in there?"

"No, we only have to pass through here," he says.

I take a deep breath and follow him. My breath catches and I freeze. I'm standing in a large room filled with gambling tables. Some of the tables are occupied by gamblers. I feel my hands clench. Why? Why would he bring me here?

Roman stops too. "It's just this room here. It is unoccupied. You can wait there for Mr. Smirnov."

A pretty Asian girl approaches with the offer of another glass of champagne. I shake my head. All I want to do is get out of this place. This is exactly the kind of place where Nigel lost all our money.

"Miss Minton," Roman prompts.

"I can't stay. I have to go," I say, and turn around to walk back the way we came. It is then I hear the loud, hearty laugh. My god! The laugh is coming from one of the smaller rooms attached to this main room. The entrance is partially covered with purple velvet drapes. I walk forward, and lifting my hand, I drag one of the drapes aside.

Everything turns silent inside me.

"Yo, I'm on a roll," a man shouts excitedly, as he reaches forward to scoop up his winnings. The croupier stands by impassively. There are two more men and a woman sitting at the same table. My eyes gaze at the man in shock. I have never seen him like this. He is at once foreign, magnificent, and frightening. Granddad once said all gamblers are magnificent when they are winning.

Oh, Nigel, Nigel, Nigel.

I never knew you. Never.

My glass slips out of my nerveless fingers and falls. I turn away and start running. My legs feel like jelly. It is a wonder they support me. Tears stream down my face. A man tries to grab me but I push him away hard and head for the door.

I don't have any idea where I'm going, but I know I have to get out of this horrible, horrible place. I run down the corridor and out to reception. I get outside. The bouncers are too shocked to react. I lift the red ropes and dash down the street.

Forty-six

Star

https://www.youtube.com/watch?v=zTcu7
MCtuTs
If You Don't Know Me By Now

Suddenly, a powerful arm grabs my arm
and whirls me around. The power of it is so
strong it jerks me off balance and I almost fall,
but I right myself and look at him with furious
eyes.

"You knew he was there," I rage
breathlessly. "You set it up."

"Yes," he admits calmly.

"Why?" I cry.

"There was no other way to get through to
you. When it comes to him you're blind."

I lift my hand and strike him across the
face. He doesn't move. I watch my handprint
leave a white mark that fills quickly with red.

We stand there staring at each other. I'm
panting hard and feeling hurt and shocked while
he looks down at me, his eyes expressionless, a
muscle in his jaw throbbing madly.

"You tricked me. How could you do that?
We were supposed to celebrate my first ever
success. I thought we were going to have a lovely

dinner together." My voice trembles with emotion.

He closes his eyes and exhales. "I'm sorry, Star."

"If you just wanted to humiliate me why did you get me to dress up? So I could look like a complete fool in front of all your staff?" I sob.

"I asked you to dress up for this," he growls. It happens so fast I don't even get time to react. He grabs my upper-arms and his lips swoop down on mine.

I know it's a terrible, terrible cliché, but my mind goes blank, the world stops spinning. The sensation is electric. Every nerve in my body sparks alive. My mouth opens helplessly and his tongue pushes in. With a muffled sound that sounds almost like a sob I suck his tongue hard, as if it is life-giving.

There is nothing but us. Kissing on the sidewalk. The kiss goes on and on until he wrenches his mouth away and gazes down at me. He is breathing hard.

I stare up at him, shocked.

My mind whirls. I feel frightened. Why am I responding to his kisses like this? This is not sex. This is something else. I am in love with him! I have been for some time now. I just refused to admit it.

But this man can never be mine.

He'll get bored and I'll end up like all those other discarded women. I can't show him how I feel. I have to protect my heart. He will trample all over it. My lips move. Words tumble out of them. Trite words. Words that have no meaning to me.

"Allowing a gambler into your establishment and letting him gamble on credit is like taking an alcoholic to a bar and telling him to help himself."

He gives a short bark of humorless laughter. "You really don't know your husband at all, do you?"

My mouth opens and more trite nonsense pours out. "I know he needs my help."

"Do you really want him back after what you saw?" he asks incredulously.

I don't think. I say what is expected of me. "He's my husband."

He shakes his head. "You're unbelievable."

"It's called loyalty, Nikolai. You should try it sometime."

The reaction I get is far worse than when I slapped him. He goes white. For a while he says nothing. Just stares at me. Then he shakes his head. Not in disgust as he had before, but as if telling himself no.

"Fuck it, Star. You want him. Go on, go to him." He jerks his head. "He's in there. Tell him all is forgiven. The debt is paid in full. Take him home and go back to playing ostrich. You're so fucking good at it."

"Nikolai?"

He takes a step back as if I could contaminate him. "No, I should have known

 289

better. Go back to him. You deserve each other," he says harshly. He looks at me with contempt. How did we get from that spell-binding kiss to this? He turns on his heel and goes back into his club.

I stand there in the street for a few more moments. Did I just imagine that? I touch my mouth. It feels swollen and tender.

I know I can't go back in there and face Nigel. I'm too confused and wounded. In a daze, I turn my head. Andrei is waiting by the car. When he catches my eye, he opens the back door. Like a wound-up toy I walk towards him. I get into the car and he closes the door.

"Back to the house?" he asks.

I take a deep breath. "No." I tell him my address.

"Look—," he begins.

"Nikolai doesn't care anymore. He said I could go. Call him if you don't believe me."

He takes his phone out and hits a button. He says something in Russian and listens. The reply is also in Russian and very brief. He glances at me in the rearview mirror. When he catches my eyes he quickly looks away. The phone in his hand goes dead. He sighs.

"I will take you wherever you want."

"Thank you."

He starts the car and drives me home. When he gets to my street, the first tears start to fall from my eyes. He stops outside my house. It is in complete darkness. I fumble with the door but he gets out and opens it for me.

"I'll wait for you here."

For a split second, I almost tell him to go on ahead then something stops me. I nod, thank him, and walk up to my house. How I loved this house. Once, when I was a different person.

I climb the steps. I touch the front door. I know where the spare key is but I don't want to go in. It feels as if I no longer belong here. I turn away from it and go back down the steps.

Then I stop halfway.

Will I regret this decision all my life? Be brave, Star. Go all the way. There is nothing to fear but a lie. It's time I knew the truth. All of it. I turn around, pick up the spare key, and enter the house. It smells different. How strange that I cannot recognize the smell of my house.

I don't switch on the light. I go through the hallway and up the stairs. My footsteps are silent on the carpet. I enter the bedroom and flick the light switch.

For a second I am blinded, then I look around me. The bed is unmade. Yeah, I expected that. I walk to my closet I open it. It looks untouched. My hands move to the end of the rail. To the very end. There it is, my school uniform. Well, not my school uniform, but an exact copy to remind him of the first time we met. Bigger obviously, to take into account that I am no longer sixteen. I pull the hanger out and bring it to my nose.

I close my eyes and exhale. It is not pain. It is relief. Now I know for sure. I don't have to guess. I don't have to regret. It's hard evidence. The decision is as clear as day. Another woman's perfume. He's had someone else in this house and asked her to wear what I thought was our thing. What I wore the very first time we met.

How stupid of me.

Nikolai and Rosa were right all along. Nigel is a pervert. It makes me feel slightly sick to think how utterly naïve I've been. What a fool. How he must have laughed at me.

Never mind. I will have the last laugh.

I hook the hanger back into its place and close the cupboard. I look around me and shake my head. Incredible. It was all lies. Every bit. I walk to the door, switch off the light and go to stand at the window. In the moonlight I see my moon garden. The glowing white flowers that I planted to bloom at night.

I turn away and go down the stairs. I know now that the yellow room will never be used. No fat baby will wear those irresistible rompers. My birds will find their food elsewhere. My garden will make some other person happy. I go out of the front door and return the key to its secret place.

"Goodbye house."

I walk to the car and get into it. "Can you take me back to the club?"

"Of course," he says in his respectful manner.

Forty-seven

Nikolai

1992

https://www.youtube.com/watch?v=OlKaVFqxERk
If You Leave Me Now

"Sit down, Smirnov," *Vasily says, nodding to the chair in front of his table.*

I don't sit. There is no love lost between us. He considers me a trouble maker and I despise him. As the second in command he looks the other way while the Director presides over an institution run on brutality and cruelty.

Right now, though, I feel nothing except pure fear. I watch him as he leans his heavy frame on the table and feigns emotion.

"I'm afraid I have some bad news. Your brother died this morning."

In my soul, I already knew what he was going to say, but it doesn't lessen the impact of his words. I feel as if I am falling into a black bottomless hole. I try to grab hold of anything I can. My head feels light. I clutch onto the table edge in front of me.

294

"I'm sorry, Nikolai. He fell over the banister."

"No," I gasp. "That's impossible. Someone must have pushed him."

He shakes his head slowly. "He didn't just fall. He jumped."

"That's a fucking lie," I snarl.

"We do not condone the use of such words in this institution," he says sternly.

"Someone pushed him."

"No one pushed him, Smirnov. He left a letter for you. A suicide note."

I stare at him in disbelief. It is a lie. They have killed my brother and now they are trying to make me believe that he killed himself. Why would he do that? "Where is the letter?" I say, my voice trembling with the raging fury that is threatening to consume me.

He takes a crumpled envelope that was sitting on his left, and holds it out to me.

I snatch it from him and tear it open. I see the handwriting and bile rushes up my throat. I try to swallow it down. Jesus! My brother took his own life!

My dear brother,

I hope you won't think I am a coward. I've tried my best to be as brave as possible. I know you are trying to escape this place. I know you can even leave tomorrow, but you are waiting

for me, because you think I'm not strong enough to scale the wall. I don't want to hold you back. So I am going to be brave and not hold you back any longer.

With all my love,
Your Pavel.

I look up from the letter. Vasily is watching me. I'm too stunned to feel anything. Not pain, not hurt, not anger. My brother jumped to his death because he did not want to hold me back!

"I want to see my brother."

"You'll be able to see him later. At the funeral."

I knew all about their funerals. They hold it at the back of the home. There is a small cemetery there and they bury all the children who die in there. There is no coffin. They are wrapped up in their bedsheet and lowered into the ground. One of the groundsmen then shovels dirt on top.

He was all I had in this world. I slam my fist into the wall. The pain comes instantly.

"I want to see him now," *I roar.*

Vasily jumps to his feet. "Calm down, Smirnov. I know you are upset and I am very sorry, but I will not allow you to destroy the property of this home. You cannot see him now. Those are the rules. If you don't stop this *behavior I'll have to ask the nurse to bring you some sedatives to calm you down."*

"I don't need anything from you or anyone else,' I say in a low growl, and walk out of his office.

****

It is winter and there is a frosty wind blowing. The two groundsmen put him on the ground. I walk forward and open the bedsheet and look at his face. Even in death he looks like an angel. A beautiful, innocent angel.

I have to clench my hands to stop myself from shaking him. I kiss his cheek. It is like kissing a frozen stone. They have kept him in a very cold place. I touch his face for the last time. My fingers touch his hair, his eyelashes, his cold lips. I kiss him again, my lips lingering on his frosty cheek.

"I love you, Pavel. I'll always love you," I whisper in his ear.

Then I stand aside and watch them lower him into the ground. I still cannot actually believe he is dead. It never crossed my mind that I would be burying my baby brother.

Why? Why? Why?

I just can't understand why he did it. I just stand there devastated. I thought I had done everything in my power to keep him safe, but I couldn't save him from himself.

One of the little girls from his class comes to stand beside me. She says nothing. When the soil has been shoveled over his body and the staff have gone, she turns slightly towards me.

I look at her blankly. I've seen her talking with Pavel. There are tears in her eyes.

"They came for him at night," she whispers.

"What?"

She nods. "He untied the knot and went with them."

"What?"

She nods. "Yes, he did that all the time. I've seen him."

"Why?"

"He didn't want them to hurt you. He was protecting you. He knew if he did not do it they would hurt you."

My head feels as if it is bursting. I want to scream. I want to break something. I want to tear open the ground and bring my brother back to life. Like water rushing in from many different sources all trying to find their level. The different thoughts in my head all rush to merge in one place.

I want revenge.
I want revenge.
I want revenge.

She looks up at me with her sad, brown eyes. "I wanted you to know that he wasn't a

coward. He always wanted to be like you. We all want to be like you."

I stare at her. Be like me. Suddenly I saw it all clearly. What a fool I have been. I couldn't even see that it was all a trick. The director had never wanted me. It was always Pavel he wanted and I had played right into his hands. I was the bait with which he used to catch my brother.

He was ready with the blow. Before my teeth could even sink into him he had already hit me. I put myself exactly where he wanted and he used me as the bargaining tool. He wanted Pavel to be willing.

It was my fault. Because of my supreme arrogance and ignorance Pavel was gone.

If I had just sucked the director's dick two years ago. If I had not tried to be such a hero. If I had compromised. If I had only sacrificed myself the way Pavel had. What a small thing it was to have done for him. I would suck the unwashed dicks of ten thousand men now if I could bring him back.

I fall to my knees and sob. Oh Pavel, Pavel, Pavel.

I will never be happy again.
I don't deserve it. Ever.

Forty-eight

Star

https://www.youtube.com/watch?v=fdHCec23BKE
Try

My heart is beating so hard and fast I have to take deep breaths to calm myself. The car comes to a stop and I quickly open the door and rush towards the club. The bouncers lift the ropes to allow me in.

"Where is Nikolai?" I ask one of the stunningly beautiful girls at the reception.

"In his office. Let me call him for you."

"Please don't call him. Just take me there."

She looks at me blankly. "I'm sorry, but I have to call him first."

"All right."

She calls him. "Er ... Star is here to see you." Her eyebrows rise. "Okay. I'll tell her." She looks at me, embarrassed. "He doesn't want to see you. He says go home."

"Please, just take me to his office. He doesn't mean it. We just had an argument. I want to sort it out. Please help me," I cry. I know I sound like some obsessed stalker but I just

can't let go. I have to make it right. I was so stupid and blind.

"I can't do that. I'll lose my job."

"Fine. Then let me just go into the club. I need to use the toilet. Did he say I couldn't use the toilet?"

"No."

"There you go then. I just need to use the toilet then I'm gone, okay."

She licks her lips nervously. "You need to use the toilet?"

"I need to use the toilet desperately."

"Go ahead."

"Thank you. Thank you so much."

"Just don't get me into trouble. Please."

"I won't. I promise."

I run through the club right past Nigel. He doesn't even see me. How could I have been such a fool for so long? I ask one of the waitresses to show me where Nikolai's office is. She points me towards the stairs. Semyon is standing at the bottom. I act cool as if I have every right to go up.

"I need to go up and see Nikolai," I say to him.

He nods. "Third door on the left."

I thank him and go up the stairs. I knock on the third door.

"Enter," he calls.

I feel my blood rush to my feet. Shit. I should have checked my make-up. Oh well. It's too late now. My hand shakes as I curl it around

the door handle and push it open. What I see inside makes my heart drop. He is not alone. The ex-model I met earlier in the evening is sitting on one of the sofas. The only consolation is that she looks as confused as me.

He looks at me with a slight frown. I could have been a complete stranger to him. "Did Maria not pass the message on?"

"Yeah she passed the message on. It's not her fault. I told her I needed to use the toilet so she let me in."

"The toilets are downstairs." His voice is robotic.

"I'm not here for the toilet."

He exhales as if he is bored. "What are you here for, Star?"

I refuse to back down. I'll say what I came here to say. "You. I'm here for you."

"Do you know what I truly find repulsive?" he asks casually.

I take a deep breath. "Tell me."

"Desperate women. I've had my fill of you. I'm in the mood to take something different home with me tonight." He turns to the dark-haired beauty sitting on the sofa. "Do you want to come home with me for a fuck, Anastasia?"

She glances at me quickly then back to him. "Yes."

He turns back to me, his eyes cutting and derisive. "There you go. I'm sorted for tonight. Now, unless you are interested in a threesome you really should leave."

I stare at him in shock. My whole world feels like it is crumbling away. He doesn't want me anymore. For a few seconds I can't do anything. I just stand there frozen. Then I turn around and walk out of his club. I don't see anyone because my eyes are full of tears. I go outside and Andrei is waiting by the sidewalk. I dash away the tears.

"Do you want to go back to Surrey?" he asks.

"No," I sob. "Take me to my friend's house."

He looks at me worriedly.

"Fine. Don't take me. I'll just call a taxi."

He scratches his head, then nods and opens the car door for me. I get in and he drives me to Rosa's apartment.

Forty-nine

Nikolai

1992

My fate is to be alone. Everyone I loved is dead.

 303

The gates are only left unattended when the bell rings. The bell only rings when something terrible happens. It has only rung twice since I have been here.

Once because a boy tried to escape and fell outside the wall. They brought him back with his bone sticking out of his leg. And the other time was when the cook accidentally burned herself very badly.

I'm not yet fifteen, but I am tall, broad, and bigger than most of the boys, and a few of the teachers. I am definitely stronger than my enemy. I watch and I wait for my opportunity. I know my enemy's movements like I know the back of my hand.

The time comes and I follow the director into the staff toilets.

Inside we are alone and I am trembling with a strange exhilaration. He has his back to me but suddenly turns and looks at me, and I see that flash of fear. Not real fear. I just startled him. He never suspects that his last breath will be at my hands. As I walk up to him I take the homemade knife from my pocket and lunge forward taking him by surprise.

He does not have an opportunity to defend himself as I drive it with all the force I can muster into the side of his neck. I step back and watch as he desperately clutches his neck. His eyes bulge and blood spurts through his fingers. He drops to his knees and screams, but all he can manage are choking, gurgling sounds.

I step forward and pull my knife out of his neck. I push him so he falls backwards. I kneel down and slash his trousers. I hold his small pale dick in my hand and slice it off with my knife. Blood gushes out like a fountain. I didn't expect it. My clothes, hair, my face, every part of me gets covered in his blood.

I stuff his dick into his choking mouth.

"Here, suck your own dick," I tell him. I look at him calmly. I finished the job I started two years ago.

They say you become what you fight. When you look long enough into your enemy's face you will become it. At that moment I become him. A murderer. I feel his life seep out of his eyes and I feel myself become more powerful.

There is hot water in the staff toilets so I quickly wash and change into the clothes I brought in my bag. Then, without another glance at the man lying still in his own blood, I simply walk out of the toilets.

I am sitting calmly in class when all hell breaks loose. Guards, teachers, cleaning women, groundsmen, are all rushing around like headless chickens.

Somebody sets the alarm off.

When the bell goes all the children must go to the assembly room. Everyone gets up and starts moving quickly towards it. I walk swiftly in the opposite direction. Outside, I don the special gloves I have made with sheets and pieces of metal, and I start to climb the wall. The broken glass shreds my clothes and skin, but I know I'm going to make it when my gloves grasp the barbed wire at the top and I carefully make my way down.

I let my legs run as fast as they can, only stopping when the orphanage is barely visible in my sight. The air is cold but I do not feel anything. I am numb. More numb than I've ever been. I am angry at this cruel world. A world that could take an innocent boy such as my brother away from me. Damn everybody. Damn this world. I will survive. I will be strong and powerful and rich. I will feel nothing. Ever again.

I don't need help from anyone. I reach out a hand, bring the cold air back in the palm of my hand to my lips and kiss it. One day my brother. One day I will revisit this place and take you back with me.

This I promise.

Fifty

Star

"Can I return the dress to you now, Rosa?" I ask as soon as Rosa answers her phone.

For a couple of seconds Rosa is too surprised to answer. "As in right now?"

I sniff. "Yes."

Her response is immediate. "Of course. Fortunately for you I'm just vegetating in front of the TV with a tub of ice cream and a whole box of tissues."

"Thank you," I say and hang up.

When we get to Rosa's apartment building I thank Andrei and tell him I won't need him again. He is a true gentleman and waits until I enter the building before he gets back into the car.

I get into the lift sniffing and blubbering. By the time the lift doors open I'm sobbing. Rosa opens her door and I walk into her arms. "I've been such a fool," I repeat again and again.

She helps me out of the dress and gives me a comfortable pair of sweats to get into. The whole time I am blubbering and sniffing and spluttering.

We sit on the sofa. She pours me a humongous glass of wine. I take it and start gulping it down.

"Whoa. Slow down. That's your lot for the night."

"I've been such a fool."

"I know, you said. How about telling me everything that happened, hmmm?"

So I tell her everything. About Nigel being there and Nikolai admitting that he had deliberately set him up. How I had defended Nigel and Nikolai had got pissed off and how I had found the evidence of another woman in my house. I finished it off with how Nikolai had told me he no longer wanted me and that he was taking Anastasia home.

"And she is an ex-model. They're probably doing it right now," I sobbed.

To my horror Rosa tries to hide a smile. "Why are you smiling?" I demand.

"Sorry. I couldn't help it."

"What's so funny?"

"You. You are so innocent. You just believe everything everyone tells you."

"What do you mean?"

"I mean. Come on. That woman works for him. If he wanted to do her he could have done it ages ago, and he certainly wouldn't still be doing her."

I stare at her. "So what are you saying?"

"I'm saying he was pretending that he was going to take her home. I bet he called her up to

his office as soon as he heard you were at reception and that's why she was looking confused. Poor thing didn't know what the hell was going on."

"Do you really think so?"

"Absolutely. No one goes to all the trouble Nikolai has gone to, to get you, for him to just turn off at the first sign of trouble. What you're telling me sounds like the ending scene ripped right out of *Gone With The Wind*." She deepens her voice. "Frankly, my dear, I don't give a damn."

"But he did chase me away."

"Yes he did. And to be honest I would have done the same thing. It is very frustrating when you try to tell someone something that is so obvious and they absolutely refuse to see it out of sheer pig-headedness. I should know, I've had to deal with it for the last seven years."

"That makes me feel so much better, thank you," I say, and reach for the wine glass.

"Well the great thing is you found out what Nigel really is. Even if nothing else comes of this. To me this whole sorry episode has still been a resounding success."

"But I'm in love with Nikolai."

"Well I have a funny feeling this story is not over. Let's see what tomorrow brings."

"I don't know, Rosa. Nikolai can be very cold and hard. You should have seen his face tonight. He just looked at me as if I was a complete stranger. As if I'm some kind of stalker."

"I don't know how it's going to work with him. He is a billionaire and they are a different species. You have to prepare for the fact that he may actually be a psychopath that has an off button and he has pressed it, but I still think you should be positive. It's not over yet in my book."

"He never revealed anything about himself to me. He was very guarded the whole time. He made it very clear that there was nothing there but the physical attraction. I don't think I'll ever see him again, Rosa."

"Let's give it some time okay and see what happens in the next couple of days. A man who only wanted to have sex with you wouldn't have walked away. He would have just banged you until he got bored. He wouldn't have cared if you were being loyal to Nigel or not."

I drain the last bit of wine. I feel completely drunk, but not happy drunk. "I want to call him," I declare.

Rosa's eyes widen. "No, babe. Not tonight. Maybe tomorrow if you still feel like that."

"What's the difference between tonight and tomorrow."

"Two reasons. You're drunk, and whatever you do tonight you'll regret tomorrow. Also, it's a good idea to give him a chance to miss you."

I nod. I miss him so badly all I want to do is ugly cry. Tonight was supposed to be a celebration.

"What about Nigel? What are you going to do about him?"

I close my eyes. I don't want to think about that nightmare. "I'll get a divorce I suppose," I say softly.

"Good." There is no mistaking the satisfaction in her voice.

Fifty-one

Star

https://www.youtube.com/watch?v=Pgmx7z49OEk
Ain't Your Mama

I wake up in Rosa's guest room with a massive hangover. The events of the night before come hurtling down on me. I tip-toe out of the room. Rosa's bedroom door is open and she is still asleep in bed. I don't know why but I go into her bedroom and stand over her sleeping form. In sleep she doesn't look so tough. Even though my head is throbbing, a rush of pure love fills my heart for her. She has been a good and loyal friend.

Without waking her up I go into the bathroom. My hair looks an absolute mess, my eyes are swollen and my face is puffy. I find headache pills in the cabinet and take them before I get into the shower. Feeling slightly better, I go to the kitchen. Closing the door, I make myself a cup of coffee and call my nan.

I ask about my dad, and when she says he is fine, I tell her I have something to tell them all and I'll be around later.

"Is it more good news?" she asks.

312

"Yeah, it's more good news," I reply. At least it will be for my dad. He'll be so glad to hear that I'm leaving Nigel.

After I end the call I stare out of the window. The view is the back end of another apartment block. The past two weeks seem like an incredible dream.

With a sigh I send Nigel a text message.

Me: **I need to talk to you.**

To my surprise, he answers immediately: **What about? Everything okay?**

Me: **Yeah. Everything okay with you?**

Nigel: **I'm doing great.**

Me: **What did you do last night?**

Nigel: **Nothing much. Stayed in. Got a take-away. Watched some telly. Missed you like crazy.**

Me: **Do you ever still feel like gambling?**

Nigel: **NEVER.**

Me: **Not even a bit?**

Nigel: **Not even a bit. All I want is for you to come back so we can start our life together again. I can't wait for you to come back, Star.**

Me: **Funny thing happened last night.**

Nigel: **What?**

Me: **I saw you in Ziggurat.**

For a full minute there is no reply. Then:

Nigel: **What do you mean you saw me there? You mean outside?**

 313

Me: **No. Inside. At a roulette table.**

My phone rings. I accept the call and hold it to my ear.

"I was not gambling, Star. I'm finished with all that. That was not even my money. You have to believe me that I was just keeping my boss company. I had to pretend. To keep him happy. You know how it works."

"Jesus, Nigel. How stupid do you think I am?"

"You don't believe me?"

"No."

"As if I would jeopardize everything by gambling again. Come on, Star. You know me better than that."

"It would seem I don't know you at all."

"Okay. I was gambling last night. I regressed, okay. I'm sorry It happens to all of us at the beginning of the treatment. I'm sorry I lied. I just don't want to lose you. I love you, Star."

"I went to the house last night."

"You did?"

"Yeah."

"Why?"

"I don't know. Just wanted to see the house."

His voice is cautious. "I don't keep it as clean as you."

"You brought someone else back and fucked her in our bedroom, didn't you?'

"Eh! No, What? What the fuck are you talking about?"

"You let her wear my uniform."

There is a shocked silence. "No, I didn't," he splutters.

"God. You're such a liar."

"I'm not lying. I swear. I don't know what the fuck you're talking about."

"How could I have been so blind?"

"I'm not lying."

"Whatever. There is no longer any need to meet. All I wanted to say is that I'm leaving you. I'll be filing for divorce as soon as I can."

"On what basis?"

"I suppose the easiest would be irreconcilable differences."

"Don't be so silly. You can't make it without me."

"I beg to differ."

"If you think I'm going to support you with alimony payments for the rest of your life you better think again. You won't get a penny from me."

"I don't want anything from you. You can have it all."

"What will you do? Live at your nan's place together with your dad, and become a clerk somewhere? I can tell you now you won't even earn enough to buy a pair of good shoes. After the good life I've given you, you won't last a day."

"I won't have to become a clerk. I'll be an author."

He laughs uproariously. "What do you think? Anybody can become an author? There are millions of people who want to be authors and only a handful have the talent to become one. I suppose in your tiny mind you imagine that publishers are just lining up to buy your book."

"My entire series has already been picked up by a publisher." It is astonishing how much pleasure and satisfaction I get from saying that to him. All these years he tried to keep me down. Well, I floated to the top, Nigel.

"Bullshit," he explodes.

"It's true."

"What? You sold your series to a publisher?"

"Well, not me. My agent did."

"Since when do you have an agent?" His voice is deadly quiet.

"Last week."

"And you've already sold your book?" he asks incredulously.

"Yeah, my agent held a mini auction for it and two publishers wanted the entire series."

"An auction?"

"Yeah. They do it for books they think will be highly sought after," I say casually.

"How much are they giving you?"

"That's very un-English of you, Nigel. You shouldn't go around asking people how much money they earn."

Nigel goes silent with shock.

"Well, I should be going. I've got a ton of things to do, but you'll be hearing from my lawyer.

"Star—"

I hang up, put the phone on the table, and bury my face in my hands.

"Well done, babe," Rosa says from behind me and comes and hugs me. "I'm so proud of you."

"My heart is breaking, Rosa."

She pulls back and looks at me. "Not over Nigel, right?"

I shake my head slowly. "I tried to fool myself last night, but Nikolai's not going to call me. Ever. I know him. He's too proud and too insular."

She looks into my eyes. "Oh, Sugar. I'm so sorry."

Too distraught to speak I can only nod.

Fifty-two

Star

https://www.youtube.com/watch?v=raNGeq3_DtM
I Want To Know What Love Is

I try to keep myself busy for the next couple of days. I know I have to start a new life for myself. I ignore all Nigel's calls and eventually I put a block on his number.

Rosa tells me I can stay with her until I find my own place and I quickly accept her offer. When she is in it is not so bad. She is funny and warm and I can push Nikolai to the back of my mind, but when she goes to work and I am left alone at the apartment, I find myself bursting into tears for no reason. I'd be peeling a pear and suddenly I'd start sobbing my heart out.

I try to write but I find that I can't concentrate like I used to be able to. Suddenly I would be thrown out of my story and my head would be filled with Nikolai. I miss him so much. At night if I have not had at least two glasses of wine I can't sleep. Sometimes I think of Miss One Penny and Ray and Celine. I went to the shop and bought a big box of chocolates for

Sophia, but then I didn't know where to send it to, so Rosa ended up eating most of it.

I go online and try to find gossip about him. There is nothing new. Which is a relief. Even though I obsessively Google him I know I would be devastated if I saw him with another woman.

****

"Who can that be?" Rosa says as she gets up to go answer the doorbell. I just slouch further into the sofa. I hear her open the door. "My, you're a big boy," I hear Rosa say, and I sit up and crane my neck to see who has come through the door.

"Can I have a quick word with Miss Minton please?"

Sweet Jesus!

That's Semyon's voice.

"And who may you be?" Rosa asks.

I try to make myself appear more presentable by quickly brushing my hair back with my hands.

"My name is Semyon."

"Well, Semyon, if you wait here I will see if Miss Minton will see you," Rosa says formally. She leaves him standing in the hallway and comes to me with widened eyes. She opens her mouth in a silent scream before saying in a perfectly natural voice, "There is a man called

Semyon who would like to see you. Shall I send him through?"

"Yes." I gulp, and jump up from the sofa.

Semyon comes into the small sitting room making it appear even smaller than it is.

"I'll be in my bedroom if anybody needs me," Rosa says, and with a wink at me, sails towards her bedroom.

"Hello," I say softly.

He nods.

"Would you like to sit?"

"No. That's fine. I won't be staying long."

"Can I get you a drink?"

"That will not be necessary either."

"Okay. So what can I do for you?"

"I just came here to say that you should go and see Mr. Smirnov. You were good for him."

My eyebrows fly up. I thought Semyon didn't even like me. He was always giving me the cold eye.

"I can take you there now."

"He doesn't want me, Semyon."

"He does want you," he insists blandly.

"You don't understand. It was just a sex thing for him. He saw me in a restaurant four weeks ago and he just thought, yeah, why not, I'm a billionaire. If I want her I'll have her, and he did. Now he's had me he'll move on to the next girl."

"Is that what he told you?"

"No, he didn't have to say it." I shrug. "But that's what it was."

"He didn't see you in a restaurant four weeks ago. He saw you in a casino two years ago."

"What?"

"I've been on your case for two years, Miss Minton. When Mr. Smirnov wants something he never lets anything stand in his way. His focus is complete. His patience is legendary. For two years he planned how to get you. He set up Ziggurat because he knew your husband wouldn't be able to resist."

I sit down on the sofa in shock. "Are you seriously telling me Nikolai set up a casino to trap Nigel so that he could have me?"

"Mmmm."

"That is so crazy."

"Yes, that is what I thought."

"So why did he send me away?"

"You'll have to ask him that yourself."

"What if he doesn't want to see me?"

"He is, how do you say in English, ah yes, dying to see you again."

I smile. "Really?"

"I know him very well, and yes, really."

My smile becomes a grin. "And you'll take me to him."

"Correct."

"Can you wait while I change?"

"Of course."

I go into Rosa's room, shut the door, and lean against it. "Did you hear?" The walls are paper thin in Rosa's apartment.

She lifts her shoulder up to her ears in a conspiratorial gesture. It makes her look like a naughty child. "Did I ever?"

"I've got nothing to wear."

"I have a wardrobe full."

"I was thinking about something demure and subtle."

"I'm thinking: something that'll blow his mind." She walks to her cupboard and takes out a pair of white shorts.

"No way am I wearing those."

"Look. You're wearing this or you're going in what you've got on now. Anyway it's the right weather for it," she says. She pulls out a button down pink top. "I don't know why I bought this. It's too girly for me, but it's perfect for you. He won't be able to resist."

"Are you sure about this? Won't it look too slutty."

"Yup. Nope you won't look slutty if you wear it with sneakers. You'll just look cute and adorable."

I change into the shorts and pink top. It doesn't look too bad. I fluff my hair out and slick on a layer of lip gloss and go out to meet Semyon.

He grins. "That is a good outfit."

"Thank you."

Fifty-three

Star

https://www.youtube.com/watch?v=qEd6
QUbK2Mw
Making Love Out Of Nothing At All

It's cool in the car as Semyon drives us to Mayfair. I lean back against the leather and try to calm myself down. I have a plan. Well, it's kind of a plan.

Yana comes hurrying into the lofty entrance hallway as Semyon and I enter the house.

"He's in the study," she says in a hushed voice.

I thank her and walk to the study. I think I am even more nervous now than when I went to look for him in the club. Then I just assumed he would take me back. What I got was rejection and humiliation. I knock on the door and nearly die when I hear his voice say what I presume must be enter in Russian.

I straighten my shoulders. I can do this. I push open the door. He is not at his desk. He is sitting on the sofa with his feet up on the low table. He turns his face towards me and freezes.

The seconds tick away while we stare at each other.

"What are you doing here?" His voice is strangely calm. There's something different about him. He looks tired. Older.

I close the door and, before I lose my nerve, start walking towards him. My sneakers make no sound on the thick carpet. His eyes trail hungrily over my body. They linger on my thighs. Thank god, the expression in them does not say thick thighs. His gaze moves up to my breasts, and up to my face.

"I was going to bring you flowers, but I heard a man would rather have a blowjob than flowers. So ..."

He blinks.

I arrive in front of him. His eyes are heavy lidded and veiled. Gently I put my hands under his calves. They tense at my touch. I pick them up and put his feet on the floor. I slide in between the table and his knees and try to push the table back. It's heavier than I expected.

Wordlessly he places his feet on the table edge and pushes it well away, before returning his feet back to the ground. I get on my knees. Slowly sinking my teeth into my lower lip. I reach out a hand.

He does nothing.

I unzip his trousers. Gosh, he is hard. Tenderly I pull his cock out. Leaning down I take his thick, gorgeous, shaft into my mouth.

Ah, how I missed him. His taste, his scent, the feel of his warm, satiny smooth skin. His head drops back on the sofa and he sighs softly. I suck him until he comes in my mouth. He looks down on me.

"The blowjob was a brilliant idea," he says softly. I smell the alcohol. He's been drinking. That's why he seems so mellow. His hand strokes my hair. "How have you been, Star?"

I lay my cheek in his lap. "Terrible. Just terrible. I can't eat. I can't sleep. I cry for no reason."

"Why's that?"

"Because I'm in love with you, Nikolai."

"I thought you were in love with your husband."

I lift my head and look at him. "No, I'm not. I was so young and gullible when I met him. I believed everything he told me and I thought the world of him. I wouldn't listen to anyone who told me different."

He stares at me intently.

"I didn't want to believe that my marriage was built on shifting sands. I wanted desperately to believe in my fairytale marriage. I wanted to be in love with him. Next year we were supposed to start a family. I cannot tell you how much I wanted that. I even know the brand of baby oil I want to use on my baby."

He looks at me curiously. "Really?"

I blush. "Yes, it's called Huile Douche. It's just wonderful. It melts on your skin and makes

325

you think of fields of flowers, fresh air and sunshine."

His lips twist. His forefinger drags down my cheek. "What a sweet little creature you are. What a shame I can't keep you."

"Why can't you keep me?"

"It would be ... messy."

"You don't have to love me back, Nikolai. You can just have sex with me whenever you feel like it. Wouldn't that be nice?"

He sighs. "It doesn't work like that, little butterfly."

"How does it work then?"

"I can't have you, Star."

"Why not?"

"Because ... because I don't deserve love."

"Why not?"

"Because I let my brother die."

My eyes widen.

"I can't forgive myself." He lifts a lock of my hair. "He had hair like yours. Beautiful. I hacked it all away, but I didn't do the thing that would have saved him."

"What didn't you do?" I ask softly.

He closes his eyes, lost in some nightmare. "I didn't suck the director's dick."

I gasp. "Oh, Nikolai. I'm so sorry. Whatever it was that happened, you were just a child too. You can't blame yourself."

"It was my fault," he says slowly.

Once I only saw a beautiful man. Now I see the pain and anguish etched into his soul.

"Tell me what happened, Nikolai. Please. Let me in."

To my astonishment he does. He tells me a harrowing story about two little boys. My heart breaks for him.

He opens his beautiful eyes and they are swimming with tears. "Anyway, you deserve something better than me. I'm a monster, Star. A criminal. I used to be in the Russian mafia."

"No, you're not a monster. You're a good man."

"I know you want to believe that I am a good man. There's no such thing as a good man in the mafia. I've killed men, Star."

"That was before. You've changed now."

He shakes his head slowly. "If someone tries to take what is mine tomorrow you will see the old Nikolai again. You do not know what I am capable of, Star. If you knew you would run away screaming."

"I don't know what you've done. All I know is the man you are today and that man is loyal, fair, and honest. That is the man I love."

"I'm hungry to taste you again, Star."

I stand up and pull my shorts down. He hooks his fingers into my panties and pulls me forward. Pushing the material aside he swipes his tongue on my slit.

"Oh my little butterfly. How I missed you."

He lays me on the couch and sucks me until I break apart. Then he makes love to me. For the first time. He makes love to me. Slowly.

Gently. With reverence. As if he is worshipping my body.

"I love you," I whisper again and again.

He doesn't speak, he just uses his mouth, his hands, his fingers, his cock, his tongue to draw the words on my body. I know he loves me and one day he will admit to it.

After we have both climaxed he looks deep into my eyes. "What is it about you? I cannot get enough."

I smile. "Semyon told me a funny thing."

"What?"

"He told me the first time you saw me was not in the restaurant." I raise my eyebrows.

"Yeah. I saw you two years ago. In a casino. You were playing Blackjack. I couldn't take my eyes off you. I wanted you so bad, I thought I would cum in my pants. You were winning and you were laughing. I thought you were the most beautiful thing I had ever laid eyes on. And then you turned around and kissed the sour-faced jerk next to you, and I thought I'd die."

"I never saw you."

"I was there because the woman I was with, I forget her name now, wanted to go. I don't gamble in casinos. That's a fool's game. I have never understood the lure of gambling. The only time I gamble is when I am in control of the odds. You didn't see me because I wanted to control the odds of getting you."

"What did you do?"

 328

"I got Semyon to find out about the jerk sitting next to you. I wanted to punch him when he gave me the news that he was your husband. And then I wanted to kiss his bald head when I found out what state your husband's financial situation was in. Your husband had a weakness. He was a massive gambler. And I knew exactly how to exploit it.

"It was like fate handed you to me on a platter and said have at it. I set up Ziggurat and I waited for him to take my bait. It was so easy I almost couldn't believe it. Like a fly to shit he came.

"Then a month ago I let myself bump into you. I didn't think the attraction would be that strong but, hell, I wanted to throw you against the wall and fuck you there and then."

"Why were you so cold to me?"

"I was afraid. I was losing control. Anything I had ever wanted I took without any emotional entanglement. It never crossed my mind that it would be different with you. It had never happened to me before. I started to hurt for you. I didn't know how to deal with it and you kept throwing Nigel in my face all the time. Some nights I wanted to fucking kill him with my bare hands."

"I never felt for Nigel what I feel for you. Not even a fraction. I was a girl when he met me. I loved him like a girl. I love you like a woman. He never made me feel the things you do. And the sex. Oh my god, the sex. To think I was going to live all my life with him and never experience what I have with you."

He smiles. "I know. The sex is amazing, isn't it?"

"You mean it's not like that with all the other women?"

"Are you kidding? Never."

I grin. Then I sober up. "Nikolai?"

"Yeah?"

"We'll make it work."

He kisses my eyelids. "We'll take it one day at a time, little butterfly."

Fifty-four

Nikolai

Two Months Later

https://www.youtube.com/watch?v=otMg
Gp7XJEE
Like I'm gonna Lose You

That morning we wake up early. Autumn is in the air and it is still dark outside. Star stretches luxuriously. I pull back the sheets to look at her naked body. I'd punished myself for years but fate sent me Star. Made her so irresistible that it pulled me out of my self-imposed hell.

In the gloom her pale skin glows. I reach out a hand and caress her smooth hip. She looks precious. Beyond anything I own or could want. I need her to know it. If I die tomorrow, I will only be at peace if she knows it.

"I want to show you something," I say.

"What?"

"Get dressed in your riding clothes. I want to show you my brother's grave."

Her face changes. Fear flickers in her eyes. I kept her in a state of insecurity. That flash of fear. That is what I need to destroy.

"Are you sure?" she whispers.

I smile gently. "Yes. It's time."

We go downstairs in the silence of the house. At the last step Star stops. "Remember that first night I came here when you stood there and I stood here."

"It's burned into my memory."

"I thought you were the most magnetic man alive. I had goosebumps just looking at you."

"I couldn't believe my own eyes. How could a mere woman be so beautiful? I had to force myself not to scoop you up in my arms and carry you upstairs to my bed."

"No regrets?"

I shake my head. "Not one."

"Give me one moment," she says, and runs lightly towards the big arrangement of flowers. She stands there for a moment. Then she picks a pure white lily. She walks back to me. "I'm ready to meet your brother."

We go to the stables and I bring Belyy Smert out of his stall while she leads Miss One Penny. We get on our horses and gallop out to the north-west part of the property.

My brother lies in the middle of a beautiful rose garden. His tomb is made of marble with an angel to watch over him. We dismount and walk together towards the beautiful structure. I hold

open the little iron gate and she walks through. We go into the stone tomb.

It is cold inside. I feel her shiver.

She walks ahead of me towards his tomb. She gets on her knees and bows her head. Now when I look at her laying the pure white lily on the smooth white stone there is a sense that life takes and then it gives. Life took him away from me and gave her to me. Blonde, beautiful, kind Star.

She looks up at me. "I love you, Nikolai," she whispers.

For the first time ever I open my mouth and say the words. "I love you, Star. I love you."

Tears roll down her face as she nods with happiness.

"I love you, Star, and I'll love you till all the stars burn away."

Fifty-five

Nikolai

Two Years Later

I am so filled with excitement I can't sleep. I just keep turning over and looking at the beautiful angel sleeping soundly beside me. Every time I look at her a warm feeling fills my entire body. I'm the luckiest fucking man alive.

Who could have imagined that a woman would bring the living corpse, Nikolai Smirnov, to heel? Perhaps because Star's not just any woman.

We waited two long years for this day to happen. I told her she could have anything she wanted. The grandest and most lavish wedding ever. No expense spared, but all she wanted was a small gathering of the dearest of our friends attending.

"What Star wants, Star gets," I said, and so she made her plan and in a few hours we'll be husband and wife and she'll be mine in every sense of the word.

And only mine.

God help any man who looks sideways at her.

Star

https://www.youtube.com/watch?v=jUe8uoKd
Hao
Without You

It's a glorious day with blue skies, and the sun is high above us when we leave for the church of St Mary in the beautiful Cambridgeshire countryside.

My father smiles at me. "You've finally found yourself a real man, Star."

"I know, Dad."

"Remember that time I was lying in hospital with a perforated bowel."

"Yeah?"

"I was terrified I would die and leave you with Nigel, but now I feel good. If I had to die tomorrow, I'd go happy. I know you'd be taken care of."

"This time does feel so different and so right."

I reach a hand across to dad and he holds it. We just sit peacefully together. It takes us less than an hour to reach our destination.

The church is a quaint and magical place. Surrounded by ancient trees and beautifully kept lawns. A stone pathway leads up to the 16th century church entrance.

I take a deep breath and my dad squeezes my hand.

"Is my dress okay?" I ask, concerned that it has become all crumpled in the journey. My stomach is in knots and my hands feel clammy.

"I've never seen you look more beautiful," dad says. Suddenly his face crumples and he begins to cry.

"Oh, Dad. Don't. Please. You'll make me cry too," I say, fanning my face frantically.

"I'm all right. I'm all right," he mutters. Whipping out the carefully pressed handkerchief from his coat pocket, he rubs it all over his face. Rosa comes bustling up the path.

"What's the hold-up?" she demands bossily.

"Nothing. Absolutely nothing," I say.

"Well, get on with it then."

I take a deep breath and we walk to the church's entrance. For a moment we stand there, as if suspended in time. Then everybody turns to look at us. My mother waves. There are tears in her eyes. I see Nikolai's tall, imposing body turn towards me and suddenly the knot in my stomach is gone.

He doesn't smile. He just stares.

The small church fills with Wagner's Bridal Chorus and my father starts walking. I follow him down the flower petal covered aisle.

This is it.

This is it.

I can't help it. I cry through the whole ceremony. I don't remember a thing. I am just so overwhelmed, so incredibly happy, so astonished that I'm marrying Nikolai.

"You may kiss your bride."

Nikolai wipes my tears with his fingers before he kisses me. Then we are hurrying out of the church. I look up at Nikolai. His light eyes are mesmerizing in the sunshine and he gives me a sexy smile. The dream becomes reality.

Fifty-six

Star

Two Months Later

I wrap the package up in plain silver paper and tie it with a yellow ribbon. Then I put it into a silver bag. Carefully, I write inside the yellow card.

> *For my darling husband.*
> *Without you there is nothing ...*
> *From your little butterfly, Star*

I get into the shower and let the water cascade down my body. The shower door opens and I smile. A large hand touches my body. I turn around.

"Hello," I say softly.

"Are you having a shower without me?"

"I had to. I'm very dirty."

"How dirty?"

"You won't believe how dirty I am."

"Oh yes, I will," he says reaching for the sponge. He pours soap on it and drags it across my breasts, under my arms, on my stomach.

"The dirtiest area is between my legs."

338

He laughs. A lovely rumble that comes from deep inside him. He runs the sponge quickly over my crotch. That is surely not the way to clean something very dirty.

"Nah, that's not going to work," he says.

"No?"

"No." He kneels down.

I sigh with pleasure and look down. God, I love this man so much.

The water sluices off his head, his face, his mouth, as his tongue swipes me gently. After I climax, he has his wicked, wicked way with me. His seed drips out of me, and the quickly moving water washes it all away.

I smile to myself. A secret smile.

We get out of the shower. I wrap myself in a bathrobe and pad into the bedroom.

"I've got a present for you." I hold out the silver bag.

His hair is wet, plastered to his head. How is it possible that I still want to have sex when I have just climaxed twice?

He takes the bag. My mind records the moment. I watch him avidly. He takes the silver package out. He unties the yellow ribbon. He tears the silver packaging. He opens the plain grey box. He takes the bottle out and looks at it. Then he looks at me.

"Huile Douche?"

"Huile Douche."

He nods a few times and I know what it is. He is speechless. Nikolai Smirnov is speechless.

"Hey, are you going to say something?"

"Do you feel all right?" he asks.

"Yeah. I'm fine."

"I'm not," he confesses. I realize that he does look a little pale around the gills.

"What's wrong?"

"I'm afraid for you. It will hurt you."

I grin. "There are seven billion people on this earth and each one was born to a woman. I'll be fine."

I take the oil from him and pour a little on his hand. I rub it into his skin and take his hand up to his nose.

He inhales. "My god, you're right. It does smell of fields of flowers, fresh air and sunshine."

I laugh. "Told you so!"

Fifty-seven

Nikolai

Seven Months Later

"Say hello to your son," the nurse says, and puts the naked, mottled creature into my arms. I stare at him in amazement.

My son.

The noises around me blur.

He is so tiny I can almost fit him inside my cupped palms. His eyes are shut and his face all wrinkly and red. His hair is still wet and plastered to his head, but it is fair. His little fingers curl and uncurl. He opens his little mouth and makes a soft mewling sound ... and my breath stops.

God, so much could go wrong.

A protective instinct so shockingly ferocious fills my chest. My heart feels as if it could burst with love for this helpless little thing.

"Nikolai," Star calls.

I look up from my son's face and gaze into the flushed face of my wife. She is exhausted, but triumphant. At that moment I love her more than I've ever done.

"You did it," I say. "You actually did it."

 341

"We did it," she says softly.

I look into her beautiful blue eyes. "No, my little butterfly. We didn't do it. You did. You made this amazing boy inside your body."

She bites her lower lip. It's an old nervous gesture. I haven't seen it in years. "Nikolai, you know how we said we were going to name him Mason?"

"Don't tell me you've changed your mind again."

She gives her head a slight shake. "I haven't changed my mind. I've never changed my mind. I've always known the name I want for our son."

I gaze at her, bewildered. We have been back and forth with a hundred names ever since we knew we were having a boy.

"I want to call him Pavel."

The sound comes from somewhere deep inside me. I didn't know I could make such a sound. It's like a cry of terrible pain. But the pain is cathartic. Like the sharp pain of a boil being lanced. Afterwards there is relief and healing.

She looks at me worriedly.

Oh Pavel. All these years I wanted to call your name but could not.

"Pavel," I whisper.

The child in my arms opens his eyes and looks at me. There is no proper focus. Just an innocent, utterly blank gaze. Then his lips move. Someone else will think it was a twitch. I know it is a smile.

Epilogue

Nikolai

Five Years Later

https://www.youtube.com/watch?v=tS26x ch5U24
Coming Home

I lift my son from his horse and set him down on the ground. I smile at him. "Ready?"

"Ready."

I tie our horses to a tree and pull the bunch of flowers from the holder on the saddle. I give him the flowers and we walk to the iron gate. He opens it and we go inside the tomb. Our boots echo in the still air.

I watch him walk to the grave and carefully put the flowers into the vase of water. He turns his fair head to look at me, and I am reminded of the first time I brought Star here. Life takes, and it gives. Life took Pavel away and left me wandering in the dark for years, but then it gave me Star and another Pavel.

"Daddy, can you tell me that story again?"

"Which story?"

"The baked apple story."

343

"Ah. That one."

He sits on the marble. "One day, Duscha
made a tray of baked apples. She put them on a
wire rack to cool. These apples were very special.
The core had been removed and filled with
Duscha's secret honey-and-nut-filling recipe.
Everybody in the family knew these were Uncle
Pavel's favorite treat. Like a bear that can't resist
honey, he couldn't resist them either. He used to
sit at the kitchen table and wait for them to cool.
He knew he couldn't eat them because we were
supposed to have them for tea. Together. But
that day, one of the baked apples was missing.
Duscha asked him if he had eaten the baked
apple.

'I didn't,' he said.

'Don't tell lies. It doesn't matter if you did.'

'But I didn't.'

'If you didn't, who did?'

'I don't know, but I didn't'

'Did you eat them, Nikolai?,' Duscha asked
me.

'I didn't eat them.'

'Did you eat the apple, Mrs. Smirnov?,'
Duscha asked my mother.

'No, I didn't eat them,' my mother said.

'Neither did I,' my father said.

'Tell the truth, Pavel. You won't be
punished,' Mama said.

'But I didn't eat it.'

'Right. If you admit it you can have another one. If you don't, there will be no baked apples for you.'

'Just say you did,' I whispered to Pavel.

'But I didn't,' he insisted.

'Just say you did it anyway. What does it matter?'

'It does matter. I don't want to lie.'

'You won't get any apple if you don't admit it,' I warned.

'It doesn't matter if I don't. I won't tell a lie,' he said.

That day poor Pavel had to sit at the table and watch us all eating our baked apples."

My son nods solemnly at this point of the story. This is his favorite part.

"Poor Uncle Pavel," he says.

"Yes, poor uncle had no baked apple. He went to bed sad that no one believed him. Then next morning Duscha was cleaning behind the oven and what did she find?"

"She found the baked apple."

"That's right. It had fallen down and rolled under the oven."

My son grins. "Now is the best part."

"Yes. Now is the best part. Everybody felt so bad that we did not believe Pavel, but Mama and Papa were so proud of Pavel because he was so honest that they decided to throw him a big surprise party. So we decorated the house with balloons and colored paper. Duscha made a whole tray of baked apples. Mama and Papa

went out and bought loads of chocolates, sweets, biscuits and cakes. The table was so full of goodies that it groaned."

My son makes a groaning sound.

I grin at him. "All the neighbors and all our friends came to the party. Everybody hid, and when Papa brought him home, we all jumped out and screamed surprise. It was a wonderful party. Everyone had a good time.

Pavel even got a present. A toy he always wanted.

"I wish I had met Uncle Pavel," my son says wishfully.

"I wish you had too, little Pavel."

My son runs up to the marble and kisses the inscription. "Bye bye, Uncle Pavel. See you next week."

We go back out into the sunshine. In the distance, I can see Star riding towards us.

"There's Mummy," my son cries.

I watch her gallop towards us. The wind is in her hair and she is smiling. It is a good life.

The End

This section is meant only for those of you who require/want more back story on Nikolai's journey from orphan to billionaire.

THE MAKING OF A MAFIOSO CRIME
LORD
Nikolai
1992

*https://www.youtube.com/watch?v=GKS
RyLdjsPA*
The Greatest

I see a sign indicating that Moscow is 110 kilometers. Further up is a gas station. I run across the carriageway to a lorry parked by the pumps. I can see the driver paying for his gas inside the service station so I quickly go around to the rear of the cab.

I untie one end of the canvas.

Checking that no one is looking, I haul myself in. It is only three quarter's full of cardboard boxes. I find an area at the rear to hide and move a few boxes around of me to conceal myself if anyone looks inside.

I hope the driver's destination is Moscow, but anywhere will do. I will find my way to

Moscow one way or another. I am so tired that I fall asleep almost immediately, and wake only when the lorry comes to a halt. The next thing I know someone is inside the lorry with me. My heart pounds as someone pulls one of the boxes that I am hiding behind. The man jumps backwards in shock at seeing me.

"Who are you? What are you doing here?" His face is tight and his voice frightened.

"My name is Nikolai. I mean you no harm. I just need to get to Moscow," I say, putting my hands up.

He turns and throws open the canvas. Bright morning light slants into the gloom. He turns around to me again, his eyes scanning my face, my torn clothes, and my cut and bleeding arms and legs. His face softens immediately.

"You are just a boy. Why are you alone?"

"It does not matter. I need to get to Moscow."

"You are already in Moscow."

I scramble to my feet and begin to walk towards him. "Thank you for the ride. I will go now."

"It is very cold outside. Where will you go?"

"I will be fine," I say.

"No. I cannot leave you to go out in the freezing cold in those ragged clothes. You will come to my home and my wife will give you some clothes and food and dress your wounds."

I look at him suspiciously.

 **348**

"I have two boys your age and would hate to see them in your place," he says slowly.

After all these years of deprivation and brutality, I am reluctant to trust an act of kindness, but he is right, I need to wash off all this blood. My clothes are badly torn and I will freeze and die in this weather. I have a promise to my brother to keep. I can't leave him all alone in that bare cemetery.

"All right. Thank you. I accept your kind offer," I tell him awkwardly.

He smiles. "Good. You will be our honored guest. I am glad to be able to offer any little help I can. You can call me Yuri," he says, coming forward to extend his hand. Up close I see into his eyes and I no longer feel any suspicion. He has warm brown eyes. I take his offered hand and shake it.

****

Yuri lives in a small apartment. They are obviously very poor. His wife, Natalya, has made a pot of stew for the family. She has a homely, kind face and does not ask any questions.

"Eat. Eat," she encourages.

It is only after I have had three helpings that I realize she and her husband are not eating. There is not enough to go around.

"I'm sorry," I tell them, embarrassed and ashamed that I have eaten all their food, but Natalya lies and pretends that she has already

eaten, and Yuri says he has a bad stomach. He will have bread and cheese later.

I realize then I cannot stay with them and accept their hospitality. I tell them I have to leave that night.

Yuri asks his wife to give me some clothes that their boys don't need. I wash in their tiny bathroom and get into the woolen sweater, thick socks, jeans, leather gloves, sheepskin coat, and a fur hat that Natalya gives me. I thank them both, and promise that I will not forget their kindness. One day I will return to thank them properly.

"You'll always be welcome here," Natalya says.

"Be careful, Nikolai. Moscow is a very dangerous place," Yuri warns.

****

The first night I sleep rough. It is freezing cold and my hands turn blue, but the second night I climb into a manhole. It is much warmer and safer. For the next few days I survive by begging and stealing. I don't need much. Just enough food to keep me alive.

Things change a little when Dmitry, the leader of a feral street gang of children called Black Bears, spots me stealing food and follows me to my sleeping place. He orders me to hand over what I've stolen. As far as he is concerned I'm operating in what he considers his territory.

I refuse and prepare for a fight.

He is tall with fearless eyes and we have a kind of Mexican standoff, but in the end, he sees that I will be a good addition to his gang and invites me to join them.

Dmitry has no family either. His father was killed on the train tracks where he worked, and his mother was an alcoholic who drank herself to death. Dmitry was sent to live with his extended family, but he was beaten regularly, so he ran away. He has lived on the streets ever since.

I fall into a pattern with them: participating in low level street crime and constantly fighting to keep the territory we roam in. We steal anything and everything we can get our hands on. What we steal, we sell for very little money, but it's enough to feed us and buy the cheap alcohol and glue that everybody in the gang is addicted to. We sleep under bridges, in parks, forests, just about anywhere we can safely lay our heads down.

I tire quickly of the daily fights, the drinking, and the lack of ambition, but I have no way to escape the quicksand of my existence.

Until fate intervenes.

While taking a shortcut one evening by a darkened alley, I hear the sound of someone crying out in pain. Stealthily, I step into the alley. Two large men are beating up a young man. It's clear he's no match for them, and is getting hurt badly. It's not my fight, but after years in the brutal cauldron of the orphanage I cannot stomach bullying of any kind. They're too busy putting the boot into the man to see me approach. One of the men stops kicking and reaches into his pocket.

For a gun!

I watch as he points it at the man on the ground. I lunge forward and smash my fist into the side of the man's temple. His legs buckle and his body staggers before he hits the ground. The other guy whirls around and squares up to me. He's really huge. At least 250 pounds. Probably more.

He snarls at me.

Staring at my face menacingly, he doesn't see the foot that crunches into his balls. He screams in agony, his face a grotesque mask as he drops to his knees. I put him to sleep with an uppercut to his chin. I extend an arm to the victim.

"Who the hell are you?" he asks.

"Who the hell are you?" I shoot back.

"Whoever the fuck you are, it's your lucky day. My name is Marat Ivankov," he says, rising to his feet while clutching his gut and wincing. He says his name like it should mean something to me. It doesn't.

"We'd better get out of here before they wake up," I suggest.

"One minute."

I watch as Marat rifles through the other man's pockets.

"What are you doing?" I ask.

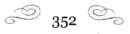

"Taking his gun," he says calmly.

"Who are these men that they have guns?"

"We all have guns. This is Moscow."

He collects both weapons, tucks one into the back of his pants, and holds the other one out to me.

I hesitate, then I reach out, take it, and copy his action.

"Come, let's get out of here," he says.

"What did you do to make these guys want to hurt you so bad?" I ask curiously.

"It's not personal. Just business. If those hired gorillas had not struck me from behind, it would have been a different outcome. It's hard to mount a defense when you're already on the ground taking a kicking."

"Who are they?"

"Just rivals," he says flippantly as if this kind of thing occurred to him regularly. "So, are you going to tell me your name or what?"

"Nikolai Smirnov."

"I live nearby. Want to come around for a drink?"

I didn't have anything better to do, besides, I was intrigued by the man.

His place turns out to be a gated house in an upmarket part of the city. As soon as we approach, his security guards rush out to help him. They want to keep me out, but Marat waves away their concerns and takes me into his home.

Whoever Marat is, he's certainly doing well as his house is like a mini palace. That night I

enjoy the best sleep I've ever had in my lavish bedroom suite. The next day over breakfast fit for a king, Marat makes me an offer. He wants me to work for him and his family. I saved his life and now he wants to repay me by bringing me into the organization at a high level.

He explains that the collapse of the Soviet Union created numerous opportunities throughout Russia, particularly for organized crime and his family is one of the most successful.

At first I am shocked to find myself sitting to breakfast and being presented with an offer to work for a violent Mafia organization, but the more Marat talks, the more I want the same. I accept his offer, and my new life of ruthless ambition begins.

****

For more than a year I get into the business of stealing cars, housing them in specialist garages that change the chassis numbers and the number plates and ship them off across the world. I also get involved in (*kryshy*) protection rackets: extorting businesses when they begin trading in the areas we control.

Yes, sometimes people die, but it's mostly rivals and those who had it coming, anyway. Marat tells me I'm a natural. I've got criminality running in my blood. I smile and say nothing. It doesn't matter what he thinks. I know why I'm doing it. Money.

Without it my promise to my brother dies.

Our financial agreement is that all the money earned by the members (*Boyviks*) passes to Marat, the Brigadier, whose position is similar to a caporegime in an Italian-American Mafia crime family. Marat is also responsible for distributing funds to the bookkeeper who then uses it to bribe government officials.

Marat's uncle, Viktor Ivankov, is the boss (*Pakhan*). The boss sits down with the power elite of the country: usually corrupt officials in high places, and the Chiefs of police to ensure we don't get any trouble.

Very quickly serious money starts to pour into my bank accounts. The first thing I do is arrive one evening, unannounced and with a bottle of expensive vodka, at Yuri and Natalya's home. The shock on their faces gives me my first sense of happiness since my brother died. I eat and drink with the family.

Again, they barely eat, allowing me to have my fill. Imagine their incredible surprise when I hand them the deeds to a house in a good neighborhood. I leave their home, smiling. They invite me to come back and visit them. I smile and nod, but I know I will never see them again.

Marat's operation was already making a lot of money for the family, but with my hard work, input, attention to detail, an intuitive feel for anything that's wrong, our earnings multiply. So

 **355**

much so, one day, Marat tells me his uncle Viktor wants to meet me.

We arrive outside the largest private house in Russia. Surrounded by high walls and electric gates, and swarming with security guards, you cannot mistake it for anything but the house of a *Pakhan*. A large man frisks me before we are shown into a cavernous library. It smells of new leather and expensive cologne. There is a large, thick set man with cold, suspicious eyes, sitting on a chesterfield sofa. He must be in his late fifties, but his skin is tight and he still has a full head of hair.

"Uncle Viktor this is Nikolai, Nikolai, my uncle," Marat introduces.

"Hello, Mr. Ivankov."

A slow smile slips into his still face. "Call me Viktor."

I nod.

"Sit," Viktor invites, pointing to the seat next to him. "We will have a drink together." He signals with his large hand to one of his staff who immediately slips out of the room.

"So, Nikolai, Marat tells me about the great things you have achieved for my family."

I shrug. "It is nothing."

His shrewd eyes gleam. "You have certainly impressed my nephew, anyway."

A bottle of Vodka and three glasses arrive. We drink and talk, and drink some more. The conversation is general, but Marat suddenly seems irritated by all the attention I am getting from Viktor. He jumps to his feet.

"I'm going out for a while," he says.

"Take two of my security," Viktor says.

"I'll be fine," Marat says sulkily.

"There is a war going on. Do not make it easy for my enemies to kidnap or assassinate you," Viktor says in a completely different tone.

"Fine," Marat calls as he walks out.

"My nephew's a little headstrong, but he's a good soldier," Viktor says calmly.

We talk for another half-an-hour. Again, nothing of importance.

"Come, let's eat," Viktor says, clapping me on the shoulder.

Though we have just met, and I have no doubt Viktor is a very ruthless man, I feel a strange bond with him. We eat the excellent food and afterwards the conversation turns to business.

"Nikolai, I do not want you to work with Marat anymore. You are undoubtedly strong and fearless, but in our field, men who know how to use a gun and their fists are many. You are too bright to be doing what you are doing."

I know a test when I see one. I nod politely. "Thank you, Viktor, but I owe a great deal to Marat, and do not wish to dishonor him, or our friendship."

He smiles slowly, pleased with my answer. "Loyalty is a good thing, but you need not worry about your friendship with Marat. In the

 357

structure of our organization, everyone works for the boss, and I am the boss of this family. Marat will be honored that he brought someone of your ability into the family, and he'll be duly rewarded."

I lift my wine glass to my lips. "What do you have in mind, Viktor?"

"I am a wealthy man with numerous business arrangements across Russia, but as these businesses grow I am less able to ensure our partners remain loyal and trustworthy. You will begin by taking responsibility for all of our clubs and gambling operations. They number over two hundred, but many are not as profitable as they should be. They need a fresh set of eyes and a sharp mind to stop the skimming."

"And for my troubles?"

"Ten percent of the profits."

I twirl the wine glass in my fingers. "Fifteen percent and one favor. The only one I will ever ask of you."

For a long while he doesn't speak and neither do I. Whoever breaks the silence is the loser. I watch as he lifts his wine glass to his mouth and takes a sip.

Then he laughs. "If you had accepted ten percent I would have changed my mind," he says frankly. "Ambition is good, Nikolai. It's what got me here. I am curious. What is this favor you want to ask of me?"

"My parents died in an accident, but I do not know where they are buried. I would like to find out where, so I can visit their graves. I'm sure you have contacts in the Interior ministry who can provide this information."

He pauses to think about my request, then he nods. "I will do this thing for you, Nikolai."

"Thank you, Viktor."

He smiles. A cold, shark-like smile. "Now we will drink to our arrangement."

****

Two days later I get a call from one of Viktor's personnel.

"Hello, Nikolai, the boss wants to see you."

"Okay. When?"

"Tonight."

"Fine, I'll have my driver take me around later," I say.

****

"Take a seat, Nikolai."

I sit opposite Viktor and watch him drink his vodka slowly.

"What am I doing here, Viktor?" I ask.

"You remember that favor you wanted? Do you still want to know?"

I raise an eyebrow, surprised at his question. "Of course, it's very important to me."

"You might not like the answers."

"It doesn't matter. I still want to know," I say with a frown.

"All that you know about your parents, Nikolai, is a lie."

I freeze. "What do you mean?"

"Your parents were not doctors. They did not die in an accident. They were KGB agents."

"How can that be?"

"Think, Nikolai. The fine house. The frequent trips away. All part of their cover. You were just too young to know different."

I jump to my feet, my heart pumping hard. "Does that mean they are still alive somewhere?"

He shakes his head. "No. They're dead. They were murdered, but even their deaths did not satisfy the State. The children had to be punished for the sins of the parents. That is why you were sent to the orphanage."

I stare at him. "What sins?"

"The KGB files show that your father and mother had passed intelligence to the CIA. They were actually in the process of defecting to the US. The KGB could never allow that to happen."

"So they stuck my brother and I in that hellhole just because they wanted to punish my father and mother?"

"I'm afraid so. You were both the innocent victims of the State's revenge."

"Their bodies, what happened to them?"

"There is no way to locate their bodies. Traitors were often buried without any ceremony."

"Now you have had your favor." Viktor stands. "I must have mine."

****

Any hope I had of finding my parents' grave died in Victor's cavernous library. I feel numb. There is no feeling in my heart. The next day I throw myself into the task of finding out where Viktor's money is disappearing to. I start my investigation with Viktor's business partners, in particular those who have been the longest with Viktor.

I find the culprit quickly, but I have to prove it, as he has been connected with Viktor's family for twenty years, and Viktor's not going to want to believe it.

I spend hours and hours collecting all the evidence I need, record upon record going back years, before I go to see Viktor. By the time Viktor's rage subsides, we both know there is no doubt about his guilt. I get the authorization to pay the disloyal snake a visit.

When we sit down it's obvious from his nervousness and body language that he knows the game is up. I calmly lay the evidence on the table before his eyes and wait for his response.

"What will Viktor do?" he asks.

"That depends on you being smart."

Beads of sweat appear on his brow as he calculates. I let him sweat a little longer before I make him our offer. Fortunately, he chooses wisely.

A speedy and early retirement.

I have him sign all the paperwork I prepared so we can seize control of all the assets he bought with funds he embezzled from Viktor.

It's only later that I find the hidden gem.

The embezzler had acquired a huge stock of privately held shares in multiple state controlled aluminum mines in Siberia, Krasnoyarsk and Bratsk. I see the opportunity instantly.

True luck is all about timing.

My timing was impeccable. Large private players with billions of funds at their disposal were seeking to monopolize the aluminum industry, buying all that they could get their hands on. We sold the embezzler's stock for more than seven billion dollars.

My percentage meant I was suddenly a billionaire.

The celebration was to be short lived for Viktor. Things were changing fast in Russia. Viktor flew in his private jet to Switzerland to count his money. It was to be his last day of freedom. Interpol and Swiss Federal police storm his plane on the runway, seizing five million dollars in undeclared funds.

They charge him with racketeering, securities fraud, money laundering and tax evasion, stretching back some twenty years. We

try to play hardball with all our contacts, but they are powerless to help him. Viktor is sent to jail for twenty years.

It is a pivotal moment for me.

For the first time, I take stock of my life. Effectively, I am the boss by default. Even Viktor wanted me to continue to run his empire, but I know the Russian authorities are clamping down on primitive organized crime, and you don't need a crystal ball to tell my future. Either a rival's bullet, a bomb in my car, or a lengthy jail sentence awaited me.

None of these options appeal so it is time to say goodbye to Russia.

I have more money than I ever imagined, and I know I have the ability to make much more. I just need a new home.

I decide on England. That would be the next chapter of my life.

Thank you for reading everybody!

Please click on this link to receive news of my latest releases and giveaways.

http://bit.ly/1oe9WdE

and remember

I **LOVE** hearing from readers so by all means come and say hello here:

https://www.facebook.com/georgia.lecarre